Welcome to Nugget:

Mining the Possibilities

This book is a work of fiction. While inspired by a small town in Arizona and the author's experiences, the organizations, characters, places, names, and events in this book are a product of the author's imagination or are used fictitiously. Any similarity to actual events or real persons, living or dead, is coincidental and not intended by the author.

Copyright © 2022 by Thea W. Wilshire.
All rights reserved.

Cover art by FayeFayeDesigns

No part of this book may be reproduced, or stored in a retrieval system, or transmitted in any form or by any means, electronic, mechanical, recording, photocopying or otherwise, without express written permission of the author. The purpose of copyright is to encourage writers and artists to produce work which enriches our lives and to use this book without permission is a theft of intellectual property. If you would like permission to use material from the book, please contact the author. Thanks for your support!

First eBook edition: 2022

Welcome to Nugget:

Mining the Possibilities

Thea W. Wilshire

DEDICATION

In loving memory of my dear friend, Kip McLaren Culver, who made our community "the last best small town in Arizona." A masterful storyteller, Kip's tales were always engrossing, usually hilarious, and invariably infused with grace and appreciation for the many small-town characters he loved … one of whom happened to be me.

"The nice thing about living in a small town is that when you don't know what you're doing, someone else does."
— Immanuel Kant

"He had to submit to the fate of every newcomer in a small town, where many tongues talk but few heads think."
— Victor Hugo

CONTENTS

Chapter 1: Blocked by a Beast 1

Chapter 2: Settling In 15

Chapter 3: Nug 22

Chapter 4: Makin Bacon 27

Chapter 5: I Love Your Cat! 34

Chapter 6: Meeting the New Boss 38

Chapter 7: The True Boss 44

Chapter 8: Meeting Crispy 48

Chapter 9: I Hate Your Cat! 53

Chapter 10: The Intruder 59

Chapter 11: My First Client 65

Chapter 12: Dinner with a Friend 70

Chapter 13: Starting to Belong 76

Chapter 14: Private Investigation 83

Chapter 15: Helping an Anxious Child 87

Chapter 16: Lock Down 91

Chapter 17: Checking In 99

Chapter 18: Hinman Makes Enemies 106

Chapter 19: Maintaining Sanity 111

Chapter 20: Maxine 115

Chapter 21: Stolen Underwear 121

Chapter 22: The Joy of a Baby's Cry 126

Chapter 23: My Mystery Dinner Guest 135

Chapter 24: Talking about Food 144

Chapter 25: Square Dancing 150

Chapter 26: The Morning After 158

Chapter 27: Processing the Violation 164

Chapter 28: Feeling Thankful 170

Chapter 29: Interaction in the Park 178

Chapter 30: Light Extravaganza 182

Chapter 31: The Wrong Car 186

Chapter 32: Getting Fit 192

Chapter 33: A Suicidal Pipsqueak 197

Chapter 34: Stopping the Madness 208

Chapter 35: Reconnaissance 211

Chapter 36: Tastes of Nugget 218

Chapter 37: Guard Cat 222

Chapter 38: The New Hairdo 227

Chapter 39: Cooking Lessons 231

Chapter 40: The Speeding Ticket 235

Chapter 41: A Bad Game of Golf 241

Chapter 42: Laying Carpet 248

Chapter 43: The Cat Finds a Home 252

CREDITS 256

ABOUT THE AUTHOR 257

Chapter 1

Blocked by a Beast

"Lord, help me!"

The desperation and terror embedded in those words would have brought a person running if my prayer was audible. However, the words shouted from my heart were barely whispered aloud to not startle the intimidating three-legged beast blocking my path. Consequently, no one came, and I remained frozen and isolated in fear.

The massive, excessively furry, feline-like thing stretched languidly across my doormat, taking the cheerful "Welcome!" message at face value. While I usually run fast and hard whenever I encounter cat-like creatures, I couldn't run this time as I needed to get into my new home. While paralyzed with fear, I was desperate for entry.

I had to use the bathroom.

"Scram! Get out of here. Pssst, shoo, be gone!" I demanded in my most authoritative voice, then pushed past my frozen terror to add a loud stomp on the wooden porch floor.

Unfortunately, my noise fell on obnoxiously deaf and fur-filled ears.

The foul creature looked like a cat but seemed too immense to be a domesticated animal. It had a nondescript pattern of brown, black, and tan fur and what looked like a black "M" in the space above its eyes and between its tufted ears. Its hair around the face and neck was short to medium length, while the hair on the body was long, the ruff around its neck was very fluffy and a little lighter in color than its body. Its coat was matted and tangled with leaves and sticks. I guessed it was either a wild animal or feral, yet it seemed not in the least bit frightened of me which unnerved me even more. Don't feral cats and wild creatures usually run away from encounters with humans?

I didn't think it was a bobcat, though it might be or a mix of some sort. I wondered if wild cats ever crossbreed with house cats? They might create something like the immense creature I currently faced. Truthfully, I wouldn't know because I've avoided all felines like the plague ever since a feral cat got into our house when I was a child. My mom was allergic, so I was given the task of removing the animal, which I did, but not before it scratched my arm so deeply I required stitches and the subsequent infection almost resulted in hospitalization. Ever since then, cats have made me edgy.

Okay, more than edgy. It's more like terrifyingly, heart-stopping phobic.

Even though the temperature was 97 degrees, I again was as immobile as an ice sculpture save for the slight tremble in my hands and my shallow breathing. The beauty of the day -- sunshine gentled by a slight breeze, the sound of mourning doves and house wrens, the intoxicating smell of a palo verde tree blooming in a brilliant profusion of yellow blossoms -- all this was lost to me in my panic.

I had to get to a bathroom but was terrified of interaction with the forbidding animal lying across my door mat. I again moved past my paralyzing fear to shout and stomp my feet to scare the animal away, but the feline (for convenience's sake, I'm simply going to call it a "cat" until I know what it is) rolled over on its side making a loud rumbling noise which might be purring but was probably growling because it was so thunderous. I could push it away from the door if I had a broom, but I hadn't yet purchased a broom. "Maybe I could use a stick?" I thought as I snuck a glance toward my yard.

The cat rolled from its side onto its back, revealing curlier fur on its belly and even longer fur around its rear end. Besides the bobcat-style tufts of hair at the tips of the beast's ears, it also had tufts around its' over-sized paws and even hair under its paws. Though I don't know a lot about cats, those can't be the paws of a house cat as they're monstrously large.

The cat looked toward me slowly and then stretched its three legs unhurriedly into the air.

Three legs... what's up with the missing leg? I wondered if it was injured. Do physically disabled kitties get special accommodation?

Would driving a handicapped three-legged cat away from my porch be considered animal cruelty?

Oh, my goodness! No matter what it might be called, I had a more pressing matter: my bladder. It was about to burst! Perhaps a neighbor would let me use their toilet? But, having barely moved to the neighborhood two days ago, I didn't know anyone yet and certainly didn't want my first encounter with a neighbor to be a request to relieve myself in their restroom.

I also didn't want to admit I had an incapacitating fear of cats. The technical term is ailurophobia, an illogical and overwhelming terror of cats. Whatever you call it, I find it completely debilitating.

As I was considering driving to a gas station or perhaps discretely peeing in my yard, the cat slowly got up and took several steps away from the door.

Yes! My hope soared.

However, this brief reprieve from terror lasted only a few seconds before the cat stopped moving, plopped down, and slowly started to clean its back left leg while acting oblivious to my presence. My hope plummeted.

This roller coaster of emotion was going to give me motion sickness.

However, now there was a four to five-foot gap between the cat and my door. While I am thin, I wondered if I could make myself even skinnier by pressing against the building to slide carefully past the creature? I flattened myself against the house to be as far from the cat as possible and slowly shuffled up to my locked door.

I wished I had closed toed shoes or long pants to help protect me from the beast, but I had dressed for the weather and not feline protection. Because I didn't want to turn my back on the cat in case it leapt at me, I tried to unlock the door while reaching behind me. The cat finally noticed me and seemed amused by my contortions. It stopped cleaning itself to watch me more closely, cocking its head to the side. This steady stare unnerved me and caused me to drop my keys.

Crud! Now I had to bend down to pick up my keys which would put my face even closer to the ghastly thing. I am quite tall, 6'1" to be exact, so this would involve a lot of courage because it required a lot of bending (people think being tall brings extra privilege, but it also has its costs). My t-shirt was starting to get perspiration spots, my brown curly hair was stuck to my sweating temple, and my heart was racing. Could I do it?

I have a history of extreme courage with animals when needed, so I tried to give myself a silent, but enthusiastic pep talk. "Come on, Zoey. You've got this, girl! You've conquered greater challenges living in a rainforest: you removed an aggressive fer-de-lance snake from the tent when you were eight and stayed calm when you stumbled upon a sleeping crocodile on the banks of the Tarcoles River. Come on now, Zoey, you can do this. It is a cat, just a feline. This should be simple."

However, my fear continued to immobilize me. I guess because a phobia is illogical, trying to use logic to fight it isn't effective.

Right when I was about to give up and shuffle back to my car, the cat mercifully got up and took a few additional steps away from the door and plopped itself on the porch again to watch my antics, making the loud rumbling noise the entire time broken up with an occasional quiet trill. Could a cat smile? It looked like it was giving me a Cheshire grin and might be amused by my terror.

Ultimately, my bladder made the decision for me: I took a big breath, bent over quickly, snatched my keys, unlocked the door, and slid inside, then began taking big breaths to slow my heart rate.

The repugnant cat didn't move, except to stretch out proprietarily, spread its toes, and occasionally flick its oversized tail.

I had moved to the little mining town of Nugget, Arizona a few days ago to start a two-year adventure serving as the school psychologist for the Nugget Unified School District. After three separate teen suicides in a 15-month period, the tiny town was rocked with both grief and a wave of hopelessness. The powerlessness quickly funneled to anger. Because all the kids were from families employed at the local copper mine, the pressure on the mining company to fix the situation was intense. So, my position was created.

It's a two-year grant situation where the mine funds the position, but the counselor is an employee of the school district. Because this region is considered a Health Professional Shortage Area, it also qualifies for a special federal student loan forgiveness program. If I am granted this, it would lessen my financial burdens by relieving $20,000 a year of my remaining $135,000 of student debt.

I am now the only psychologist in an 85-mile radius and the only licensed mental health provider for a 50-mile radius. The town's last licensed counselor, Mr. Smith, angrily left nine years ago and no one else has been willing to come here since then. The story is almost unbelievable to me, but the local folks not only believe it, but appear to take it in stride.

They say a mentally ill young man was court-ordered to therapy but didn't go. He proceeded to murder the nephew of the district judge's wife. She was so furious about this injustice; she became relentless in her demands for her husband to "just do something!" To quiet her, he finally issued an arrest warrant for Mr. Smith as an accomplice to the murder, something he loosely linked to "dereliction of duty" even though Mr. Smith was not even aware of the court-order to treatment and had never met the young man. Given the seriousness of the charge, the judge gave instructions for the counselor to be taken into custody immediately.

Mr. Smith was respected and involved in the community, so the arresting officer felt terrible when he called him out of a Wednesday night Bible study to take him to the police station. The humiliation of spending a night in jail was beyond what this conscientious and highly educated professional could bear. Never mind the foundless charges were dropped immediately and a local attorney offered to sue the state on behalf of the innocent counselor, Mr. Smith was done with this foolishness! He packed up his family and moved to another state within the month.

Not surprisingly, the judge lost his position in the next election cycle; however, he kept his marriage intact. On some days he wondered if he had come out ahead.

Nugget is a fascinating little town, different from anywhere else I have lived. This high desert community is nestled among the foothills of two mountain ranges, in a small bowl-shaped valley. Its 4200-foot elevation makes it cooler than low desert locations which means it sometimes gets snow in the winter, but it still can push the thermometer over a hundred degrees in the summer. This had been the case for the past two days. I felt like I might melt.

When it cooled in winter and was blessed with occasional precipitation, the craggy mountain peaks around Nugget might wear a sprinkling of snow well into the start of spring, making some of the residents unconsciously crave something covered in powdered sugar. Not surprisingly, donuts sell well when this happens.

The small town is surrounded by national forest, large mining tracts, federal Bureau of Land Management tracks, and an Indian reservation. Unfortunately, being landlocked means the town doesn't have the option of expanding into its neighboring regions. However, it also means the region is blessed with amazing natural resources. Mountains, desert, rivers, streams, lakes, waterfalls, canyons, and pine forests provide lots of opportunities to explore on foot, mountain bike, horseback, and ATV.

I thought I would like my new home and looked forward to time spent hiking, canyoneering, and kayaking. I love adventures and know this region would offer many options to me. But my path getting here was surprising, even to me. I wasn't looking for work when the president of the Nugget school board heard about me from his wife's cousin's husband's friend and recruited me to the position despite my resistance every step of the way.

The phone call was so surprising, it was crystal clear even now.

"Good morning, this is Dr. Zoey Trost at the South Central Special Education Department. How may I help you?"

"Good morning, Dr. Trost. My name's Don Hernandez and I'm the board president of the Nugget Unified School District's Board of Directors."

This rang no bells for me, so I hoped more information was forthcoming.

"Good morning, Mr. Hernandez. To what do I owe this call?"

"We're looking to hire a child psychologist for our school district and wanna bring you out to Nugget for a job interview."

"Excuse me?" I stuttered with surprise.

"We've had several suicides among our student body and received special funding to hire a psychologist for the next 2 years, with the possibility of extending the position beyond that. We've been looking for candidates and your name came to us. Your dissertation chair recommends you with the highest praise."

My former professor?

"We'd like to bring you out in the next two weeks for an interview."

"Oh, well, this is a surprise, Mr. Hernandez, and a tremendous honor." I was trying to quickly process how this call was unfolding. To say I was surprised would be an understatement. However, even thinking fast, I knew I didn't want to leave my life in Los Angeles. I had never been happier in my adult life with a wonderful apartment only two blocks from the beach, incredible friends, a great church, a challenging job, almost-complete-recovery from a bad break-up, and all my family within an hour's drive.

My answer was crystal clear to me, "Thanks for extending this offer to me, Mr. Hernandez, but unfortunately I am not looking for a new job at this time."

"We'd still like you to come for an interview, Dr. Trost. We'll pay for your flight and cover all your expenses."

His refusal to accept my "no" was beginning to feel rude and I think my voice began to reveal my irritation. "That's very generous, thank you. However, I'm not looking for work and need to respectfully decline."

I didn't realize Hernandez Automobiles was the most successful car dealership in Copper County, AZ. Besides being an astute businessman, Mr. Hernandez was a stellar salesman.

"I need to apologize. Please forgive my lack of communication skills. I'm learning," he humbly admitted.

I wasn't sure about what he was apologizing, but of course I'm going to support someone asking for help. I opened my heart a bit to support him in his learning process, but I wasn't sure yet what the lesson was.

[Did I mention he was a successful salesman?]

"I must not be making this clear. We'll cover your plane ticket, the rental car, and two nights at a hotel. We'll even provide a per diem for meals. You'll have no expenditures, you'll get a nice trip out of it, and all you have to do is sit for a job interview."

Besides being out of the blue, this offer sounded too good to be true. I've found things that seem unbelievable usually have hidden hooks and catches. I seriously doubted this was a real job interview.

"Sir, be honest, is this a time share sale? It sure sounds like it."

He laughed heartily and agreed. "Yes, it does, doesn't it? But, no, not a time share. Dr. Trost, our students need help sooner rather than later and we've been looking for a while for the right person to join our team. We think you're a perfect match and want to bring you out for an interview. That's all. No cost, no pressure, nothing to lose."

"Let's back things up a bit. Where did you say you are calling from?"

"Nugget Unified School District."

"Okay, but where is Nugget?"

"Oh, excuse me, yes, that's important," he chuckled a bit. "We're a little rural community in Eastern Arizona. You can look us up on a map… we're in a lovely location and have a great community. I think we're the best kept secret in the state."

"Alright, Eastern Arizona, hmm," I tried to process this information quickly and out loud. "I have never been to your region, and I like to explore new places; however, it feels unethical to use your school district's money to fund my travels when I'm not looking for another job."

"We'd still like you come out for an interview, Dr. Trost."

"Mr. Hernandez, I don't think I can be clearer. I am not looking for new employment. If you are fully aware I am considering this an all-expense paid vacation and not a job interview, then I'll come."

He shocked me with his response: "Great! We're so looking forward to meeting you in person."

He gave me the name and number of a woman at the district office, Delvinia Standford, who would help with travel arrangements, and we talked about dates. They were in a bit of a rush to get things in order before the school year started and I was surprised to learn Arizona schools opened almost two months prior to California schools.

Right after I hung up with Mr. Hernandez, I called my best friend.

Welcome to Nugget

"Hey, Sarah, can Ron watch your kids next week so we can go on a three-day adventure?"

"I'm sure he can. Where are we going?"

"Eastern Arizona."

Once in Arizona, I had five interviews which should have warned me away from the job with increasingly dramatic descriptions of overwhelming need and a paucity of resources, but instead I found myself so excited by the prospect I couldn't sleep. I spent time praying instead of slumbering most of the night.

To my shock and Mr. Hernandez's pleasure, I called and accepted the job the next morning.

My family couldn't understand my decision and even I was a bit mystified by how this was unfolding. I had no prior rural experience, no exposure to mining or desert topography, never desired to live in Arizona, and seemed extremely happy with my life in Southern California. My older sister, Katrina, allowed it might be a fun adventure. My mother didn't really have an opinion one way or the other, but thought it was probably motivated by me trying to move away from my ex-fiancée who cheated on me with one of my best friends. However, Alberto, the man who raised me and whom I considered my father, didn't like the sound of this adventure, and challenged my decision repeatedly.

To be honest, I think Papa wanted me closer for our weekly lunch dates.

Alberto joined our family when I was only three and we've shared a special bond since our first encounter when I left my distracted mother's side on a street in Agujitas, Costa Rica and climbed into the lap of a friendly stranger at a sidewalk café. As he tells it, I clutched his shirt with my right hand, popped my left thumb into my mouth, snuggled into his chest, and promptly fell asleep. He didn't want to wake me, so he slowly finished his meal and then patiently waited with an unknown sleeping child on his chest for 45 minutes until my mother frantically approached the dashing stranger with a dimpled smile. This decisive act, what Papa called his "divine appointment," was the origin story of my parents' relationship and we heard it told and retold frequently over the years.

Papa was my biggest supporter and cheerleader. He had more patience than my mother, so early on he took on the task of raising my older sister and me. This involved such mundane tasks as combing out our unruly heads of curls, hair made even curlier by the constant humidity of our Central American locale, and such elevated tasks as coming to Father-Daughter dances when we moved to the United States. He would take my sister and me out walking and with him on errands. He played endless childhood games and sat through countless "tea parties" with our stuffed animals. But, most importantly, he showed the most empathy to my childhood health challenges.

Our bond was cemented through pain.

My intense leg and arm pains started at age seven. Because he had seasonal work, he was my primary caregiver and grew intensely protective of me. At first, my discomfort was attributed to my quick growth and being taller than every kid in my grade and even some of the teachers. Papa would hold me for hours, rubbing my extremities and making hot water bottles to try to ease the pain and stiffness. As the ailment worsened, he took me to all my doctor's appointments and treatments. The physicians looked for joint stiffness and swelling, but I didn't fit into most of the conditions they knew. When local doctors couldn't figure out what was going on, my parents took me to specialists in San Jose, the capital and biggest city in Costa Rica. There I was given a reluctant diagnosis of juvenile idiopathic arthritis.

My mom read everything she could find on this condition and felt this was a foolish and inaccurate diagnosis as my pain, stiffness, and clumsiness worsened as the day went on. Additionally, I did not have joint swelling, and I never had a fever or a rash. She worked to quickly finish her doctoral research so we could return to the United States for additional medical consultations. Alberto was so embedded in our family, there was no thought about him not joining us. He and my mom married quickly to help with his immigration.

However, even back in the U.S., Western medicine brought little relief. Papa was the one who refused to believe we had exhausted all our options. He found traditional Latin American healers, *curanderos*, to treat me with herbs and folk medicine. I believe these treatments, bound up with his focused care and deep compassion bathed in constant prayer, brought about a miraculous recovery. The western physicians said traditional healers were quacks and my recovery was impossible; consequently, this proved I must have been misdiagnosed.

Regardless, Papa's years of deep love and consistent care had awarded him an important voice in my life decisions. His approval was important to me.

In his heavily accented English and with impeccable logic, he challenged my decision to embark on this Arizona adventure.

"Zoey, mi hija (*my daughter*), what are you doing? I researched this place and uncovered scary statistics about single women in remote settings. This is peligroso (*not safe*) and remoto (*too far from home*)," he added decisively.

"Papa, living in remote areas has never stopped our family before. Why would it do so now?"

When his initial words didn't sway me, he pursued the idea of fiscal stewardship. "You'll likely make less than you'd make working at a school in Los Angeles. Don't you want to pay off your student loans sooner, mi amor (*my love*)?" he pleaded.

"The pay is comparable, the cost of living is less, and there are student loan repayment opportunities for working in remote areas to which I can apply," I countered. "These loan repayment programs aren't available in L.A."

As he continued to object, I thought I should pull my trump card, so I stated, "Besides, I prayed about the opportunity and really feel God is directing my steps toward this little school district."

There are fewer surefire ways to shut down a debate than invoking God or your culture (especially if it is not the same as the person with whom you are arguing). Unfortunately, this was not the case for my papa in this situation.

He countered by appealing to me as a father saying, "No, I am your padre (*father*) and God is our heavenly padre, so I know he's on my side with this one. Besides, I cannot protect you over there!"

"You can't protect me in L.A. either, Papa," I countered. Which was true. "L.A. has more gangs, traffic, crime, and natural disasters than Nugget. Also, people can die from tripping while getting out of bed.

There are no risk-free ventures, no perfectly safe locations, and no guarantees about life."

Papa scowled, grumbled a bit, and shook his head slowly. He wasn't accepting my logical explanation, so I countered with history.

"Our family is famous for being intrepid explorers and doing the unexpected. When Mom moved alone with two small children to a tent in the rain forests of Costa Rica, everyone thought she was crazy. But her archeological work proved ground-breaking, she earned her doctorate, and, even most importantly, we all met you. This is small potatoes compared to her actions."

He continued to glower, but I thought the tightness of his mouth might have relaxed a bit, so perhaps I was getting through to him.

"Papa, you always told us to live our lives bravely and that's what I'm doing." He seemed to remember this saying and could appreciate I took his words to heart. I decided to add another, "You also told us to say 'yes' to adventures."

He nodded once and gave a big sigh.

I decided to push my advantage and end strong in this discussion, so I shifted to impacting the world through living our passions. This has always been a driving force and pinnacle of purpose for Papa and, consequently, all my family.

"I love counseling and helping kids, and my lifetime struggle dealing with physical pain makes me uniquely qualified to understand pain in any form. I want to make a difference in the world and yearn for my work to be meaningful. I can't imagine a better place to practice my skills as a psychologist than in a tiny town where the resources are few and the needs are large. I'll be vigilant about safety and won't make foolish choices."

He shook his head morosely and responded, "Demasiado tarde, mi amore." (*"Too late, my love."*)

He felt my decision to go was already fool-hearted.

Despite what my papa thinks, I'm not utterly naïve about my new season. I know it will be far from family and at times possibly scary. It will be hard work, perhaps overwhelmingly so. The schools where I will work will have few outside resources (at least compared to most U.S. cities), which will require more professional ingenuity to help the children and families with whom I will work. All in all, I know there will be many challenges in this new venture; however, to be honest, I didn't expect the challenges to surface this quickly.

Even more importantly, I didn't expect my first big challenge to involve my kryptonite: a cat.

During the next few hours, I kept sneaking peeks at the intimidating feline behemoth lounging on my porch and discovered he felt no compulsion to leave my property. When he noticed me looking his way, he gave me long, slow blinks which felt a little threatening to me. My little house was so diminutive I didn't have a back door and, despite my phobia, I was not willing to climb out a window to avoid the beast if he decided to cement himself to the porch. If he didn't move, I needed to figure a way to chase off a cat, particularly an intervention which could be done from as far away as possible.

¡Que Dios me ayude! (*God help me.*)

SIGN ON THE WINDOW OF PILGRIM'S PHARMACY:

There's a fine line between crazy and free-spirited and it usually involves a prescription

WEATHER REPORT IN THE NUGGET NEWS:

```
Heat wave hits the Southwest:
Thermometer rose to "You've got to be
            kidding!"
```

Chapter 2

Settling In

To get ready for my new job, I decided to move to Nugget two weeks before work was scheduled to begin. This would give me time to unpack, work on my rental house, and get to know my new town.

There weren't many rentals available in Nugget and the one I found that fit me best was in poor condition and phenomenally dirty. It didn't look like any care or upkeep had happened in at least 25 years and, when asked, the landlord refused to do any of it. I found out later he was the new owner and had recently inherited the house from his aunt. He wanted the income from a rental, but not the work. I couldn't find another rental that was better, so I offered to do some of the work if he would credit me this labor toward rent. He agreed to half the second month's rental fee if I did the work myself. While this wasn't much for what would be several big projects, I would have done it without the credit just to live in a semi-decent place, so I took his offer.

I devoted my first week in Nugget to cleaning the rental house thoroughly, shampooing the carpets, repainting the living room, and sanding the dreadfully splintery front porch. I hoped to explore my new town and the surrounding area in the second week. As it ended up, a week was barely enough time to get all the house projects done and led to the discovery of several plumbing issues. I called the landlord and left a message asking for help with the repair needs, but he was mysteriously unresponsive.

I also had not factored in how overwhelming the heat could be and found I did not want to try to bike or hike when the temperature was over 100 degrees. What's up with Arizona starting the school year the first week of August and ending the first week of May? It was too hot to breathe. In California, school didn't start until the last week of September and ended the last week of June. This seemed infinitely better to me, though maybe the heat was part of the reasoning behind their early start. I'm not sure.

I figured out if I wanted to run or hike or bike, I had to get up at the break of dawn before the air began to sizzle. I'm not great in the morning but tried to get up early for this reason. It also helped with the outdoor work I was trying to accomplish. I finished up Sunday afternoon and headed over to the laundromat to wash all my clothes, towels, drop cloths, rags, and other laundry dirtied by the many house projects.

Because a lady at the laundromat said I shouldn't miss the Nugget Historical Museum, I made a point to swing by. I was met by two friendly and talkative seniors who absolutely loved the town. The man seemed more focused on mining and geology while the woman seemed hooked in with the people of the past. They were both knowledgeable and interesting. From them I learned an unbelievable amount of information about Nugget.

They explained the town is rich in Old West history and lore. The remoteness and unforgiving topography made it one of the last places in the continental United States to be settled by white and Hispanic people in the 1870's and Chinese settlers in the 1880's, though it was not uninhabited before this. The Native American history goes back multiple centuries and the people who lived here fought long and hard to keep the newcomers from intruding on their homeland. The entry of the U.S. Cavalry shifted the axis of power and crushed the opposition, so the new guys stayed.

First renowned for its silver reserves, miners quickly discovered this was more copper country than anything else. Mining built this community and the mining industry had explosive growth in the late 1890's when the railroad finally reached Nugget. The wealth of copper in the early 1900's resulted in some fabulous buildings by top architects of the day. These architectural gems anchor the present-day historic downtown and add to the flavor of the community.

However, even with the riches from the mines pervading the community and centerpieces of famous architects in the downtown, the little town remained wild and wooly. Outlaws and famous Old West lawmen and their ladies called Nugget home. Arizona was the last of the lower 48 to become a state for good reasons, primarily related to places like Nugget. The community fought tooth and nail against the territorial president's plan to outlaw prostitution and gambling to try to make Arizona more "presentable" and "state-worthy". Ultimately, Nugget lost, Arizona won, and the citizens of Nugget eventually felt the United States of America was a better place for their addition.

My new museum friends shared that Nugget has produced famous state and national politicians, musicians, scientists, mathematicians, artists, athletes, ranchers, and innovators in many fields. They boasted some of the mining solutions proposed by Nugget workers a century ago are still used throughout the world in extractive industries to this day. I wondered if having time underground to think coupled with the isolation of this place may have helped inspire creativity across these many disciplines, particularly with necessity serving as the mother of invention. This level of success across so many disciplines also could be linked to the spunky, "can do" spirit of the people who choose to live here.

Or maybe there's just something in the water.

One of the most pivotal events of the last 100 years was when the highway formerly traversing through the center of town bypassed the community. Even though it only moved half a mile south and there were lots of signs inviting people to enjoy a quick detour, car traffic and subsequent business traffic tanked. Restaurants, gas stations, and hotels closed. The community had always thought of itself as a mining town but realized through this unfortunate change it depended on pass-through tourism more than anyone could have imagined. This was when the population went from 7,200 to 4,700 people. If you add the people living in the small neighboring town of Odessa and in the unincorporated county land, the region almost hits 8,000 people.

What an interesting place!

As I prepared to leave, the female docent recommended I check out their "gift store" which was a single bookcase near the entrance. There were a few books about Nugget history, a half dozen historic postcard reproductions, and something she called copper splash. This was really fascinating and something I had never seen before. The miners sometimes spill or purposefully splash molten copper on a cooler surface and it takes on unique shapes and colors as it cools and hardens. I bought a small, heart-shaped piece for my mom's birthday which was coming up.

I felt anonymous in my new hometown because I knew no one yet and I was used to the lack of interaction common among residents of large metropolitan areas. I did not realize any newcomer to a small town stands out like a palm tree in a corn field. There is no anonymity and newbies are the topic of intense observation, as well as discussion all around town. This started to become obvious to me during my second week in Nugget.

People were genuinely friendly throughout Nugget and strangers struck up conversations with me at the Nugget Hardware Store, Jimmy's Dash and Go Market, Pilgrim's Pharmacy, and the Gas Up fuel station. Most folks commented on the heat, but all seemed hopeful the expected summer rains would bring some relief. One woman took the time to educate me about how droughts and monsoons create unique dangers and warned me about flash floods during monsoon season "because you're new to the area and probably don't know this sort of thing."

Several people recommended I try a local fast-food joint renowned for its' "world-famous" chicken nuggets, a place with a huge sign proclaiming it to be "NUG's Nugget Nook in Nugget, AZ."

To my surprise, the food lived up to the hype.

The chicken nuggets were mouthwateringly good and offered a choice of regular or extra crispy breading which encased a moist and succulent interior. However, as delicious as they were on their own, it was the sauces which truly sealed the deal. I'd never had anything like them, particularly NUG's secret sauce. After my first visit, I kept thinking about that fantastic food and went back two more times.

Maybe it was because I was becoming a repeat customer, people seemed to look at me differently and I must have felt even more approachable to them. One man stopped by my table as he was leaving the restaurant with his small children and said, "Hey, I know you're new to town. Welcome to Nugget. Please be aware we don't tolerate big city driving in these parts. Remember, you're in Nugget now." He then nodded while offering a half smile and exited the restaurant.

After he left, I tried to make sense of what he meant by "big city driving." I didn't have a clue. It seems my perplexity was obvious and communicated through my knit brows and confused look. The folks at the table across from me must have been listening because the older gentleman signaled to me, smiled graciously, and then explained, "We drive the speed limit, we use our blinkers, and we completely stop at stop signs." He seemed to feel his description was an adequate explanation as he smiled broadly and then returned to his extra crispy nugget meal with honey mustard sauce.

While he felt the matter was done, I was still confused. I drove the speed limit, used my blinkers, and stopped at stop signs… didn't I? I had never had a speeding ticket in Los Angeles and had learned to drive there. The City of Angels taught you early on to drive assertively or you wouldn't be allowed into traffic. Also, it wasn't safe to drive slowly, or people would become angry and possibly aggressive. For this reason, the freeway speeds were always ten to twenty miles faster than the posted limits.

Was my Los Angeles-trained driving style inappropriate in this setting? Are there big town and small town driving modes? I would have to watch myself to see if I handled the road differently than the people around me. It seemed both of those men were aware of my driving and, as weird as it felt to me, they seemed to think this was not unusual.

I finished my meal, threw away my trash, and stopped into the women's room to wash grease off my fingers. While at the sink, a woman came out of a toilet stall and looked at my face in the mirror before flashing a big smile and stating enthusiastically, "Hey, I know you!"

I looked at her and found she wasn't even vaguely familiar. I quickly scrolled through my mental Rolodex to see if she fit among my college contacts, church friends, camp co-workers, graduate school colleagues, former work mates, or even past neighbors and friends. I came up blank.

She then continued, "You did five loads of wash last Sunday at the Fluff and Fold!" before nodding once, smiling at me again, and exiting the bathroom with a "Nice to see you again" like we were old friends.

My mouth was open and my eyes incredulous: she was right. I had done five loads of wash. But who notices or keeps track of other people in public settings? Who counts the number of loads of laundry a stranger is doing? How many other people were watching me and making notes? This must be linked in some way to the two men who tried to nicely educate me about my driving. What other matters were happening around me of which I am unaware?

The realization shouldn't have been a surprise, but somehow it was: I was no longer in Los Angeles.

GRAFFITI MESSAGE SCRAWLED ON HIGHWAY UNDERPASS:

Cannibal = someone fed up with people

FOUND IN THE NUGGET NEWS OBITUARY SECTION:

No deaths this week, but several people are sick so we're watching and waiting.

Chapter 3

Nug

Newton Ulysses Green hated his name. When he was ten, he joined a touch football league, and his coach was a former Army sergeant who called all his young men by their last name. Going by "Green" wasn't the problem. The difficulty started when they distributed uniforms and he called out "Green, Newt" causing every boy on the team to split their sides in laughter. Newt felt like his face was on fire!

A normally laid-back kid, he was so upset by the experience he wouldn't eat dinner after practice and put himself to bed early which worried his parents immensely. He tried to come up with a way to soften the embarrassment of his name but couldn't figure out how to accomplish this with his current moniker. Consequently, he decided he would change his name entirely and vowed to accomplish this if it was the last thing he ever did.

He liked the name Brian, so at first, he told his friends and family he was changing to this new name. However, his mother took grave offense. She told him in no uncertain terms, "I named you Newton Ulysses Green and that's that. My 12 hours of blood, sweat, and tears delivering you gave me naming rights. I have not revoked my privilege, nor do I plan to do so."

Newt didn't know his parents had squabbled for almost eight of the nine months of pregnancy about his future name, so his mom was ardent about the subject. She was a science teacher and felt Isaac Newton was the best scientist of all time, so she fought for "Isaac" as the baby's name if he was a boy. However, this was the same name as a kid who had ceaselessly bullied his father in grade school, so he refused to allow any Isaac in his home. She then switched her campaign from Isaac to Newton.

His father was a Civil War reenactor and had many famous generals he wanted considered which is where the Ulysses came from. He agreed to Newton if she would agree to Ulysses. She did. Newt later learned his father had also nominated other Civil War first names, including Clement, Pitcairn, Erasmus, Jubal, and Ambrose. When those were considered, Ulysses was a gift by comparison.

Newton's Uncle Stanley was a master negotiator. He was the one who suggested a compromise.

"Young man, your mother really fought to get your name, so I don't see her backing down on this. But what I've found in life is there is always another way. When you encounter an insurmountable wall, you can continue to ram it or take a different strategy and go around the wall entirely."

"I don't understand," frowned Newt. "If she won't let me change my name, how can we 'go around' that?"

Uncle Stanley lowered his voice to a conspiratorial whisper and motioned Newt closer. "Instead of changing your name, you can begin using your initials." When Newt still didn't understand, his uncle further unpacked the idea for him. "You can go by N.U.G. or Nug. Would that work for you?"

At first, Newt wasn't sure, but the idea grew on him, especially after Stanley explained using his initials would quiet his mom as her naming privilege would still technically be honored this way. He shared his uncle's suggestion with his best friend, Kenny, and a few of his closer buddies and they thought the nickname was cool, so he decided to make Nug his new handle.

Newt carefully told all his friends, teachers, pastor, coach, and family his new name was "Nug", and he would only respond to this title from today forward. Most people had no problem with the transition, but his mom held out the longest. However, when Nug simply would not respond or acknowledge any comment directed to him using his old name, she eventually acquiesced as well.

Perhaps linked to a lifetime of being called "Nug", he found he simply loved chicken nuggets. When his Uncle Stanley passed away and willed him $15,000 with the suggestion he start a new business, Nug carefully considered his business options: Toy store? Drycleaners? Comic book sales? Pool supply store? Fudge shop? Doggie day care? He vacillated for a month before firmly landing on his most passionate of passions: chicken nuggets.

Nug's Nugget Nook was born!

He planned to start small, but because his building was less than half a block from the high school and the kids were allowed off-campus for lunch, his business exploded. He quickly had to hire staff to accommodate the lunchtime rush for his nuggets which then spread into a return crowd for dinner. To free him up to cook, Nug asked his best friend, Kenny, to handle the front of the building (welcoming guests, overseeing the staff at the ordering counter, keeping the interior dining space cleared and clean) as Kenny was a natural and great with people.

The great food coupled with wonderful hospitality only made the customer base grow faster and the natural word-of-mouth promotion went viral. Within the first month, Nug doubled his nugget order from the food supplier and then a month later doubled it again. When he discovered some locally sourced organic chicken options, he switched to these, and his business doubled again.

He offered the traditional BBQ, honey mustard, ranch, and spicy buffalo dipping sauces, but also introduced his own world-famous Nug's Nugget Nook secret sauce. This was made with some mysterious mixture of mayonnaise, ketchup, pepper, and garlic powder which was spiced up with Worcestershire sauce. There may have been additional undisclosed ingredients as no one in town could replicate Nug's secret mixture. The sauce was highly addictive and sublimely delicious. About a third of his customers swore by the secret sauce and some would eat the mixture straight off a spoon.

He offered both regular and extra crispy chicken nuggets in 3, 6, 9, and 12 packs. Sometimes the football players would down 24 or 36 nuggets each! Besides incredible chicken nuggets, Nug opted to only include French fries, shakes and sodas on his menu. No burgers, fish, or tacos (though everyone knew some of his customers took his nuggets home and made their own soft tacos with them). He wasn't interested in offering his customers a quantity of selection, but rather wanted quality of production for a few top-notch items to be his banner.

With the community's love of his business and my new addiction to his nuggets as further support, he had succeeded beyond his wildest dreams.

MESSAGE ON THE TIPSY STEER BAR'S LIGHTED MARQUEE:

Soup of the day: Whiskey

HEADLINE IN THE NUGGET NEWS:

Cougar falls through skylight and eats 72 chicken nuggets:
"I'm glad he left me the secret sauce or I'd be really fuming."

Chapter 4

Makin Bacon

My landlord remained nonresponsive to my repeated messages about what seemed like serious plumbing concerns, though I noticed my deposit and rent check were cashed. I tried to reduce my frustration with extra-long runs up and down the hills of my new neighborhood, but I encountered multiple cats along my route which invoked my feline phobia and caused me to cross the street to stay away from them while trying to calm my breathing and pulse rate. Consequently, running only helped a little bit.

I needed to do something tangible, so I decided to try to get some professional help for my plumbing issues, with or without the involvement of the landlord. A guy at the Fluff and Fold laundromat named Tom suggested I go to SureFlo Plumbing and Fixtures Shop. He said to ask for Makin Bacon and to say he sent me. I thought he was pulling my leg with this odd and amusing name, so I smiled slightly and gave a little huff.

"Nope, no joke. That's his name," responded Tom seriously to counter my disbelief.

I had just stepped into the shop and walked to the counter when a hefty man with thinning hair wearing worn jeans and a work shirt with the name patch "Makin" grabbed my arm with a smile and a quick, "Brace yourself!" just as the door banged open. A middle-aged man in threadbare clothes stepped into the shop, screamed at the top of his lungs, turned twice in a circle, stopped, and looked vacantly around the shop.

"It sure is nice to see you again, Carl," Makin said amiably to the newcomer. "Looks like you got yourself a haircut. You look fine indeed. Thanks for stopping in and be sure to come back again now, you hear."

Carl focused on the speaker, smiled, gave a slight nod, turned, and quietly left.

Seeing the shock on my face, Makin gave a soft laugh, and explained, "That's our Carl."

"Your Carl?"

"Well, not *my* Carl, but *our Carl*, you know Nugget's Carl. He stopped talking eight or nine years ago and wrote the town a note explaining he was abducted by aliens, and they stole all his words. The docs at the V.A. tried to get him on some sort of crazy person pills, but he refused. Then, Tracy down at Pilgrim's Pharmacy, she's Cora Miller's daughter, the one who went to U of A, was smart enough to start calling the medication 'Alien Recovery Tablets' and Carl has been taking them faithfully ever since. He started to shower again and only yells a few times a week now, so they seem to really be helping."

My new town continued to surprise me. Carl was one of several unique Nugget characters I had met in the past week.

"Now what can I do you for? I love to help folks because 'each time you flush a toilet, you put food in my family's mouth'." Makin gave a guffaw.

It seemed like a joke he had used before.

"I have both a small and possibly big problem. Because I've left multiple messages for my landlord and not been able to get any response from him, I thought I would stop in and try to solve the issues myself."

"Well, if your problems link to water or sewage, you have definitely come to the right place. Hit me with your list, little lady."

I smiled at the "little lady" reference as it was an adjective I stopped hearing in sixth grade when I grew taller than all my teachers, could no long find pants long enough or buy shoes where all the rest of my classmates did, and began to hit my head getting into cars. I nodded once, then started to share my repair list.

"Okay. First, my kitchen faucet is leaking badly and the sink drains really slowly, and I don't know how to fix these issues."

"Sister, you got to know Nugget is famous for our hard water. All the minerals make the water taste great, but the deposits are hard on pipes and fixtures. I can swing by this afternoon and fix that for you."

Welcome to Nugget

"My address is…"

"Oh, sweetheart, you don't need to tell me. I heard at church a young woman from Los Angeles moved into the Reynold's old place. Then, at the Rotary luncheon, another person said you're working for the school district as a head shrinker. I also heard at the Roundup Bar about your massive three-legged cat. So, I know where you live, sister."

I still was not accustomed to the lack of anonymity in a small town and blinked while I tried to take this in. Also, how did he know about and why did he assume the gargantuan tufted-ear creature was my cat?

"Now, partner, you said you had a small and a big problem. I'm guessing the leaky faucet is the small challenge?"

"Yes, it is." I recovered enough to smile slightly before continuing. "I also think the sewage pipes may be disconnected under my house. These huge hairy pigs keep breaking into my crawl-space entry at night and then hang out under my house. There is a bad smell coming from there and when I pointed a flashlight under the house, I noticed a lot of moisture and a pipe laying there. Maybe those pigs knocked something lose?"

Laughing, Makin patiently explained the creatures are called javalinas and they're not really pigs, but collared peccary. "More like boars," he added. "Honey, I've been wondering why the hillside coming down from your house looked so green and figured something plumbing-related would come my way eventually." He smiled and nodded.

"Now, I know Evelina Reynold's great nephew inherited her house and he is a notorious skinflint. If the plumbing is disconnected, it could be a large repair and he'll balk at the expense but let me come up and look at what we've got going on. If repairs are needed and he won't pay, we can call Mark over at All State as he insures the property and he will make sure the repair gets done. Mark is one of my Ringtail Cat Lodge brothers." He winked, nodded, and then looked at me knowingly as if this reference meant something.

"So, don't you worry none, we'll get you taken care of. By the way, as a head shrinker, I'm curious if you give out Alien Recovery Tablets?"

I laughed and shook my head, "No, I'm a child psychologist, not a psychiatrist. I don't prescribe any medication. I'm more of a 'feelings doctor' for kids."

"Well, I'll be dipped! The local kids sure could use some help. Glad you decided to come out to our little hamlet. By the way, you being a doctor and all, do you know how a doctor and plumber are both alike?" He paused expectantly waiting for an answer before he finished with a twinkle in his eyes, "They both bury their mistakes!"

He was still chuckling at his own joke as I left the shop.

Later I learned Makin Bacon was the only licensed plumber in a hundred-mile radius, though lots of handymen will help with plumbing issues if needed. Makin had been teased since he was a kid about his unique name. He adored the attention and merriment this produced. In fact, he loved to make people laugh more than anything else in life.

As a young boy, he learned humor could pull his clinically depressed mother out of her doldrums and it could make kids laugh at school which made him popular. He told jokes as a volunteer M.C. for the Christmas Light Parade downtown and as the auctioneer for the annual cattle grower's steer sale. His friends knew he wanted to be a stand-up comedian but couldn't bring himself to leave Nugget. For this reason, his vocation was plumbing, and his avocation was comedy.

Makin's wife, Elizabeth, had grown up being called Betty. When they started dating their senior year of high school, Makin was a lineman on the state champion Nugget High School football team and Betty was the smallest of all the cheerleaders. He started calling her Little Bitty for her diminutive size and because he couldn't help teasing the people he loved. Three years later, he went down on one knee with his grandmother's diamond ring and asked, "Elizabeth Ann Hawkins, will you marry me?" Before she could answer, he added, "And from here forth be known as Bacon Bit?" She laughed and cried simultaneously, said "yes", then kissed the goofball who was now at her height. Amazingly but not surprisingly, he got her to agree to name their kids Eaton Bacon and Lovin Bacon.

The kids did not find this as humorous as their father did.

People all over town smiled just saying the Bacon family names which warmed the cockles of Makin's heart. Additionally, because the monikers were so unbelievable, local folks shared the Bacon names with their family and friends from outside the area. Folks from outside Nugget usually didn't believe the names were true at first and laughed at the silliness of it all, sometimes even referencing the oft repeated urban legend of the Texas twins named Ima and Ura Hogg. However, when they learned the Bacon names were real, their incredulity turned to shock realizing someone purposefully did this to their kids. Some of the folks even had a little admiration for the audacity Makin displayed through his naming.

It also usually included at least a little pity for the poor kids with no choice in the names they were given.

Makin was true to his word and came by later in the afternoon. After a few jokes ("Someone broke into our local police station and stole the toilet. Right now, the police say they have nothing to go on…" and "Why shouldn't you play poker with a plumber? A good flush beats a full house every time"), he fixed my sink faucet and clogged drain in under five minutes and confirmed my suspicion the javalina had disconnected my sewer line. He also called my famously tightwad landlord while still at my house and, as predicted, the skinflint refused to fix the problem, saying this was likely a hoax to con him out of money. He stated he was out of town for several weeks and would ask an elderly neighbor if she would crawl under the house to confirm there actually was a problem. Makin just shook his head, then called his ringtail cat brother, the local insurance agent, as soon as he hung up.

I learned later the elderly neighbor was named Maxine and she was outraged at the audacity of the request and refused on the spot. "Have me crawl under his house? Well, I never!" It took a couple days and threats to call in the Copper County health inspector, but finally the pipes were repaired.

A few days later, I enjoyed a gully washer of a storm that seemed to be over as soon as it started but managed to drop buckets of rain. Earlier, when a guy at the laundromat told me what desert monsoon rainstorms entailed, I thought he was pulling my leg; however, it was true. I loved the temperature dropping, the smell of greasewood, and how refreshed everything seemed just after the rain. This was yet another unexpected joy of my new home.

When the rain stopped, I walked downtown on a now bright and beautiful Saturday morning to pick up some milk and eggs at Jimmy's Dash and Go Market. Before going to the market, I decided to look for a novel in my new favorite hangout, a little independent book shop called "Bound to Please." The shop is in a small brick building tucked into the corner of a tiny courtyard with a fountain and terra cotta planters filled with flowers. When I first discovered the store, it felt serendipitous, like discovering a secret garden of books. Now I felt happy just walking up to the door.

After I selected a new book (Fredrik Backman's "my grandmother asked me to tell you she's sorry"), I couldn't wait to start the book, so I delayed the market for a bit and sat outside the No Doze Café at a small metal table painted bright red and read my book while enjoying an iced mocha. At one point, I looked up and saw the unkempt Carl walking down the sidewalk toward where I was sitting. Remembering Carl was "Nugget's Carl" and starting to feel more at home here, I decided to introduce myself and proudly claim my new Nugget residency.

"Hi, my name's Zoey. I'm new to town. I think you're Carl, right?"

When he took a half step backward, looked deeply concerned at my statement, and seemed worried I knew any personal information about him, I quickly explained, "I was in SureFlo the other day when you came in and Makin told me your name."

I knew Carl would not verbally respond, but habitual courtesy made me pause to give him the opportunity to reply. He didn't.

"Well, I just wanted you to know who I am. Nice meeting you, Carl." I nodded, purposefully averted my eyes to relieve the pressure he appeared to be feeling and reached for my drink before returning to my book.

I didn't see an incremental smile creep across Carl's face as he slowly turned and walked away.

PLAQUE ON MANAGER'S DESK AT THE MINER'S RESERVE BANK:

"The key to savings is to live below your yearnings."

HEADLINE IN THE NUGGET NEWS:

Maxine Edwards' locally famous bicolor gladiolas win top honors at Arizona State Fair

Chapter 5

I Love Your Cat!

"You hoo!"

I had just arrived home and was climbing out of my car with a take-out bag of Nug's Nuggets for dinner. At what sounded like an airy whisper, I looked up to see an elderly woman with a huge smile, waving me down by waggling the fingers of her right hand while her left hand firmly gripped a yellow cane with lime green polka dots. She seemed to be hurrying to get to me.

Dressed in a bright orange sweat suit, the lady appeared about 5'1" and may have been as wide as she was high. Her fly-away hair had a faint blue tinge where it poked out from under a fluorescent pink patterned scarf. Her color scheme was only missing shoulder pads and leggings to fully represent the 1980s. But, more important than her fashion sense, she fairly radiated joie de vivre and good humor. She looked like sunshine in a track suit.

Approaching at what seemed a fast pace for cane-assisted walking, she continued until she stood surprisingly close to me and then rested her hand on my forearm. I realized I was now acting as her anchor and holding her up. She smiled broadly while trying to catch her breath with big gulps of air and then released my forearm long enough to hold up her index finger in a "wait just a minute" gesture and took a half dozen additional gasps.

When she could finally breathe a little easier, she proceeded in a breathy, quiet voice to say, "I've been watching for you and I'm really glad to catch you. I wanted to tell you something important: I just love your cat!"

She smiled and nodded to emphasize her statement while taking a few more gulps of air to offset the breath she invested into that sentence. After this, she seemed to catch her stride and, though her speech was still breathy and quiet, she started a continuous stream of consciousness recital that provided few breaks for my involvement.

"What an absolutely beautiful creature! Those green eyes just slay me. I've never seen such an immense cat and I love his long pointy ears, his little – well, not so little -- tufted toes, and super fluffy tail. It's almost like he's a tail with a cat attached to it." She laughed at the imagery she painted. "He's also so affectionate! He wants to be a part of all I am doing, loves to touch me with his paws or his body, and talks all the time in his little funny way." She paused to catch her breath and smiled and nodded, perhaps expecting I had the same experience?

She then continued, "He's been coming over every afternoon when I take my coffee break and I like to think I'm his safe house of sorts, a place he can come in for a little bit and cool off when the afternoon is scorching hot." She looked at me with a smile and nod. "Your little sugar bug watches 'I Love Lucy' with me from the Turner Broadcasting Network. Do you know about the TBN channel? They show old, classic movies with some of my favorite actors like Marlon Brando and Paul Newman. Ooo, Paul Newman's blue eyes just make me swoon. Do they do that to you? Maybe when you watch 'Cool Hand Luke'?"

Before I could tell her I'd never heard of the movie, she continued joyfully.

"So, any hoo, your sweet angel keeps track of the time and comes over and then starts chattering at my screen door until I open it for him." She seemed both amused and delighted by the cat's attention. "Then he trots right in like he owns the place and sits beside me on the couch. He usually puts one paw or his head on my leg and just purrs and purrs. He rumbles so loudly, even I can hear him!" She giggled at the thought.

"I just love him! What a treasure. Did you train him to do the thing with the door and his paw?" She looked expectantly at me but didn't pause long enough for me to answer.

"We have our little routine. I have my Sanka with 2 sugar cubes in my Viva Las Vegas mug and he has a small saucer of milk. Well, it's more like a shallow little bowl than a saucer, but you get the idea, right?"

She patted my forearm and looked me in the eyes. I managed to quickly smile and nod. "So, I put both of our treats on my TV tray, the harvest gold one from a set I bought with S&H green stamps back in 1977. The old Stop and Shop, it was the former store in the Jimmy's Dash and Go building, gave stamps with purchases and you saved them in a little booklet. Have you ever heard of green stamps?" She looked expectantly at me before giving a shake of her head and looking away while answering her own question. "No, you probably haven't. You're too young to know about green stamps."

This endearing little dynamo was a pleasant surprise, and I had a sense my chicken nuggets might get cold before I could eat them.

"My goodness, your little darling loves his milk. He laps it up lickety split and then is intent to clean his whiskers and face after the treat. He makes me laugh out loud watching him work to keep up his debonair appearance."

"Debonair" was not a word I had ever associated with the giant, long haired, messy, three-legged creature.

"So, yes, what I wanted to say was welcome to Nugget and I love your cat. Thank you for sharing your sweet dumpling with me."

She turned to go and then realized she never introduced herself. "Oh my, where are my manners? I'm so sorry, sweetheart." She patted my arm again. "I am Lucille and I live next door."

Her smile grew even bigger, and she spread her arms suggesting a welcome embrace as she summed up the situation dramatically, "We're neighbors!"

The sun seemed to shine a little brighter and my day immediately improved.

SEEN ON A SIGN BOARD OUTSIDE ROBERTSON'S FLOORING:

The inventor of the doorbell did not own a chihuahua

AS SEEN IN THE NUGGET NEWS:

Cookie dough explodes in woman's underpants while shoplifting: "I will never steal anything with chocolate chips again. They're way too painful."

Chapter 6

Meeting the New Boss

Even though I am not a morning person, I woke up bright and early for my first day of work. The sun was shining, the birds were singing, the air was lightly scented from the palo verde flowers outside my window and the temperature was a perfect 85 degrees. I found myself eager to head to the school district office, meet my co-workers, and begin this new adventure.

I went for a long run through the hills of Nugget and only saw one cat in someone's driveway across the street, so I felt blessed. Upon my return, I was a little confused when I found a pair of men's underwear on the sidewalk outside my home. Then I became a bit alarmed when I realized those had not been there when I left for my run. This concerned me for several reasons. First, who would bring underwear to my house? Second, why would a person be carrying dirty underwear this early in the morning?

I didn't want to leave them there but thought I should get gloves or a paper towel or something to pick them up, so I kicked them to the side of the walkway for now. Knowing my tendency to overthink just about everything, I did not want this little mystery to follow me into my new workplace, so I gave myself permission to let this go and return to it after work. I showered and ate a hearty breakfast of steel cut oats with pecans and apples, lightly sweetened with local mesquite flower honey.

To make a great first impression, I dressed in my new favorite professional outfit of navy pants, a bright pink Tencel blouse, and a beautiful blazer with navy and pink accents. I felt loved as I closed the clasp on the *Mi Amor* gold heart necklace Papa had given me. I looked in the mirror and smiled back at my reflection. Finally, before leaving the house, I reviewed my inspirational quote for the month from

Welcome to Nugget

Catherine of Siena, "Be who God meant you to be and you will set the world on fire." I had carefully copied this thought onto a sticky note before putting it on my refrigerator.

This year, the staff were asked to start a full two weeks before the children came to school to set up classrooms and attend new state-mandated trainings. I knew the campus would be quieter than normal which was fine with me. I was hoping to get a better feel for the schools, meet the staff, and figure out how to best set-up a referral system for children, as well as how to divide my time across all the grades.

I drove a whopping five minutes to get to the other side of town (within the posted speed limits at all times) and easily found parking. This was yet another indication this was NOT Los Angeles. I noticed the parking lot contained giant pick-up trucks and a few SUVs, but no other compact hybrid vehicles like my own. Unlike the big city, these trucks looked like they were used as work trucks, with hay in the back of some and mud-splattered sides for others. Most truck owners I knew in Los Angles were young white collared men wanting to appear manlier as they drove to their office jobs.

None of them owned a horse.

I was 30 minutes earlier than the school superintendent, Mr. Swanson, had said I needed to be there, but being early could only work in my favor so I gathered my brief case and insulated lunch bag, locked my car, and headed into the school district office. I had been in this building for my interviews, so there were no surprises, and I was grateful to see the animated receptionist who had greeted me before when I was waiting for my interview a few months ago.

"Girl, you did it! Umm, umm, umm. Yes, indeed, you got yourself the job!" Her words were accompanied by a look with sparkly eyes, a smile spread ear to ear, and couple of dimples from the depth of the smile. She also moved from behind her desk to give me a big welcoming hug with her brightly colored African-print caftan flowing as she moved.

I liked this little lady who could make me feel loved, respected, and safe with a single look.

"It's good to see you again, Delvinia," I said with sincerity. "I'm pretty excited to get started. I know I am early, so I hope Mr. Swanson is available."

She dropped her voice and quietly relayed, "Now listen up, sugar. There've been a few changes in the past month. Mr. Swanson, bless his sweet little heart, is no longer working here. His wife got a great job teaching out-of-state at the university over in Albuquerque, so he gave notice unexpected like. It took everyone by surprise. This was a couple weeks ago. The school board hired a stranger to fill the position lickety-split." She paused and looked over both shoulders before continuing even quieter. "We think this man is a friend of one of the board members, but he's not from around here, so we're not sure. His name's Dr. Hinman and wouldn't you know he's starting his new job today just like you."

I was surprised by this new development as I had confirmed my employment and first day plans with Mr. Swanson just three weeks earlier. I liked Mr. Swanson and felt he would be a great boss. I wondered what this new person would be like.

Delvinia grabbed my arm and said, "Oh, speak of the devil, guess who's entering the building?"

I heard footsteps and turned to see a tall, thin man in his mid-50's wearing a deep frown. I immediately thought "military." His shoes were polished so shiny you could see your reflection in them, and his gray suit appeared tailored specifically for him. He looked fit, sported an extraordinarily short haircut, and had thick-framed black eyeglasses.

"Good morning," I said.

He didn't reply but stopped and scowled in my general direction.

"My name is Zoey Trost, and this is my first day."

"Are you the psychiatrist, Ms. Trotter?"

"No and yes," I said with a smile. "I think you are referring to me, but I'm actually a child psychologist not a psychiatrist, and my name is Dr. Trost."

He glowered, folded his arms, looked me up and down, took note of my briefcase and lunch bag, then confronted me with a glare as he pointed at the wall clock, "Are you usually this late for work?"

His question shocked me, and I stammered out an "Excuse me?"

He gave a look of disgust and slowly shook his head. I had a feeling I had just failed some sort of test. This surprised me and I tried to recover.

"I believe I'm actually early. Mr. Swanson said to be here at 9:00 am."

"Mr. Swanson does not run this school district, I do," he responded icily. "You will be here ready to start work no later than 8:00 am every day. Not 8:01 or 8:03, but 8:00 o'clock. Is that clear?" he asked sternly.

Yikes! This was not starting well. I replied with the only acceptable answer in this situation, "Yes, sir." While I didn't usually add a "sir" to my answers, it felt appropriate with this person.

He continued to scowl at me and concluded with a "You're dismissed Ms. Trotter" as he turned toward his office door.

I didn't want to speak to him again but needed a little clarification. "Excuse me, sir," I uttered tentatively. "Mr. Swanson told me he would brief me, introduce the staff, and show me where my office is. Will you be doing my orientation or will someone else show me where I will be working?"

He turned back and fixed me with a look of unrestrained hostility. After an uncomfortably long pause, he curled his lip and quietly spat out, "Doctors!" He shook his head dismissively, then met my eyes with an intense stare which broached no challenges. Without breaking eye contact, he ominously warned, "I will be keeping an eye on you, Ms. Trotter, and I WILL take note of your behavior. Be aware I won't tolerate entitlement or insubordination. And, to answer your question, of course I will NOT be doing an 'orientation' for you. My schedule is too demanding for that sort of thing."

He seemed to notice Delvinia for the first time. "You, there. What's your name?"

When I looked over at her, this was a different woman than had greeted me moments earlier. This one appeared unusually calm, radiated a just controlled anger cloaked in professionality, and felt almost dangerous. In my head, I could hear the buzzing of warning you might experience if you approached a hive of Africanized bees.

Delvinia was sitting up ramrod straight and appeared considerably taller than her actual 5'3" height. She lifted her chin and didn't blink when she made eye contact matching the intensity he had just given to me. She replied slowly and emphasized each of her words, "I am Mrs. Delvinia Rogers Standford. I am the district receptionist and executive secretary to the superintendent."

I noticed she did not say "your secretary".

"I have been employed with this school district for 26 years and I will be addressed as Mrs. Standford, SIR."

My eyes bulged, and I think I stopped breathing. I didn't know you could say "sir" in a manner which made it sound like an insult, but she pulled this off while still appearing completely professional. I gave a quick sideways glance over at Dr. Hinman to see if he could feel the insult of this particular "sir." I was growing anxious how the situation might further escalate.

But he was either clueless or aware and didn't care because he replied with a dismissive, "Whatever. You will do whatever is necessary to get Ms. Trotter to earn the obscene salary she found some way of negotiating." This held the insulting suggestion I would not work without close supervision or that I cheated the district by accepting the salary they offered to me.

I also was trying to figure out both what had happened for him to find me so distasteful at a first meeting and how he could be hired into a position of such responsibility if he displayed rudeness of this magnitude. I sometimes find it challenging to turn off my "psychologist" analysis of both people and conversations.

He continued directing Delvinia with, "Also, you will hold all my calls for the morning. That's all." He then entered his office and shut the door firmly.

Delvinia and I slowly turned to look at each other with speechless disbelief.

**MESSAGE ON FRONT WINDOW OF
AL'S SHOE REPAIR:**

We're fully committed to your care:
We'll heel you, save your sole, and
even dye for you

AS READ IN THE NUGGET NEWS:

It's so hot, farmers are feeding ice
to chickens so they won't lay hard
boiled eggs

Chapter 7

The True Boss

Everyone knew Delvinia ran the Nugget Unified School District. From the most recently hired janitor to the staff at the Arizona Department of Education, everyone understood Delvinia was the woman who knew who was who, what was what, where was where, and why was why. As the head driver at the bus barn summarized quietly to me while Delvinia was speaking to another staff member, "She knows where the bodies are buried." Delvinia was intelligent, had excellent social skills, displayed surprising wit, and was graced with a razor-sharp memory.

Last year, the state-elected Superintendent of Public Instruction had contacted Delvinia to consult on a policy impacting rural schools. While she had Delvinia on the phone, she begged her to finish college and then get a graduate degree so she could take over leadership at the local and state level. She also offered Delvinia a job with the state Department of Education at any time if she ever wanted to move to Phoenix explaining, "We will create a position for you if you'll come work here."

What she didn't know was Delvinia was already a few steps past her recommendations. Because she didn't want anyone to treat her differently or to push her into a position she was not ready to take, Delvinia had quietly taken classes and earned her bachelor's degree (with highest honors), but never told anyone except her husband and best friend, Joyce. Now she was enrolled in graduate school finishing up her Master's in Education with a 4.0 grade point average.

I was lucky to have Delvinia introduce me to other team members. In her brightly colored flowing dress and chunky jewelry, she moved through the school grounds with grace. She gave me a tour of the district building and the attached elementary and junior high schools, introduced me to all the staff and many of the children, and reassigned me to a nicer office than had originally been assigned explaining with a huff, "I was told to 'do whatever is necessary' and I find this necessary."

She appeared to love everyone (except maybe Dr. Hinman) and was utterly adored in return. Her smile and laughter felt like gifts, and she seemed to bestow these presents on most of the folks with whom she interacted.

I made appointments with the school principals and then met briefly with the guidance counselors to set up our referral system. We also scheduled individual appointments to talk about their concerns for students with needs kids should be seen first. I was given times to present my services to all the teachers at staff meetings and then set up meetings with the Director of Special Education, the woman starting a new alternative school for the district, and the local juvenile probation officer.

Dr. Hinman glared at me once from a distance, but fortunately didn't interact with me. I found his animosity unsettling and was not sure how to proceed or if I had any culpability related to the tension. Also, his refusal to use my name was something Delvinia and I discussed after she noticed him glaring my way. While I wondered if he had a bad interaction with a personal therapist, Delvinia thought he was trying to establish power over me and others by renaming us – she said he did this to other staff today and not just me. I decided to take her word on this.

I unpacked my play therapy resources and a few important reference books, made sure I had the right password for the computer, and watched Delvinia fast track my name plate so the sign on my door proclaimed this the purview of DR. ZOEY TROST. I think she might have had in mind countering Dr. Hinman's continued refusal to use my correct name or acknowledge my doctorate.

I was grateful she had my back and felt like I had been selected for the winning team by being in her good graces. She reminded me of a G.K. Chesterton quote I had once written into my journal, *"There are no words to express the abyss between isolation and having one ally. It may be conceded to the mathematician that four is twice two. But two is not twice one; two is two thousand times one."*

SEEN ON THE MEAT WITHOUT FEET BAIT SHOP MARQUEE:

It's been a rough week, but I didn't need bail money and I don't have a body count, so it could have been worse.

AS READ IN THE NUGGET NEWS:

After 42 years, 5 kids, 12 grandkids, and 4 greats, couple decide to make it official and tie the knot: "I almost had a heart attack when she finally said 'yes'!" states the new husband. "I never knew my parents weren't married," exclaimed shocked middle-aged daughter.

Chapter 8

Meeting Crispy

Those hairy pig-creatures came back. Dang it, what did Makin call them: Harehenas? Havahollas? Hevalines? Never mind! Tusked boars, I'm going with tusked boars if I'm asked. Anyway, those things came back. They got past the wooden crawl space cover I jerry-rigged, had a party under my rental, and now my house smelled like sewage again. I needed Makin to come back.

With the weather cooling down a bit this week and only in the low 90's, I decided to walk to SureFlo. However, I was surprised to discover another pair of underwear, this time a lacy woman's pair, crumpled on my patio. What the heck? Like I had done with the men's pair, I kicked it out of the main thoroughfare and planned to pick it up with gloves and throw the undies away when I returned home.

As I walked to town, I stopped to take in the view, greeted dogs behind fences, and smelled the flowers. I smiled at neighbors and was pleased when total strangers waved at me as I passed. At one point, I saw Carl in the city park and waved, but he didn't acknowledge me, which was okay given it was Carl.

I was starting to like living in a small town.

The bell hanging over the SureFlo door jingled when I entered, and Makin looked around the corner from his office.

"Hey, Zoey! Glad you came in. My wife, Bit, was talking to me this morning and she says I have two faults: I don't listen and… well, something else." He guffawed and slapped his knee. "What can I do you for, sister?"

"Hey, Makin. I think those hairy pig creatures may have knocked out my sewage pipes again. Do you have time to come check?"

"Well sure I do. How about…" He stopped midsentence and seemed to be thinking or listening or something.

"Oop," Makin said with raised eyebrows, "I sense a Crispy problem coming our way." He looked slightly over his shoulder, and I felt a little nervousness in my stomach.

I stood in the lobby of SureFlo Plumbing and thought of all the random and non-ending litany of plumbing issues I had experienced with my rental house: detached pipes, leaking sewer lines, clogged drains, mineral build up in the pipes, and dripping faucets. During each of those headaches and endless plumbing discussions, I had never heard Makin reference crispiness when talking about my pipes.

"'Crispy'? What's a 'crispy problem'?"

I heard a fast-clacking sound like an experienced journalist working a vintage typewriter. I leaned to my right to try to look around Makin's considerable girth to ascertain what was making this noise. While I was peering behind him, Makin crouched down near the floor as he explained, "No, Zoey, not a 'what', but a 'who'." He stretched out his arms in anticipation as the oddest-looking little creature came sliding around the corner, running at full speed, its tiny nails causing the staccato sound. The small dog leapt into Makin's arms and began to frantically kiss or more accurately, noisily slurp his face and neck.

"Meet my dog, Crispy," Makin said as he tried unsuccessfully to twist and turn his face away from the hyperactive tongue. "Though if you want to use his proper given name, he should be addressed as Sir Crispy Bacon, the Great." Makin laughed.

The little dog's appearance was comical. His physique was slim with long legs like a mini-greyhound, his face looked squashed with bulbous eyes like a French bulldog, he was covered in wrinkles like a Shar-pei, and his wiry fur was darkly marbleized. The little creature was making a bizarre wet huffing sound like an overweight man with congestive heart failure topping out on a flight of stairs.

I had never seen a dog quite like him.

Makin kept the energetic dog behind a swinging half door built into the SureFlo customer counter, but it was obvious the dog was friendly and trying to get to me. He was wagging not just his tail, but the entire back two-thirds of his tiny body.

"Well, hello, Crispy," I said to the comical little pup. The huffing noise increased as the dog began to fairly crackle with anticipation of making my acquaintance.

"May I pet him?" I asked Makin.

"Oh, no, not a good idea," Makin quickly countered. With a frown and while shaking his head, Makin dropped his voice and unhappily explained, "Crispy has a licker problem."

"'Liquor'? Did you say Crispy has a liquor problem?" I said with surprise. I looked at the little dog and noticed his long tongue drooped out the side of his mouth as he continued to breathe both through his mouth and his squashed little nose.

Was the dog drunk?

"Makin, you don't give your dog alcohol, do you?" I asked with disbelief. I thought of all the things Makin might do for a laugh, but I'd never thought he was cruel or destructive. Giving an intoxicating beverage to a dog would constitute canine abuse.

"No, I don't give him anything, this is all his decision. The whole family has tried to work with him on this, Zoey, but he simply can't hold his licker."

"Makin, this is horrible. I've never heard of an alcoholic dog before. Well, I take that back… one of my clients told me she had trained her dog to drink with her when she was at the absolute bottom of her alcoholism." I paused as I remembered this client and her remarkable courage in embracing sobriety, but my recollections of the client and her long ago dog were interrupted by the presence of the very real little dog dancing excitedly in front of me.

"But your dog? My goodness, Makin. It must be dreadful." As I further considered this unlikely situation, my eyes grew wide with horror, and I began to shake my head. "How in the world do you treat canine alcoholism?" I wondered out loud. "I've never heard of a 12-step program for dogs."

"No, I don't know of any either," Makin agreed with a deep look of despair and a continued slow shaking of his head. "He's really bad off, too. Even though I'm not a trained counselor, I think it would definitely be considered an addiction for him."

"Makin, be honest: is he drunk now? Is this why you don't want me to pet him?"

"No, not exactly, Zoey. It's just his licker problem is really out of control, and I don't want him bothering you." Makin looked hopeless when he added, "But if you really want to meet him, well, maybe we might a could give it a try." At this, he slid the bolt and nudged the swinging door open.

With no warning, Crispy catapulted forward with lightning speed and began to lick my sandaled feet, ankles, and shins with a ferocious and desperate commitment. I looked down at him with a horrified fascination. What just happened? Am I really being licked obsessively by a tiny dog straight out of a Dr. Seuss book? How much spit can a little dog generate? How was he moving so quickly? I couldn't even see his little tongue as he slobbered all over my lower legs.

I might have kept looking down, but when I heard a stifled grunt, I looked up to see Makin red with his efforts to not explode in laughter. However, like a suppressed sneeze, he simply could not keep it in and began to laugh so hard he bent over and even slapped his knee while rocking in amusement.

I looked at him incredulously, then slowly looked down again at the little dog lapping the lotion off all the skin he could reach while generating copious volumes of saliva. It was a slow realization, but I finally caught on the "liquor" about which I had been concerned had been "licker" all along. I snorted once at my own gullibility, then slowly shook my head at how I had fallen so completely for Makin's prank.

Moments later, a growing smile began to spread across my face. When I looked up at Makin again, his joy was so contagious I began to giggle. This quickly turned into deep belly laughter. At this point, Makin's glee had grown to the point where he was laughing so hard, he wasn't making any sound and tears were running down his face.

I couldn't fault him: it was funny.

Crispy continued to lick like a demon-possessed ant eater while we shared a moment of silliness and laughed on.

SIGN BY DRIVE-UP WINDOW AT MINER'S RESERVE BANK:

Don't go broke trying to look rich.
Act your wage!

HEADLINE IN THE NUGGET NEWS:

```
55-yo great-grandmother unexpectedly goes
              into labor:
   "I thought it was just indigestion"
```

Chapter 9

I Hate Your Cat!

"You!" shouted an elderly woman from the house directly across the street from my rental.

Her intensity startled me, and I quickly looked behind me to answer my question of "Was she talking to me?"

Almost as if she could hear my thoughts, she shouted, "Yes, you!" pointing a gnarled finger at me while marching quickly over to my car. I had pulled in from work, but not even gathered my briefcase and lunch bag yet. The woman was tall and thin as a bird, wore a gray polyester pants set at least half a century old, and had her white hair twisted up into a large bouffant. I had an image of a stork straight out of a 1950's cartoon and wanted to smile but somehow knew it would not be wise.

"I want to talk to you about your horrible cat!"

Oh, no. Not this again.

I felt I needed to clear the air immediately as she seemed furious, so I quickly explained, "Hold on, he's not my cat."

"Oh, no, you don't, Miss Smarty Pants! You think you can fool an old lady and avoid responsibility by denying you own a cat who is so clearly yours. I won't be duped by a con artist!"

Wow, this was going downhill fast. With dread, I wondered if she knew Dr. Hinman.

I didn't even know her name, but before I could begin an introduction, she proceeded to vehemently outline the cat's offenses.

"Your cat is peeing on my hydrangeas and roses! Your cat dug out my petunias! Your cat tipped over my watering can, flooding my prized geraniums. And, as if to add insult to injury, your cat jumped up and pulled my personals down from the line, then played with them like a toy!"

Personals? Line? What was she talking about? Did she mean something like a personal ad? But what would an ad be doing on a telephone or clothesline?

She saw my look of confusion and dropped her voice to explain, "My intimates." Still not making sense to me, she hissed in an angry whisper, "My underclothes!"

Wait, is she saying the cat stole her underpants?

I was trying to process what she said while recovering emotionally from the shock brought about by this elderly stranger's unexpected and intense attack. The picture of the furry behemoth jumping up to pull underwear off a clothesline was an image I wished I didn't now hold. Underwear and a cat, truthfully? What an odd combination. But then I considered maybe it provided a clue to the mystery underwear and panties I was finding near my house.

In what was becoming a barrage of thoughts, I then shifted to the litany of offenses she accused the feline beast of committing: destruction, flooding, and theft. A picture of mayhem by a creature many other people consider entirely loveable (though not me, of course). The immense amount of damage purportedly inflicted by one cat: was it even possible? Not that I want to ever defend the beast, but could she be giving him a bum rap?

Then I went back again to the odd detail: underwear.

My head flooded with questions: What would a cat do with underwear? How many pairs did he take? Did she get her underwear back or are they still at large? Really now, where would a cat take underwear? Is he a repeat offender? If he truly stole her "personals", has he done this to other people? And most importantly, how do I proceed from here and get away from this angry woman?

Before I could open my mouth, she interjected, "And don't even try to pull off a three-legged 'handicapped cat' excuse!"

I hadn't thought of this fact, but a good defense attorney probably would have gone there immediately.

She shook her head with disbelief as she declared, "Your cat is so long, he can jump higher than any cat with four legs."

Welcome to Nugget

Pointing her gnarled finger at me and using it to emphasize the next sentences, she fairly shouted the next lines. "Keep your cat out of my yard! Lock him up and throw away the key. This will be the only time I let you off the hook so easily, missy."

This was easy?

She then gave a dramatic close by adding, "I will expect full financial recompense for any further damage that creature… no, let's be perfectly clear, YOUR cat does!" She then turned abruptly and stomped off, leaving me stunned.

In a quiet voice heard only by me, I responded, "He's not my cat."

I walked down the hill to get my mail (why did they put my mailbox across the street and down the hill?). Lucille greeted me a few minutes later as I made it back into my yard and said she was at her kitchen window and watched our neighbor marching over to my house earlier. With a little giggle, she stated in her breathy voice, "I hope Maxine wasn't too harsh."

"Hmm, so her name's Maxine?"

"Oh, yes, sweetheart. She's famous in these parts. She can suck the joy out of an ice cream parlor during a birthday party." Lucille laughed appreciatively as if this was some sort of accomplishment. "You know, I don't think I've ever seen her smile or heard her utter a kind word about any person or situation. If they gave such a thing, she could win a crown for negativity." Shaking her head slightly, she added, "Bless her sweet little heart!"

"Well, she was pretty angry at me and accused that darn cat of all sorts of mischief. She didn't give me even a sliver of an opening to say a word in my defense, so I just took her barrage of criticism."

"Oh, sugar, you've just got to know this is all about her and not at all about you. She is one of the soggiest wet blankets I've ever met and that's saying a lot."

"She clearly does not like me, and I didn't even get a chance to give her my name."

"Don't take it personally, sweetie. Maxine is set in her ways, so any change throws her for a loop. I figured she would have a long list of complaints sooner rather than later with any new person who moves into town."

"I feel like I should avoid her from now on," I replied truthfully.

Lucille seemed to think I was joking and laughed in her breathy way.

"Sweetheart, Maxine has had a really hard life." She looked sad as she reflected on all Maxine had survived and shook her head with pity. After a big sigh, she continued, "Actually at every stage of her life things have gone about as bad as they could go, and she's just weathered it all as best as she could. When her mom died, when she had to shelve her own dreams to raise her younger siblings, when she married a handsome con man, and so much more." She looked my way with eyes wide with wonder, "Truly she is a remarkable survivor if you pull back far enough to see the big picture."

In a truly non-Lucille manner, she paused and then spoke more to herself, "I better stop here. I probably shared more than I should've when I remember the pastor's sermon on gossip a few weeks ago." Even more quietly, she concluded, "My goodness, I hope I didn't say too much."

Too much or too little, I found her information insightful. With this background knowledge, there was a slight softening to my perspective, and I could feel myself reconsidering my resentment toward this unpleasant senior citizen. I considered the difficulties this onerous woman had endured and felt a little bit of empathy and compassion toward her, a remarkable shift considering my earlier feelings of intense animosity after being unjustly attacked. All the same, I wasn't going to go out of my way to interact with her. She felt toxic, unpredictable, and draining, like an emotional black hole.

I also realized Lucille was a real treasure, even with her meandering storytelling, and I hoped we might become friends. I thought of a G. K. Chesterton quote stating, "We make our friends, we make our enemies, but God makes our next-door neighbor." I shot a quick arrow prayer up to thank God for Lucille, then I thanked Lucille for sharing the story, explained I really needed to get home, and smiled as I turned to go.

"Of course, you need to get home, sweetie. I bet your precious kitty is eagerly waiting for you and probably ready for his dinner."

I didn't tell her I wasn't feeding the beast and never planned to start.

SIGN AT THE MEAT WITHOUT FEET BAIT SHOP:

If you have a better fish pun,
let minnow.

FROM THE WEEKLY ARREST LOG IN THE NUGGET NEWS:

Smith, Eric Patrick, 33, resides in
Odessa –
Failure to appear/Unlawful possession of
wild javalina/No lights on skateboard.

Chapter 10

The Intruder

As a precautionary measure, I kept my new broom out on my patio in case the giant cat returned and again blocked my front door. I looked for the beast when I ran each morning and, for a little while, saw neither hide nor hair of him. Foolishly I started to relax. Then, two weeks later, I walked into my home, put my briefcase down, tossed my keys on the counter, turned toward my living room, and screamed.

The cat was in my recliner!

I froze. How should I proceed? I could run out of my house, but then what would I do… wait for him to leave? He didn't seem to react when I screamed, except to roll over on his back and stretch lazily. He began to make his rumbly sound, blinked slowly several times, and stretched his toes out revealing his scary-looking claws. Was he trying to threaten me with his display?

When he moved, I noticed several pieces of colored cloth under him. What was he laying on? I peered more intently and finally realized he was resting on several pairs of my underwear! I was so shocked; my outrage overrode my fear. I looked the creature square in the eye and spoke to it, "Now wait a minute, cat. This is going way, way too far. You have no business being in my home, but then messing with my underclothes just adds insult to injury."

He seemed to purr even louder after my admonition and gave a few quiet trills. I couldn't tell if my limit setting might have caused a little remorse, if he felt proud of his actions, or if he just liked the attention I was giving him.

I flashed to my initial interaction with Maxine and her seemingly off-the-wall accusation of the cat stealing her underwear. My disbelief about her statement being true was shifting. I also felt a twinge of empathy realizing how she must have felt when the cat involved himself in such an intimate part of her life.

Something was gnawing at my unconscious and seemed important, so I started to think a bit more: I know I put the underwear in my dirty laundry basket, so how and why did they end up in my recliner? "Wait!" my brain finally screamed as I suddenly realized this situation had to involve more than underwear and a huge terrifying cat.

There had to be a human assisting the cat!

Someone had to be involved to let the cat into my locked house, go through my laundry basket, and move underwear into my living room. If a person came into my locked house, they might still be here!

My brain and body were flooded with adrenaline and all my senses were heightened. I didn't hear anything from the back rooms, but the silence didn't mean the person wasn't lying in wait for me. I needed to get out. I was clear headed enough to grab my phone as I raced past the only-mildly-interested, resting cat to get out of my house. I called 911 and reported an intruder had been in my home and might still be there. I wasn't sure about the presence of another person, but I was sure of my own absolute terror!

Dispatch kept me on the line while radioing an officer. Though it felt like hours, the police car pulled into my driveway in minutes. Officer Jacy Peshlakai got out and introduced himself, then I tried to explain the situation with the cat being in my house and my concerns about a possible intruder. He agreed with my assessment and appeared to take the matter seriously which gave me a modicum of relief (in other words, on a scale of one to ten, my anxiety level went from a ten to a nine).

With a frown and a twitch of his facial muscles, he directed me to step aside, then pulled out his flashlight and unsnapped his gun safety strap before resting his hand on his service revolver. I watched through the window as he systematically checked each room, closet, and under the bed before coming outside to announce the house was clear. With a little embarrassment, I then told him about the underwear being moved. He kept a professional demeanor, but the left corner of his mouth may have moved upward toward a smile. He seemed perplexed by the idea of underwear being an item of focus. He agreed it suggested someone had been inside sometime today.

Officer Peshlakai then carefully walked the entire exterior of the house, looking at the window jams and door frame to see if there was any evidence of someone breaking into the house. Still being highly spooked and not wanting to be alone, I made myself his shadow and followed him every inch of the way. After thorough examination, he told me he found no evidence suggesting breaking and entering.

"Who else has a key to your home? A realtor or a maintenance man, perhaps?"

"No, I don't think so. Well, the landlord has a key, of course. But he lives in Georgia. This was his aunt's house and he recently inherited it, but I don't think he was planning to be in the area as I had to express mail my down payment to him last week at his Atlanta address."

We both paused to think a little more.

"Also, doesn't a service person need to ask permission before entering a residence?" I asked. "I know this was the law in California. Is it the same in Arizona?"

"Yes, it is." He grew quiet as he continued to look around and consider options, "This is curious indeed," he finally added thoughtfully. His comment made me immediately think of the "curiouser and curiouser" comment by Alice in *Alice in Wonderland* and I giggled a bit as I blurted this out, then felt embarrassed about inserting silliness into a serious situation.

Anxiety can have strange effects on my judgment.

We reentered the house together and I pointed out the intruding cat who had continued to relax in my recliner during the officer's site investigation. Officer Peshlakai said it looked like a friendly cat and began to pet the creature who purred appreciatively.

"This is one gorgeous cat! A Maine coon, right? He's huge. I don't think I've ever seen a larger cat in my life."

"I don't know. He's not my cat."

"He's also polydactyl!"

Because I looked confused by this comment, Officer Peshlakai pointed to the beast's front paw resembling a giant mitten. "See the two extra toes he's got? Those are super cool! Ernest Hemmingway loved polydactyls and I've heard half the cats at his former home now have multiple toes."

I didn't know quite what to do with this information but tucked it away in the mental file I was keeping on the beast. Perhaps it would help me figure out eventually if the creature was a cat or not. For me, the jury was still out.

Officer Peshlakai brought me back to the present when he asked, "Do you know how he lost his fourth leg?"

"No, he's not my cat. I don't know anything about him."

"Oh, so he was already missing a leg when he started to hang out with you?"

"Yes, I guess so."

Hang out with me? Is that what the cat was doing? That's a new take on this. However, more importantly to me, it seems like Officer Peshlakai heard this creature was not my cat, so maybe I'm making some progress in setting the record straight.

"Well, he sure seems at home here. Are you sure he's not your cat?"

"Yes!" I replied sharply, then caught myself. I don't care how much stress I was holding; this fine officer did not deserve my ire. I toned down my intensity and continued, "Yes, I'm sure he is not my cat. I don't own a cat and don't want a cat. I don't even like cats," I sputtered at the end.

Why do people keep assuming this is my cat?

"Well, you may not want him, but he appears to want you, so you may be given little say in this matter," he teased while now scratching under the cat's chin and rubbing his belly. The thunderous purr appeared to get even louder with the extra attention. The cat put his paw on the police officer's arm and seemed to knead a bit. "Yes, this is one fine feline," Officer Peshlakai added appreciatively.

"If you like him, you're free to take him home," I suggested hopefully.

"Nah, my wife is allergic. I love cats and would have a whole posse of them if I could."

My mouth started moving before my thoughts could catch up and I blurted out, "A posse of cats is called a stare."

"Well, that's a fitting name," he responded while looking intently at the creature.

While I was kicking myself for blurting out more nonsense, I figured I had little to no pride left, so I might as well ask for help getting the feline out of my domicile.

"Officer Peshlakai, do you mind helping to remove the cat from my house?"

"Not at all," he said as he pulled the huge feline up into his arms. I watched the cat snuggle against his chest, laying its head on his shoulder proprietarily as he carried it gently outside. He gently fingered the cat's extra toes and the creature seemed to like this (of course). I overheard him quietly praising the cat the entire time he held it which elicited even bigger purrs, a few trills, and more snuggling from the beast.

After watching the cat's shameless affection, I started to realize why people think this cat is so fantastic: besides having extra toes and a thunderous purr, the beast is a huge flirt!

SIGN IN THE MEAT CASE AT CASTANEDA'S DELI:

Bacon is duct tape for the kitchen

HEADLINE IN THE NUGGET NEWS:

Man runs out of gas on interstate then sets up camp stove to make pancakes

Chapter 11

My First Client

I got my first referral in the first hour of the first day of school for the students. A seven-year-old second grader named Miguel refused to stay at school if his mother left, insisted he had a headache and stomachache necessitating a return home. Additionally, he threw a loud tantrum both in the classroom and the school hall when Mom twice attempted to leave. After Mom called her work and explained with exasperation her unexpected delay, she and Miguel were escorted to my office by the elementary school vice principal.

The little boy was a chubby cutie pie with big chipmunk cheeks, a well-scrubbed face, hair combed and parted carefully to the right, dark brown eyes, and a serious expression. He appeared to be wearing brand new school clothes: crisp jeans, a nice shirt still showing the fold marks from the package, and bright white shoes. His mom, Estrella, was dressed in the mom-on-the-run uniform of yoga pants and a comfortable t-shirt with slip-on mules. She appeared young, pretty, and utterly exhausted.

After introducing myself, I explained what my role was at the school and then quickly shared with Estrella and Miguel information about confidentiality and its limits (i.e., things are private, except for suspected child abuse, elder abuse, and suicidal or homicidal threats). As Miguel discretely scooched even closer to his mom, I asked them to help me understand what was going on.

Estrella explained Miguel loved school, was an excellent student, and had never had any issues separating from her in preschool, kindergarten, or first grade. She seemed stymied by what was happening today. Miguel was unable to share any insight into what was happening for him to not want to be away from his mom and he wouldn't meet my eyes as he quietly sniffed at the end of what had been a dramatic crying jag. I asked Estrella if anything had changed between the end of the last school year and today.

At this question, Mom revealed Miguel's dad had left the family two months ago and she recently was injured in a car crash necessitating hospitalization for a few days while Miguel and his younger sister stayed at their grandparents' house. When she returned, Miguel refused to sleep in his own room. When she insisted he could not sleep in her bedroom, she said she began to find him sleeping on the floor just outside her bedroom door rather than in his room or bed. She reported he followed her all the time now, even waiting for her when she used the restroom, was constantly trying to be in physical contact with her (she discretely pointed to his thigh glued against her leg), and she felt like a prisoner in her own home with her new lack of privacy.

Using play therapy and art resources, I explored how Miguel felt about the changes at his house and discovered he felt responsible for his dad leaving because he had not done the chores his father wanted him to do on the last day his dad was in the house and his dad had been upset with him just before he left. He also felt responsible for his mother's care because he was now the "man of the house" and believed he had failed to do his duty during his mother's car crash because he was playing at a friend's house and not there to help mom care for his baby sister. He was certain his mother would die or disappear if he did not watch over her and stay near her to protect her.

Mom was shocked to hear how Miguel felt and suddenly had more understanding for why he was shadowing her so closely at home. She tried to lift the inappropriate responsibility he felt for dad leaving and her car crash. They cried together, but Miguel couldn't immediately step out of the role he felt he had to do. We discussed ways to help Miguel manage his anxiety when apart from Mom, ways to slowly separate him from his mom, and ways to reinforce his return to the classroom. I shared various interventions associated with cognitive behavioral therapy and how successful this was to address separation anxiety in children. At this time, I did not tell them a small proportion of kids also required medication to treat the debilitating anxiety which was limiting their existence. We would visit this concept in the future only if necessary.

Because we were already halfway through the school day, I worked with Miguel and his mom on relaxation techniques, then asked Estrella if she could remain at the school until the school release time. She called her boss again and explained what was going on.

After pulling the teacher out of the class for a few minutes to explain the plan, Mom sat for 90 minutes at the back of the class and then 30 minutes outside the classroom where Miguel could see her. We set up a quick reinforcement menu with prizes he could earn by staying in the classroom. These included favorite foods and toys like Transformer vehicles, Buzz Lightyear pencils, bubble gum, Legos, fruit roll-ups, and Pokémon cards. We also discussed an exposure plan for increasing his time away from Mom. Estrella and Miguel would meet with me for a few minutes at the end of the day and for 20 minutes before school tomorrow to implement a more in-depth intervention.

Though anxious, Miguel remained in the classroom for the rest of the day, repeatedly checking to see if his mom remained within sight.

At the end of the day, I heard from four other teachers about crisis situations they felt they had with kids in their classrooms: the kindergartener who refused eye contact and hid under a desk the entire day making animal sounds, two kids who were so hyperkinetic they were on task for less than 5% of the day, and one fourth grader who appeared compressed with sadness. She was silent, withdrawn, and may have been crying during lunch. I set up observation periods for the next day in each of the classrooms and gave three of the teachers some quick intervention ideas they could implement.

I wrote my clinical notes documenting all the work occurring today, as well as notes about the kids for whom teachers had concerns. Then I locked up my records, put away the art supplies, straightened my office, and locked the door. Delvinia saw me down the hall and called me over to her desk.

"Girl, how'd your first day with the kids go? What do you think of your new position?"

I was grateful for her support and responded from the heart, "Wow, Delvinia, I love this work, this place, and these people. I believe

I have a lot to offer the community. This is exactly the reason I got into my profession and, to be honest, I think I may be a good match for this place."

She smiled knowingly and lovingly affirmed, "Yes, sugar. I believe you are."

SIGN POSTED ON THE NUGGET HIGH SCHOOL CALCULUS CLUB BULLETIN BOARD:

Why do we put round pizza in a square box and then cut it in triangles?

HEADLINE IN THE NUGGET NEWS:

Teen high on methamphetamine starts fight with park bench (The bench wins)

Chapter 12

Dinner with a Friend

"Yoo hoo, Zoey!"

It was Lucille waiting at my gate as I drove into my driveway.

"I tried to guess when you would be home and that made me think of all my friends who have been teachers and when they got home. But it was different for each of them, so I wasn't sure what this might mean for you and when you'd get home. Plus, it being the kids' first day, it might be different anyways."

I took a big breath. Lucille could take a while to get to her point, but it was usually worth it to wait out the process.

She continued, "Then I thought I'd just come over and be here to greet you. Of course, your furry hunk immediately came out to make me feel welcome while I waited. He's been the perfect gentleman." She smiled as she pointed to the massive cat rubbing against her polyester sky-blue pants as he made a slalom course of her legs.

All this monologue seemed like a lead-in to a more important matter. After a brief pause, what this was became clear. Lucille's eyes grew wider and then she asked with breathless excitement, "I wanted to come over to hear about your first day with the kids you'll be helping. How did it go?"

Her big smile and eager curiosity made me feel important and loved which was even more a gift following my ongoing interactions with Dr. Hinman and Maxine. Really, how easy it is to make a difference for good in the lives of others.

Before I could answer, she looked over my shoulder and added, "By the way, our mailboxes are the only two down the hill and I like to decorate mine for each season. In honor of your new job, I included yours." She pointed over my shoulder toward the mailboxes. "Our

Welcome to Nugget

boxes now are done up with a fabulous back-to-school theme," she announced proudly, then smiled with satisfaction.

When I first moved in, I had noticed the elaborate patriotic decorations on the mailbox next to mine and now saw both her box and mine were embellished with A, B, Cs and 1, 2, 3s, as well as apples and blackboard cut-outs and actual pieces of chalk taped to the mailbox handles. I wondered how the postal delivery person felt about the new chalky grip.

"Even more important, Zoey, I thought you might like to be treated to dinner to celebrate the real start of your new job," she announced in her breathy voice coupled with an even brighter smile. Her enthusiasm was contagious, and I found I was now looking forward to dinner, something I hadn't even considered until now.

"That's so sweet, Lucille. Thanks. I'd love to join you for dinner." I was touched she kept track of my schedule and important dates which might impact me, grateful for her kindness, and emotionally lighter with her interest in my life. I almost felt a bit teary with her tangible act of love in offering me dinner. "What did you have in mind? Do you need me to bring anything?"

"Oh, no, sugar. I have everything we'll need. All you need do is decide if you want chicken or beef cup-of-noodle. I have both of those choices and plan to compliment them with some nice Jell-O cups, you know, the ones they give out with the Meals on Wheels deliveries." She raised her eyebrows with pleasure and seemed to think I would know what a treat this was. She added, "I can't always eat all they give, so this is from my stash." She gave me a wink like a rebel who is fighting The Man and winning.

"Hmm, sounds delicious, Lucille. Thanks. I think I'll take chicken ramen."

"Will do, buckaroo," she replied cheerfully. "Oh, I almost forgot the best part: I also have the good cookies they sometimes give out when Jimmy's has to clear the shelves of bread and baked goods after they reach their 'sell by' date. Do you know those get marked down and then actually thrown away if not purchased?" She shook her head in frustration before continuing, "What a shame. All that wasted food and just think of all the people who might've benefit from having it. I heard there're people starving to death among the refugees trying to escape war in the Middle East and political dictators in Africa and in lands with drought and floods and such. Boy, we sure do have it good in America, don't we?"

Again, she paused a nanosecond as if I could jump in that quickly with a word. I just smiled and nodded, knowing she needed no encouragement to continue.

"Anyways, before they gotta throw away all those cookies and loaves of bread, and because they're still good and just can't be sold, they bring them to the senior center, and we can take as much as we want for free. No cost at all!" She bounced a little bit and clapped gleefully even while managing to keep her cane close with a wrist strap.

"They buy more of the cheaper type of cookies, you know the generic Oreo style, so we usually get those, but today I got the marshmallow cookies dipped in chocolate. I think they're called Mallomars. Have you had the pleasure of those delicacies?"

I shook my head and knew they were in my future.

"Give me about 20 minutes to get on home and heat up the kettle for our noodles, then come on over to my place."

I nodded and added, "Perfect, Lucille. That will give me time to get out of my work clothes and put my things away."

"By the way, I found two pairs of your panties on the patio. Maybe you dropped them coming back from the laundromat? I put them on your door mat so you could find them easily."

I knew they were not mine and cringed to think of Lucille touching what were now two more pairs of mystery panties and tried to imagine how she bent over to get them with her cane and sizeable stomach. I also realized I was glad they had been women's underwear and not men's, concerned she might think my morals were loose. Finally, I again wondered where these were coming form.

"One more thing, sweetie. Don't forget to bring your little darling."

Fortunately, I didn't have to bring the cat as he happily followed Lucille home to help her with her meal prep. When I came down 20 minutes later, the tea pot had just come to a boil. The overly warm house was brightly lit, and the TV was loudly announcing a quiz show in the next room. Her kitchen table was set for three with brightly colored plastic placemats, plastic plates with desert scenes, mismatched silverware, an assortment of fast-food take-out napkins, and a cheerful plastic flower centerpiece. There was a bowl on one of the place settings for the cat and the other two had Flintstone water glasses.

All in all, it looked great.

Lucille had left her cane at the front door and was using the counter for extra stability as she slowly moved around the kitchen. I was a little worried watching the massive cat shadow her every step as I hoped he wouldn't be a tripping hazard, but she didn't seem to mind and kept talking to him as she worked. When she grabbed the kettle to pour water into the cups of noodles, her barely contained curiosity could be held no longer and she started to ask questions even before moving the cup of noodle Styrofoam containers to the table. "So, tell me all about your day. sweetheart. Are you making lots of friends among the staff? Did you see any clients yet?"

I told her about Delvinia and how the teachers offered me a warm welcome. I also shared how the job started with Dr. Hinman. She asked questions and appeared spitting angry at the disrespect he had shown me and others as she learned more. I had a sense he wouldn't be safe if she and her cane met him in a darkened alley. She knew of Delvinia by reputation and sang her praise concluding "she's worth her weight in gold." She predicted if anyone could put Dr. Hinman in his place and stand up for the staff, it would be her. Lucille seemed particularly tickled to hear my office had been upgraded.

I explained I had seen one client and received several referrals but couldn't share anything about them. After I explained the legal and clinical reasons for confidentiality, she seemed to respect my silence about my clients, particularly in a small town where privacy is next to impossible to maintain. In her eyes, this added an element of mystery to my work, and I felt like I was being given the respect of an international spy or someone who might say, "I could tell you, but then I'd have to shoot you."

We enjoyed our food, and she included the cat in the conversation as we ate and talked. I was surprised he seemed to respond with quiet little trills when she asked him a question and, on two occasions, seemed to point at the milk when he wanted a little more. She praised his clear communication and always rewarded him with not only milk, but a little pat on his head. Each time she touched him, I was appalled to see tiny bits of hair flutter off him and land on the table. I had to look away when I realized how much hair was already on the table and how much the hair on the table bothered me.

I also had a sense we were starting a positive ritual we would repeat often as I explained who the players were, what the drama of the day was, who said and did what, and how the day ended. She made my life sound more exciting than a soap opera and made me feel like a star.

My urgent need to touch base every day with my out-of-state family felt reduced by several notches. This was good.

**SIGN NEAR WATER BOWL OUTSIDE
SUREFLO PLUMBING:**

Water bowl for dogs or really short
people with low standards

AS READ IN THE NUGGET NEWS:

Mayor bucked from stallion and breaks leg
at annual round-up:
"That was a mighty fine horse."

Chapter 13

Starting to Belong

The work of a therapist can be draining and, if not proactive about self-care, the counselor can become vicariously traumatized by the issues experienced by one's clients. For me to stay well and to be effective in the work I loved, I knew I needed physical health, social support, and spiritual food. I also realized my craving for friends my own age was moving toward loneliness and, when I was tired, the loneliness was flirting with depression.

Something unique to me, though, was my pain condition. Once it was "cured" in my childhood, my parents were proactive in pursuing health, researching inflammatory foods or situations that might cause inflammation, and pursuing all means of enhancing the immune system. Even with all these prophylactics, I did have flare ups, usually followed by longer periods of remission. When the pain came, I withdrew from my regular life and stayed home. Because I missed a lot of school, I was set-up by the school district for "home schooling" which involved a lot of quiet reading and reflection. I think this isolation impacted my social development and I grew comfortable being alone, even though I am an extrovert by nature. I also overthink most situations. While I can analyze people and social situations easily as a psychologist, I have been working for years to catch up on my own relational skills and letting things go mentally.

For all these reasons, I tried to proactively pursue wellness.

I ran faithfully and tried to get seven to eight hours of sleep a night for my physical health. I also ate healthfully which wasn't hard. My mom had been a real health nut and raised us with the motto, "Let food be thy medicine or medicine will be thy food." I think it was her rift on something Hippocrates might have said. She served us lots of organic fruits and vegetables, was evangelistic with her opposition to processed foods, and urged us to avoid all prescription drugs. She didn't have to add anything about alcohol or nonprescription drugs as avoiding those went without saying.

Besides my efforts at physical health, I tried to keep up my physical appearance and quickly learned no one in town knew how to cut curly hair and, if you wanted something besides Western wear, most people went into the big city to buy clothing. There are some costs to living in a small town, though the benefits seemed to balance this out. Also, as I was learning from the referrals I received for kids needing services, as Mayberry-like as this little town appeared at first glance, there were darker elements running just below the surface for some families. Small towns are not immune to family dysfunction and mental illness.

For my own emotional and relational health, I tried to connect with other staff at the school, but most of them were married with children and their time was devoted to their families. It was hard to build a new social support system and I really struggled with loneliness for the first few months of moving to Nugget, so my best friend, Sarah, came out from Los Angeles three times to bolster my social reserves. My phone calls with her and with Papa helped keep me grounded as my "over-thinking everything" tendency kicks into high gear when I'm feeling down which tends to make the situation worse.

I also tried to find a church home and visited a half dozen churches in the area, including First Congregational, Ebenezer Baptist, St. Luke's Episcopal, and the Zion Abyssinian African Methodist Episcopal Church. Most were tiny congregations (15-30 people) in large older church buildings, and I was half the age of 90% of the attendees. Even though my faith background was evangelical protestant, I also visited Our Lady of the Hills Catholic and the Church of Jesus Christ of Latter-Day Saints for good measure and to give every church in town a try.

I finally decided to attend First Congregational because there were a couple of younger families there, they planned a potluck after church for the following week, and one young family invited me to go to Nug's Nugget Nook with them after service (yes, I am fully aware I was using chicken nuggets as a tool for spiritual discernment and, no, I don't want to reconsider my decision). It felt good to be with a family again, I liked Kim and John and their three young kids, and I saw a glimmer of hope on the friendship front as Kim seemed like someone with best friend potential. Also, her sharp wit made me laugh hard and often.

Besides church, there weren't a lot of activities for a young single woman in town outside of drinking and karaoke at the local bars. I wasn't comfortable inside bars particularly with the substance abuse work I was doing in the community, so I felt I needed to branch out and try new activities. I looked for community sports leagues and found these were all focused on kids and the only adult league was bowling, but then the bowling lanes shut down two months after I moved to Nugget. I sat in on lectures with the historical society and talks put on by the U.S. Forest Service, went to the rodeo, looked for volunteer opportunities around town, attended every parade and street fair listed, investigated classes at the junior college, and reached out more to my neighbors.

Little breathy-voiced Lucille was my favorite in the neighborhood, and we began to share at least one meal a week, frequently with the cat joining us at her insistence (she continued to set a little plate for him and he had an assigned chair at the table). I could track the passage of each season as she continued to decorate our mailboxes for each holiday. The Back-to-School theme had recently been replaced with a birthday cake and balloon decor when Lucille learned we both had birthdays in September.

It was usually during our dinners that I learned more about her life. She shared stories about her dad's role as Chief Executive Officer of the mine, her beloved nanny, her privileged childhood, the six months long "Grand Tour" of Europe she took with her mother after high school, and her interests in entomology (insects!). She told me about meeting her husband, Milton, and their whirlwind romance, as well as her family's disapproval of him and subsequent shunning when they married because he was both Catholic and Irish. I also heard about their attempts to have children and her two miscarriages. She was an endless fount of stories, and these were always conveyed as long versions with all the tangential thoughts she would include as she recounted an incident.

Invariably, Lucille wanted to hear about work and wanted the latest report on the underwear we suspected was coming from the big cat (she and I both had spotted him on different occasions carrying a pair of underwear in his mouth). Regardless of the identity of the thief, the "underthings bandit" continued to pilfer the neighborhood and bring his loot to my home. So far, none of it appeared to be Lucille's.

Lucille also loved to hear about my life and asked all sorts of questions, chief of which was why I was still single (she and my mother both felt this was a big deal). I told her about past boyfriends and my most recent two years dating and then one year engagement to James Robert Hastings, III, a man whose mother called him James, his Yale fraternity brothers called him Jim Bob, and his friends and I called him Treye (for being the third of the James Robert Hastings). I shared how we met during graduate school at Pepperdine University where I was pursuing my doctorate in psychology and Treye was finishing law school. When she learned how I discovered him being unfaithful to me with one of my best friends, she was hopping mad on my behalf and even stopped watching one of her favorite TV shows, Gunsmoke, for a month because the lead character was played by another man named James.

Lucille was a true friend and beloved companion, even with our 45-year age difference. However, I really missed having friends my age.

Fortunately for me, Kim and John started to invite me to spend time with their family. We were eating at Nug's after church when I mentioned I was heading to the laundromat later in the afternoon to do my wash. When asked why I went there instead of doing my laundry at home, I explained my rental lacked a washer/dryer hook-up. Kim frowned, shook her head, and immediately came to a decision.

"Nope, no more laundromat. From here on out, you bring your clothes to our house and wash them here." We discussed it and I gratefully began doing laundry on Friday night which also allowed me to join their family night. This always included pizza and a Disney movie. My honorary inclusion in family night felt like a tremendous honor and my loneliness started to fade.

As we became even better friends, I started to hang out at their house several times a week, sometimes in the evening after work and frequently on the weekends. I was head-over-heels in love with their little girl, Olivia, and sometimes took all the kids to the park or on a picnic to give Kim a break. The kids were always up for an "adventure" and usually asked me to tell a story or two of growing up in a tent in the rainforest.

I think this family more than anything helped me overcome my homesickness, combat loneliness, and maintain my sanity. But it was more than just these friends. The town became my friend, too.

I loved to spend an hour or two browsing the shelves at Bound to Please, trying to figure out the focus of whatever new section the owner added for the month (i.e., the "Poisoned Pen" section focused on murder mysteries and "Boomerang Books" were reissued best sellers). I could now go into No Doze and ask for "the usual" and the staff there would start working on an iced mocha if it was a hot day or a vanilla latte if it was cooler (in other words, any day under 75 degrees). Most of the checkers and baggers at Jimmy's knew my name and I discovered I could greet them by name now without looking at their name tags. When I saw Carl about town, he would make eye contact about half of the time now when I waved at him. Like the locals, I began salivating just thinking of Nug's secret sauce for his chicken nuggets.

I didn't catch on at first, but then it hit me: I belong. Nugget had become my hometown.

I felt myself relaxing and starting to smile when people waved at me as they drove past, strangers started up a conversation in the parking lot of Jimmy's Market, and the postal delivery woman left me a note alerting me to check the air pressure on my back left tire. My curly hair and how hard it was to cut became a regular topic when I stopped at Gloria Jean's Diva Salon and Boutique.

The cherry on the top was walking home from a trip to No Doze for a latte and having someone in a big truck start honking enthusiastically. I looked around to see who the driver was honking at and realized I was the only person on this section of the street. This, of course, immediately made me nervous because I was taught in Los Angeles to avoid eye contact with strangers when walking or driving.

However, as I was starting to learn, there are few strangers in small towns. When I didn't respond to the honking, the driver pulled over suddenly which terrified me even more until I realized the person jumping out of the truck with a huge smile was Makin. Crispy was in the passenger seat, licking the window.

"Zoey, you have to see my new tattoo! It is awesome!" exclaimed Makin with enthusiasm.

While I tried to get my heart to return to a normal rate, Makin hustled over to me and then quickly bent at his waist. This confused me until he pointed repeatedly to the top of his head and started laughing. Finally, I saw why he was so excited and started to smile. Makin had just gotten a tiny grazing goat permanently tattooed onto the edge of the bald spot on the top of his head. His giggling was contagious, and I started to laugh which only made him laugh harder which made me start to laugh harder until tears came to my eyes. He stood up, slapped his knee, and then did a little victory dance.

"This is totally awesome!" he proclaimed proudly in lingo he must have borrowed from his kids.

I kept smiling and nodded as I wiped the tears from my face and watched him do a little jig on his way back to his truck, kick up his heels, jump back in the truck, pat Crispy on the head, then look back and give me a wink accompanied with a huge grin.

SIGN IN THE BREAK ROOM AT CRUZ AND SONS' FUNERAL HOME (TACTFULLY TAPED WHERE NO CUSTOMER COULD EVER SEE IT, BUT STILL TAKEN DOWN ALMOST IMMEDIATELY BY GRANDMA CRUZ):

*Don't take life so seriously.
It's not like you're going to get out alive.*

AS READ IN THE NUGGET NEWS:

`Odessa teens arrested for selling tickets to heaven`

Chapter 14

Private Investigation

Joyce Humphrey had worked as a lunch lady for 32 years. She enjoyed cooking food for the elementary students, watching them grow up, mentoring a few, and then cooking lunch for their kids, too. One of "her" kids was an intelligent young woman who signed on to be a lunch lady when she graduated high school. Joyce wanted more for her, pointed out how smart she was, and challenged her to go to the local community college while working at the school. When the young woman replied, "Why should I? You're smart and you never went to college," Joyce realized she was right.

She enrolled in Copper County Community College that afternoon.

Joyce had never used a computer before and, while nervous at first, quickly discovered they were fascinating. In fact, though more than twice the age of any of the other students, she started helping the other students when they encountered computer challenges and then surprised all her new college friends by deciding to get a certificate in Information Technology. She spent hours each evening reading about computers, as well as taking them apart and putting them back together. She also discovered she loved exploring the internet.

Joyce heard the staff complaining about Dr. Hinman's rudeness and lack of productivity. This was heightened when she got more information from her best friend, Delvinia. Because of this and her computer proficiency, it was Joyce who stepped up to be a private investigator for the staff.

She did online research and discovered Dr. Patrick Hinman had no training in education and had never worked in a school setting. He had just retired from the Navy after 20 years as a procurement specialist.

He was called into this position by a school board member who used to be his college roommate 28 years previously. They randomly crossed paths and Dr. Hinman happened to mention he recently retired just after the board member had gotten an emergency phone call about the unexpected departure of Mr. Swanson.

While he was more than ready to retire from the Navy and take on the equivalent of a full-time job golfing, his family didn't support his plans. He was quite clear when he explained he didn't want another job and felt his Navy retirement would provide adequate support, but his wife was even clearer when she insisted he work for a few more years to support their twin daughters' graduate school expenses. Medical school and law school tuition were not cheap.

She may have also wanted him out of the house to get a break from his negativity and criticism.

To avoid her persistent nagging, he reluctantly agreed to go to the Nugget School District interview, but he did not plan to get hired. In fact, he did all he could to sabotage the interview, including emphasizing his lack of experience, being short and almost rude to the interviewers, and asking for what he felt were unreachable hiring stipulations. However, his attempts to not get hired didn't work because the Nugget School Board was desperate and, at that point, were just looking for someone with a heartbeat and the appearance of higher education.

When the board agreed to an obscene salary and an unheard of "two years pay if fired" clause in the contract, he reluctantly accepted the position and moved to Nugget with a bad attitude and even worse comments about this tiny mining town in Eastern Arizona. He stayed in town Monday to Thursday and rushed back to the big city as soon as he could on Friday afternoon. He was determined to do as little as possible for a job he didn't want until his daughters finished graduate school in about two years. He then planned to move back "to a real city with a proper golf course" without any undo harassment by his wife or financial responsibility for his adult daughters.

Dr. Hinman did not like children; actually, he didn't like anyone. He preferred to be on his computer rather than interacting face-to-face and would send an email to communicate rather than call or speak directly if he could help it. He refused to hold customary monthly staff meetings or to keep up with the traditional "From the Desk of the Superintendent" newsletter to let the employees, parents, and students know where the school district was heading.

He didn't want this job and planned to do as little as possible while employed.

With his bad attitude and abrupt communication style, he immediately ostracized everyone employed under him and then quickly proved himself a jerk to every person in town as well. He even managed to offend the bartenders at both The Tipsy Steer and the Roundup Bar which, if you think about it, is certainly saying something.

Because he allowed no one to use his first name and insisted he be called "Dr. Hinman" by teachers, car mechanics and restaurant servers alike, his staff and the townspeople quickly began to call him "Dr. Inhuman" or "Dr. Hellman" or more frequently just "Hellman." Of course, this was done behind his back and he appeared unaware. Though he may not have cared one way or the other as he didn't like this town or its' residents and wasn't trying to be liked.

Joyce later learned his PhD was in Military History and entirely unhelpful for his position.

OVERHEARD AT THE NUGGET SENIOR CENTER:

"I think senility will be a fairly smooth transition for me."

AS READ IN THE NUGGET NEWS:

Traffic Stop Results in French Fries: Police tried to stop an intoxicated driver, but he instead entered Nug's drive-through and ordered fries for himself and the police car behind him. "Darn it! When you need fries, you need fries!" [The check-out clerk said he requested extra secret sauce.]

Chapter 15

Helping an Anxious Child

I planned to check in on Miguel who had been doing well at remaining at school during the school day and again focusing on his lessons rather than worrying about his mom. We had implemented a stopgap for him where he wore one of his mom's rings on a string around his neck under his shirt. He could touch this if he needed a little bit of comfort and a tangible reminder of his mom's presence.

I had several new referrals, including a fourth grader named Johnny whose teacher was extremely concerned about his mental state. She wrote in her referral he never smiled, did not play with other kids at recess, rarely spoke, avoided eye contact, and had an exaggerated startle response. He also had dark circles under his eyes and seemed to be always on edge. I planned to check on him today.

However, my plans for the day were sidetracked when the junior high called about four seventh-grade girls who were found cutting their forearms with a razor blade in the bathroom. I went over to the school immediately and most of my day was spent there. I got to my office 15 minutes before the final bell and wanted to at least get a quick look at the fourth grader and introduce myself to him. I had about five minutes in the classroom before the day was done.

When I got to the classroom, Miss Geller quietly pointed out Johnny. He was an extremely thin little boy, wearing worn clothing that appeared a little too short for the pants and too tight for the t-shirt. His clothing was dirty and his tennis shoes had a large hole in the right toe. His hair was a bit long, his face appeared drawn and tense, and is eyes darted around the room assessing the situation constantly.

As the kids were lining up to leave, the little boy seemed acutely aware I was glancing at him and seemed to grow more anxious by the moment. I decided to introduce myself to try to relieve his apparent worry and, with a quick nod from the teacher, gave the little boy a smile and motioned for him to step out of line for a moment so I could speak quietly to him alone.

"Hi. My name is Dr. Trost and I'm a feelings doctor for kids." Upon hearing this, he furrowed his brow and his eyes reflected terror. To reduce his anxiety, I quickly added, "Don't worry, I don't give any shots. I just talk to kids." My words didn't seem to relieve his concerns at all.

"Johnny, your teacher thought you and I might be good friends. I'm hoping we can get to know each other by spending some time playing with the toys in my office. Would you like to do that?"

He didn't respond or look at me, but his eyes widened, his face paled, and he stared at the ground instead of making eye contact.

I was watching him the entire time I spoke and found anxiety radiated off him like heat. His breathing rate increased, and I was worried he might hyperventilate. I had never had a client respond in this extreme manner to my introduction or invitation to work together. This seemed like something bigger than just anxiety, but I hadn't been given all the pieces to the puzzle yet to make sense of it. My gut suggested child abuse of some sort.

Because the class was getting ready to walk to the buses, I suggested Johnny take several big breaths and told him he was free to rejoin his fellow classmates in line. He did so quickly and without a word.

It seemed like my presence stressed him out, so I waited in the hall for his teacher to return to her classroom rather than walk with the class to the bus stop. She came back about 10 minutes later.

"Hey, Dr. Trost. Thanks for checking on Johnny," Miss Geller commented with a small smile. Her look became more serious when she followed with, "What did you think?"

"I can see why you were worried about him. That's one really anxious little boy. I'm glad you caught on to his needs and made a referral for counseling." Even though my words were reinforcing her connection to her kids and resourcefulness, she didn't seem to relax when given this affirmation and her brow furrowed and her mouth tightened as her concern for Johnny showed on her face. She seemed like a sensitive and empathetic teacher.

I knew I needed a lot more information to be able to help Johnny, so I asked Miss Geller, "Do you have any idea what might be causing him so much worry? Has something happened to him or his household? Has he been hurt in some manner?"

"I wondered that myself," she said. "I spoke to both his second and third-grade teachers, and they said he was always quiet, but didn't seem as anxious in their classrooms as he appears to be in mine. I found it interesting neither could identify a single interest for him as he was present but seemed invisible. Last year's teacher didn't have any information about things that might have happened over the summer and said she had no contact with Johnny's father and limited interaction with his mother, someone she described as painfully shy."

"Have you met his parents?"

She shook her head and replied, "No, they didn't come to our 'Welcome to Fourth Grade' introduction night two weeks ago and then didn't respond to my follow-up email."

"I'd really like to get them involved and ask if they have seen any increase in sadness or worry for Johnny. It would be interesting to know if he acts this way in all settings or just at school. I also want to ask if something traumatic happened over the summer. Are you okay if I reach out to them or would you like to be the bridge to connect us?"

"Please let me introduce the idea to them. I really want to build a relationship with them as co-educators of their son. I planned to ask them to come talk to me about my concerns for Johnny and I will try to make this happen in the next few days if possible. At that meeting, I'll let them know I referred Johnny for additional support."

I nodded. "Your plan makes sense, particularly as you try to build an alliance with his parents. Please let me know how I can support you in this process."

We smiled, I offered my hand, and we shook on her plan.

MOTHER OVERHEARD AT JIMMY'S MARKET:

"Don't look at me in that tone of voice!"

AS READ IN THE NUGGET NEWS:

Mother collapses & child calls 911 after unsuccessfully trying to wake her by slapping her with pizza

Chapter 16

Lock Down

After the last bell a few days later, I got an urgent call from the office saying I was needed at Miss Geller's classroom immediately. I left my notes and hurried down the halls.

As I neared her classroom, I could hear an angry man threatening Miss Geller.

"How dare you make accusations about my son! You are just a girl and have no right to treat him like this. I will not allow him to remain at a school that disrespects him and disrespects my family!"

"No, Mr. Canazuela, it's not like that at all!" Miss Geller tried to interject. I rounded the corner and was grateful most of the children were already heading home. It was just Miss Geller, Johnny, and a small, wiry man who appeared to be Johnny's father standing just inside the classroom door. Her facial expression and posture suggested she was feeling intimidated by the man.

To try to defuse the situation and give her a little bit of space to regroup, I smiled and interjected cheerfully, "Hello there. My name's Dr. Trost. May I help in any way?"

Mr. Canazuela looked at me briefly when I first started talking and then angrily looked away and refused to acknowledge my presence. He appeared to grow angrier, and spit was flying when he asked Miss Geller in an even louder voice, "Is this the head shrinker? You said you were going to refer him for counseling, but you already sent my kid to this quack, didn't you?"

As he spoke, he stepped toward Miss Geller leaning in with his chest while forming fists with both hands. HIs posture, coupled with his enraged expression, suggested he was about to explode, and I was worried he might hit Miss Geller or me. During the nanosecond of processing his escalation, I was also aware Johnny appeared to be holding his breath with a terrified expression on his face. He seemed even paler and smaller than he had seemed yesterday.

I think Mr. Canazuela saw Johnny at about the same moment and shifted his rage from Miss Geller (a woman substantially shorter than me) toward his son (a boy substantially shorter than Miss Geller). By comparison, he towered above the child. He reached out his hand and grabbed Johnny by the shoulder, yanking the little boy toward him while saying, "Come on! We're getting out of here."

Johnny appeared paralyzed with fear, and I thought I could suddenly smell urine. My quick professional judgment said it was not safe for him to be going with this enraged adult.

Just as I made that assessment, Mr. Canazuela lowered his voice and became even more menacing when he whispered to Johnny in Spanish, "Sabes lo que has hecho, ¿verdad? Has matado a tu perro. Estarás sosteniendo su correa cuando sea golpeado hasta la muerte y luego iré por ti." (*"You know what you've done, right? You've killed your dog. You'll be holding his leash when he is beaten to death and then I'm coming for you."*)

It was clear he did not think either of the "white girls" standing nearby could understand him and perhaps thought we couldn't hear him make these quiet threats and proclamations.

Unfortunately for him but fortunately for Johnny, I understood.

Before I could think through my actions, I somehow straightened up even taller than normal, stepped toward the little man, and interjected in clear and commanding Spanish, "¡No te detengas!" (*"No! Stop!"*) I watched shock and disbelief pass over the father's face when he caught on I just spoke to him in Spanish.

I then continued in Spanish in a calm manner, but with a steely strength that would not be cowed and explained, "Senor Canazuela, soy un reportero por mandato legal. Eso significa que debo involucrar a los Servicios de Protección Infantil oa la policía cuando sepa de abuso infantil potencial o real. Su intimidación emocional y amenazas de violencia física constituyen abuso. Sus palabras por sí solas son suficientes para que los Servicios de Protección Infantil saquen a Johnny de su hogar." (*"Mr. Canazuela, I'm a legally mandated reporter. That means that I must involve either Child Protective Services or the police when I know* of potential or actual child abuse. Your emotional intimidation and threats of physical violence constitute abuse. Your words alone are enough for Child Protective Services to remove Johnny from your home.")

I watched distress flood his eyes at the mention of the police before rage obliterated his fear. He put his arm roughly around Johnny's neck as he continued to yank the little boy toward the door while commanding, "¡Vamos rápidamente, inmundo pedazo de basura!" ("*Get moving, you filthy piece of trash!*")

As he hurried down the hall, he paused briefly to look over his shoulder at me, narrow his eyes, then simulate firing a gun at me with his fingers as the pistol. I stopped in shock, and he smirked before continuing.

I directed Miss Geller to call for campus security while I called 911. I spoke to the dispatcher as I hurried to the school office where I gave the vice principal a quick summary of what was happening. Because the principal was at an out-of-town meeting and he was acting, he initiated lock down procedures based upon the homicidal threats and called the district office.

The school secretary quickly asked, "What do you need me to do?"

"Get Johnny's address and any information about the parents we can relay to the police.

"I'm on it!"

As she pulled Johnny's student file, I moved to the school's glass entry door and observed Mr. Canezeula use two hands to lift Johnny and then forcibly throw him into the front seat of an older, blue pickup truck with a bashed-in left rear bumper and broken signal light. He then jumped behind the wheel and peeled out of the parking lot, almost hitting a young mother holding the hands of two small children as they walked to her car.

I gave the police dispatcher the vehicle information I had gathered and the address and names the secretary had obtained. She asked for a clear spelling of all the involved staff and a number to reach each of us. I gave her both the school office number and my cell phone number. She said an officer was on the way to the school to take my statement while other units were dispatched to try to find Johnny and his father.

After disconnecting with the police, I felt shell shocked and vibrating with both fear and adrenaline as I walked back into the school office. The office was silent, but full of people with a shocked school secretary, a frightened and shaking Miss Geller, an angry Vice Principal wanting to protect his student and staff, and several other teachers gathering with curiosity at the office door because they could hear the commotion in the hall but weren't sure yet what was happening. The security officer hurried into the office a few seconds later.

"The guy got away with the kid," he reported.

We all knew that.

He then added, "I'm going to patrol the perimeter of the school in case he returns." I thought that was a silly thing to do until I thought about Mr. Canazuela threatening to kill his family and shoot me. Suddenly, his plan didn't seem like over-reacting, and I was grateful for our security guard's military experience.

"Now what?" the Vice Principal asked me.

I wasn't sure what to say as this was a novel situation for me, so I simply stated the little I knew and explained, "The police are sending an officer to take our statements while other units are looking for Johnny and his dad."

At that, we were all quiet for a few seconds before everyone started talking at once. None of us had ever experienced something like this nor been trained specifically for this situation. People were sharing with anyone within ear shot what they had seen and heard in a gushing torrent of adrenaline-fueled energy. Fortunately, two police officers showed up about two minutes later (a period that felt like 20 minutes) and asked people to stop sharing.

The older officer explained, "I know this was traumatic, but we would really appreciate you not sharing your stories with each other until we get your statements first. Sometimes in high stress situations like this, one person's story can become another person's experience and we want to get your testimonies before they are influenced by the accounts of others around you."

This made sense, but it was hard to not keep repeating to ourselves and others what we had just experienced.

The Vice Principal asked the officers, "When will we know if Johnny is safe?" The others in the room quieted quickly, nodded that they also wanted to know, and looked intently at the officers.

The younger one said, "As much as we're able, we'll keep you apprised of the situation as it develops."

We couldn't ask for more and people quietly looked at each other and nodded upon hearing his response.

The two officers conferred quickly and decided the younger officer would go with Miss Geller to look at what was referred to as "the crime scene" and get her statement, while the older officer started taking our statements. The younger officer joined him after about ten minutes. They both pulled out small tape recorders and asked for private space to interview. The Vice Principal gave up his office and opened the principal's office for the younger officer after he finished at Miss Geller's classroom.

While they interviewed us, their police radios were giving steady updates, but in police code so none of us could figure out what was happening. At one point, the older officer pulled out his cell phone and conferred with someone on the other line. He was taking my statement at the time, and I asked if he had any updates which could be shared with the team. He nodded assent, then opened the principal's door, knocked on the door of the vice principal's office and indicated to the other officer through the window for the door to be opened. Once this happened, he began to talk while the waiting staff crowded into the main office.

"The suspect's vehicle has been found abandoned in a ditch. We have one team staking out the Canazuela home in case they go there and several other teams looking for Johnny and his dad on foot. Both the Highway Patrol and Sheriff's Office have sent officers to assist."

When it was clear he had no more to say, the staff started to excitedly talk with each other about this development and what it might mean. The more optimistic on the team interpreted them on foot as meaning they couldn't go far while the more pessimistic staff felt this meant it would be harder to track them down. With the amount of fear each of us was carrying, all argued like their opinion was fact.

The officer came back into the principal's office, closed the door, and finished taking my statement. He then had several questions I answered as well as I could.

Most of the statements had been finished among the staff when the police radios squawked another coded message. Whatever this was, it brought the older and younger officers out of their smaller offices on the run as they headed to their car.

"Wait! What happened?" yelled the Vice Principal to their departing forms.

"Johnny's been found in an empty lot on Seventh Street. He's injured and an ambulance is on the way. Someone, we believe it is the suspect, shot a police officer. Now all hands are on deck to find the assailant."

They got into their squad car and peeled out with the lights on and siren blaring.

We regrouped in the office and tried to figure out what to do next. I wanted to go to the small local hospital, assuming that is where they would take Johnny. However, other staff suggested I should not be near the child or alone until the suspect had been apprehended. This was logical, but frustrating as I wanted to act or do something, not wait stewing in my fear. The vice principal called police dispatch asking if we were free to leave the school. She must have paged the officers who did our interviews because she got back on the line quickly and said we could leave. As I prepared to head home, Delvinia burst in with a worried expression and everyone stopped what they were doing as she carried an aura of authority and professionalism. She started speaking to me first.

"Zoey, are you okay? What's happening here?"

I filled her in, and she asked several good questions. She said the first responders were looking after Johnny and her focus was on safety for the team and the other students. She praised the vice principal for his quick thinking and implementation of lock down procedures and then discussed further safety strategies with him. Delvinia also stated neither Miss Geller nor I would be going home alone. She offered her house to both of us, but one of Miss Geller's friends said she could stay with her instead. That left only me.

"You leave your car here, Zoey, and come with me in my truck," Delvinia directed. "I don't want you alone, even in your vehicle, until that man is found. I'll bring you back for your car when the risk has passed."

I didn't question her instructions and felt immense relief a competent, caring person was making decisions with my best interests in mind. It felt like I had been holding my breath for 90 minutes and I could finally breathe again.

OVERHEARD AT THE NUGGET SENIOR CENTER:

"Whenever I'm sad, I just think about how the Welsh word for microwave is 'popty ping'."

AS READ IN THE NUGGET NEWS:

Nugget Fire Fighters Wash Cars Outside Nug's As Fundraiser for Local Boy with Leukemia

Chapter 17

Checking In

When I was safely at Delvinia's house, I was still on an adrenaline high and found myself pacing in her living room. She made us each a cup of herbal tea, asked her husband if he could handle the dinner arrangements, and then just let me walk as long as I needed to do so. I didn't tell her I could feel my muscles tightening, a precursor for my pain disorder, but tried to focus on my breathing to relax my body and walking to keep my muscles from locking up.

Delvinia told me she had several phone calls she needed to make to check on the unfolding drama and to communicate with the school board and that made me think about my phone. I wondered if either Kim or Lucille had heard anything about what was happening. I decided to be proactive and reach out to both.

Unfortunately, when I pulled out my phone, I realized it was on silent. I had no calls from Kim, but over a dozen from Lucille. I decided to call her first.

When Lucille answered, she was in a bit of a panic, so I was glad I rung her first.

"What's going on, Zoey? Are you okay?" Lucille's breathlessness was pronounced, so I knew she was concerned. "I've been calling and calling, but nothing. I heard it was something with a gun and a psychologist, so I knew it had to involve you. I've been so terribly worried!"

And with that she started to cry.

"I'm so sorry, Lucille," I said sincerely. "Thank you for looking out for me and I'm really sorry you were worried." I heard her harumph in the background and felt I needed to give her a bit more detail. "I was trying to help a threatened child be safe, then working with the police, and then Delvinia came to get me and took me to her house. I didn't realize my ringer was off until just now."

"Well, you hear about school shootings and then I watch CSI, that crime scene investigation show, and there's so much violence in the world and there's just so many guns around now. Things can be scary and unpredictable." I heard fear and frustration and impotence all wrapped together in her voice.

"You need to let me know sooner if this happens again!" she commanded angrily.

I think she could get mad at me now since she knew I was okay.

"I hope this never happens again or anything like it, Lucille," I answered honestly, "but, if it does, I promise to check in with you sooner in the future." My pledge placated her, but I could still hear her breathing heavily. I thought I better talk a bit more to give her a chance to catch her breath and because I really wanted her to know more about what was happening to help her understand my failure to check in. I also found focusing on Lucille right now helped lessen my fears and loosened up my body a little bit.

"It's been awful. A scary man threatened to kill a child and then threatened to shoot me. Now a little boy is hurt, and a police officer has been shot. Law enforcement is actively seeking the shooter, but he's not been caught. This situation needs so much prayer, Lucille."

"I have been praying, Zoey. Praying like nobody's business."

I knew she was speaking the truth and I couldn't think of another person, except perhaps my papa and mother, who would pray harder for me.

She then added, "I'm also taking matters into my own hands to help the Almighty. I have a .357 magnum loaded and within reach. I pulled out my bathrobe tie so I could strap the gun to my waist to be ready to defend you and your home. However, the gun kept falling out which probably wasn't the best with it being loaded and all."

"Did you have the safety off?" I asked with concern.

"Of course I did! How can I defend us if I can't shoot?" she asked with disbelief I would even ask such a silly question. "Anyways, I shifted and took some of the plastic grocery bags I got from Jimmy's Market, doubled bagged two of them for a little extra strength, put the gun in the bag, and hung it on my walker handle." She sounded proud of her solution and, though likely slow on the draw, I knew she'd shoot to kill. She assured me of this when she said, "You don't have to worry at all, Zoey. I am watching out for you, your cat, your house, my house, and our neighborhood, too."

I could just imagine her with the bathrobe tie and then the Grab and Go shopping bags on her walker. With sudden clarity, I realized a holster might make a great Christmas gift. Also, I would need to call before I go to her house over the next few days.

"By the way, I also went up and told Maxine what was going on. She has an arsenal up there and I bet you didn't know that in addition to being an award-winning gardener, she's also one of the best marksmen in town."

"Maxine's a marksman?" I asked with disbelief, then kept processing what Lucille said, "She has an arsenal? Really?"

"You've heard of the NRA, the National Rifle Association? She's won so many of the NRA's Turkey Shoots they asked her to not compete any longer to give someone else a chance. But this is Maxine, so she wasn't going to let anyone, especially some good ol' boys, tell her she couldn't shoot with the rest of town," Lucille chuckled as she remembered the incident. "She offered to take off her high-powered scope which made them feel like the others with their scopes stood a chance. But wait until you hear this, she got an even higher score that year and won again even without the scope! Isn't that amazing?" I could tell Lucille was amazed and, to be honest, I was impressed, too.

Lucille continued with her story, "So the Nugget NRA board had to get creative, and you know what they did? They changed their club bylaws so officers were forbidden from competing in NRA shooting contests and then voted Maxine in as their secretary." Lucille had enough breath back she could belly laugh at the image of dour Maxine dutifully attending all the NRA meetings with a pen and notepad.

"Any hoo, she's armed to the teeth now. She loaded up a bunch of firearms and has the pistols at hand and rifles leaning against most of her door jams. I was impressed as I watched her strategically prepare for potential armed conflict." Lucille relayed this information like it was reassuring, but I was still trying to take it all in.

"If there's a crisis, you always want Maxine on your side," Lucille advised.

I believed her.

"Oh, I almost forgot. She offered to loan you a spare if you don't have your own gun." Lucille then dropped her voice a bit as if she was embarrassed to relay the next sentence, "She thought you might be the type of person to not have a firearm." After getting this distasteful statement out of the way, she bounced back to her regular good humor, "Now that's downright neighborly, don't you think?"

I was shocked. No, I did not have a gun and, with my family history of both a great-grandmother and an uncle committing suicide using guns, I did not want a gun in my house. However, now was not the time to discuss this.

I wanted to get off the phone and tried to close the conversation with, "Lucille, I'm calling to let you know I am safe. I'm sorry I missed your calls and I appreciate all you're doing to keep our neighborhood safe. I'm at Delvinia's house now and will probably stay here until they catch the bad guy."

"Thanks for letting me know, sweetheart. Oh, one more thing, I have your cat at my house and will keep him here tonight, so don't you worry at all about him."

I hadn't even considered the cat.

My next call was to Kim. She had not heard about what was happening.

"Tucker has had projectile vomiting for the past six hours. I've not been aware of anything besides puke."

"Well, there was a threat against a child, I tried to intervene, the father became enraged and said he was going to hurt the child and me, and then the police were involved. But I wanted to let you know I was okay."

"Is the threat still active? Do I need to keep my kids home tomorrow?"

"The police are actively looking for the suspect. If they've not found him by tomorrow, I bet classes will be cancelled."

"Which kid, Zoey?" Kim asked with concern.

"I'm sorry, Kim, I can't legally reveal that. But you'll probably hear the name around the community in no time flat."

"I'm glad you're okay, Zoey. Sorry to be out of the loop."

I later learned Johnny had been in Gunnar's first grade class a few years ago. They knew each other and Gunnar had included him in his class-wide birthday party invitation, but Johnny did not socialize much in school and went nowhere outside of school that Kim was aware.

Mr. Canazuela wasn't apprehended until 2 am after a brief shootout with several officers, but no one else was hit. Officer Peshlakai had been the law enforcement officer hit by his earlier shot, but fortunately, the bullet mostly grazed his upper left arm. When Mr. Canazuela was taken down, he was still holding his firearm, but was out of ammunition. Several officers speculated he was trying to get shot in a "suicide by cop" manner rather than captured.

Because the police chief had received a courtesy notification by the federal Drug Enforcement Administration a few months prior that they were conducting an undercover investigation of Mr. Canazuela, they were notified as the manhunt was underway and they sent officers for support. By the time he was apprehended, the DEA had been assisting in the operation for about five hours and they took the suspect into federal custody.

Over the next few days all sorts of information came out. First and most importantly, we learned Johnny had facial injuries, a broken arm and rib, and a closed head injury after being beaten senseless by his father. His brain swelling put him in critical condition and he had been flown almost immediately to the trauma unit at Phoenix Children's Hospital.

We also learned Mr. Canazuela was involved in the Sinaloa Cartel and he was primarily responsible for overseeing the movement of drugs between Mexico and Canada. He was using Indian reservations whenever possible to hopscotch north to Canada to keep the bulk of the drugs in sparsely populated areas with smaller police forces. It was ingenious, but also scary. Who would have imagined an international drug cartel would have an operative in a tiny town like Nugget?

We also learned he was extremely abusive toward his wife, Johnny, and the other children in the home. However, because Johnny was the oldest child, he tried to protect his mother and his younger siblings which made him a greater target for his father. The FBI revealed Johnny had extensive prior injuries (like bruising, broken bones, burns, and lacerations) in various stages of healing which indicated he had been suffering abuse for a long time. I was heartbroken for the child, but also encouraged by how much of a survivor he had already proven to be. I prayed he would make it through the grievous injuries he had just endured.

MESSAGE ON THE TIPSY STEER BAR'S LIGHTED MARQUEE:

Nothing says "I mean business" more than a shopping cart in a liquor store

AS READ IN THE NUGGET NEWS:

Officer Peshlakai Released from Hospital: Chief exclaims, "It's folks like Jacy that bring honor to law enforcement"

Chapter 18

Hinman Makes Enemies

As I usually do with any case referred to me that takes a dramatic turn, I reviewed it carefully to see if I could have done anything differently to catch on to Johnny's abuse sooner or to prevent further injury. While I suspected abuse with the amount of anxiety the child displayed when he met me, there were no visible injuries, and I didn't have anything tangible to report. I had hoped to query for this when I started working with the little boy. It was hard to not feel slightly responsible when child abuse is my area of expertise.

Dr. Hinman made it worse by insinuating something to this effect at a staff meeting the next day. "Ms. Trotter is specifically trained in this area and could have stopped this, but she did not," he said to the entire team. Then he zeroed in on me and said, "I've learned you had a referral and did nothing. You could have intervened, but instead your dereliction of duty made this happen and a child is facing permanent brain damage because of you," he almost smirked with his last statement.

Miss Geller and the vice principal angrily jumped to my defense and shared how things actually played out. They spoke to my professionalism and lauded my ability to stand up to this dangerous man while trying to help Johnny. I saw people shooting hate stares at Dr. Hinman as they were talking, but he didn't seem to be listening to anyone else as he had already created his own "story" and he wasn't going to be swayed by the truth.

It was still hard to not take some of this to heart as a failing on my part, even though I knew his position was totally bogus. I think if I believed I had some control or could have done something different, I would feel like I could prevent this from happening in the future and

Welcome to Nugget

this would help quell some of the fear I was still carrying about the incident.

I also considered whether I should stay in this job with the leadership not only firmly against me, but also virulently attacking and undermining my credibility. I don't care how outrageous a lie, if it is told often enough, it begins to smack of truth. Also, if you're going to lie, the more outlandish the better because it will catch people's attention and they will keep thinking about it.

However, as I considered quitting, I was stopped by Miss Geller. She pulled me aside and still appeared angry at Dr. Hinman. "Dr. Trost, do you have a minute?"

"Sure, and thanks for speaking up for me in there, Miss Geller."

"Please call me Amy."

"Thanks, I'm Zoey."

"I just wanted to share something you may or may not know," she looked at me for permission and I nodded.

"I am Jewish and my grandmother shared her outrage about the atrocities of the Holocaust, as well as her admiration and gratitude for those courageous enough to stand up against evil. One saying she taught us kids was 'If you save one life, it's as if you've saved the whole world.' This is a longstanding Jewish tradition, but it applies to more than just Jews."

She stopped again to see my reaction and I nodded, still listening to her.

"I don't care how obnoxious Hinman may be, his opinion is not the truth. What you did with Johnny was save a life. Please know how important your actions are and how impactful your courage is to him and all of us."

I was shocked and a little teary. I didn't know how to respond.

She didn't wait for a response, but added, "Zoey, I admire you and am grateful you stepped in." With that, she grabbed me for a quick hug before turning to leave.

When Delvinia heard about Dr. Hinman's caustic accusation, she was angrier than I've ever seen her. Her body quivered with rage and her pupils dilated.

"That cowardly excuse for a man didn't have the decency to show up at the school while this event was unfolding and did nothing to assist the staff or ensure students were safe. Later, his moral decrepitude was highlighted when he lied to the school board saying he was leading throughout the experience. Now he has the audacity to try to undermine you. Oh, heck no!" She was sputtering in anger and her dark face grew darker with emotion. "He thinks he can throw you under the bus to deflect attention away from his own complete failure as a leader and a human being. Well, Zoey, know this for a fact: he threw more than a person under the bus. He just threw a match in his own powder barrel to bring about his occupational demise."

Delvinia's professionalism was legendary, but she was so angry, I wondered if she could hold it together. I felt she might go looking for Dr. Hinman immediately to confront him publicly for his cowardice and lies, particularly as she stepped into the role he should have had to monitor the situation, check on the staff, and report to the school board. Fortunately, her friend, Joyce, joined us at that moment and could see how angry Delvinia was and stepped in to talk her down.

She put her left hand on her hip and with her right hand she emphasized her opinions, "Honey, that man is as useful as a turd floating in a punchbowl and as intelligent as your average bowling ball. Del, he is not worth confronting and, besides, we both know he won't listen or change anyway."

Delvinia valued Joyce's opinions and knew she loved her. They had been best friends since second grade and were now closer than two coats of paint. Their families used to socialize regularly, especially with both of their dads being the only black men employed at the mine in the 1960's and 1970's. Their dads and their families had endured regular prejudice, supported each other through life challenges, and managed to thrive despite the opposition they withstood.

Delvinia knew Joyce had her back in all situations, so she could speak to a place in Delvinia' heart. At Joyce's admonition, she reluctantly agreed, "You're right, Jojo. You're right."

"Ummm, I'm going to just savor your last statement for a moment," Joyce said as she closed her eye and tilted her face toward the heavens. "Okay, that was nice," she added before jumping back into the situation at hand. "Del, you are the smartest woman I know. Go at this strategically. This is war, girl. War!"

"Um hm," Delvinia nodded as she considered her friend's words. Her brain was processing information so fast, I expected smoke to come out of her ears. You could see when she landed on her plan of attack as her face relaxed slightly, her tense shoulders dropped, and she gave one decisive nod.

"I'm going to the school board," she said with resolve. "I'll write things up, testify at a meeting, or whatever else they need. This has gone on long enough and that bully needs to be stopped."

"That sounds good, Del. In the meantime, don't you have like a kajillion hours of sick leave? Why don't you head home to cool down a bit before you cross paths with that whackadoodle? Besides, with how much he depends on you to do his job, that would be greater punishment for him today than anything you might say to him or about him."

"You're right, Jojo. I have over a thousand sick leave hours. Maybe it's time I use a few."

We all nodded at the wisdom of this plan.

As Delvinia gathered her purse, she muttered to herself, "That dipstick will need to answer his own phone and possibly do a little work for a change."

She then strode quickly and confidently to her truck.

GRAFFITI IN ALLEY OFF MAIN STREET:

Didn't go to the gym today, but the cashier at Nug's was named Jim, so I was close.

AS READ IN THE NUGGET NEWS:

"Tom Johnson, who asked to remain anonymous, gave the police a detailed description of the suspect."

Chapter 19

Maintaining Sanity

Kim became both my best friend and a great sounding board for my small-town experiences. Besides spending time with her family, sharing meals, and going out each month to get manicures and/or pedicures, we made a point to talk in person or by phone each day. We shared our daily experiences, offered opinions about current events, revealed our life passions, and – most importantly – kept each other up on our family relations.

It turned out Kim had a mother-in-law from hell who fit every negative MIL stereotype on the books.

Marge Winthrop was a woman who valued appearance, propriety, and public opinion. She had a privileged upbringing, attended a prestigious college, and married a banker. Besides the respect from his employment, Hal Winthrop was also an elected official, president of the Rotary Club, and involved in many charities. Marge was proud of his accomplishments and spoke of these frequently among her friends at church and the local country club where she visited daily to either swim or play tennis. Physical appearance and fitness always have been important to Marge.

Marge lacked tact and probably wouldn't have seen the necessity for it if confronted about its absence. She knew she had a lot of wisdom to share and so many people made wrong decisions when lacking direction. She believed she was always right and, if anyone dare challenge her position, she simply grew louder until they came to their senses. Truly the world was a better place when gifted with her continually expressed opinions.

Because Kim was not her birth child, Marge knew she would have a lot of correcting to do to bring her in line with Winthrop standards which, though high, were expected of all family members. Marge felt the standards were particularly important to enforce for people like Kim, an interloper who snuck into the family through marriage. Marge harangued Kim about her weight, criticized her parenting style, and even objected to the number of children she and John had. Marge was always disparaging about the state of cleanliness for her house, the types of food she fed her children, her fashion selections, and even the music she listened to. There was no area of life Kim was doing correctly, per Marge.

As I heard additional stories of Kim's interactions with Marge, I grew angrier at Marge's behavior and amazed at how much hurt one person can cause. I was also impressed with how longsuffering and patient Kim could be toward her insufferable mother-in-law. After a few interactions of my own with Marge, I grew even more impressed with how calmly and respectfully Kim interacted with Marge, even as she taxed her patience daily both at home and in the community.

After surviving one of her visits, Kim and I recovered in her den with glasses of wine. I was so impressed with her tolerance I asked her, "A lesser woman would have blown her top at Marge, but you were kind. I wasn't even the focus of her ire, and I was ready to push her off a tall cliff with a short rope. How do you remain patient with her?"

Kim replied serenely, "I do yoga to relieve stress."

John was passing her chair when she said this and he stopped short, guffawed, turned his head toward her, and gave her an incredulous look. Kim saw his expression, sighed, and slowly shook her head. She knew her gig was up.

"Just kidding, I drink wine in yoga pants," she reported quietly and more honestly. "Though I did try yoga once," she added in her own defense while looking pointedly at John.

John smiled, leaned over her chair, and kissed her forehead. "You're my rock star," he whispered and then went to his office to play Minecraft, his own version of mother decompression.

As we kept talking and poured a second glass of wine, Kim shared several sayings from her mom she had put up on her bathroom mirror. She said she frequently reviewed these words internally during interactions with Marge. These included wisdom like, "You don't have

Welcome to Nugget

to attend every argument you're invited to", "She hates me simply because he loves me," and "Your mood should not dictate your manners." Kim added a saying of her own, "I am thankful for all the difficult people in my life as they have shown me exactly who I do not want to be."

As we poured another glass of wine, Kim shared her other stress management strategies which included talking with me, watching The British Baking Show, yelling at the top of her lungs when driving alone on the freeway, and exercising her newly acquired hobby of knife-throwing. She invited me to try her new sport, so we headed to the back yard.

She had put up a big 4' by 8' piece of plywood in the back yard with concentric circles drawn as a target. I tried chucking the throwing knives and found it both surprisingly satisfying and more difficult than I expected. I only got one of six throws to stick. My inexperience coupled with the wine probably didn't help and may have played a part when one of the knives bounced off the wood and barely missed impaling Kim's thigh. We didn't have to say a word, just looked at each other, collected the knives, and then headed inside.

One other coping strategy Kim occasionally used was a well-timed act of subtle rebellion by doing something she knew would drive Marge batty. While some would call these actions "passive aggressive", she called them "maintaining my sanity." This is what motivated her and John to plan their engagement party at Nug's Nugget Nook and not the Country Club (Marge had a conniption) and the time she used an empty Hershey's chocolate syrup bottle as her water canteen when the Winthrop's participated in a walk-a-thon at the Country Club.

She shared the satisfaction of seeing Marge's exasperation in one of these thoughtfully planned "acts of thoughtlessness" could last her months.

AS OVERHEARD AT THE NUGGET LAUNDROMAT:

"The divorce rate among socks is absolutely ridiculous"

AS READ IN THE NUGGET NEWS:

According to a recent survey, 100% of people are willing to answer surveys.

Chapter 20

Maxine

Despite the stress of the last few days, today had been a good 8-hours of work. Miguel's mother stopped me when she was dropping him off at school to thank me for continuing to meet with her son and to tell me he was doing much better now. She said his father had moved back home which helped Miguel, though she now had to figure out how or if she wanted to repair their relationship after his infidelity. I knew she could handle this and told her so. She gave a tired smile but seemed to be sitting up straighter as she drove out of the school parking lot.

I was able to help a fourth-grade girl who had been traumatized by a car crash she was in recently, then checked in with a depressed sixth grade boy who was grieving the death of his dog. I was glad to hear he was finally sleeping and eating regularly. I did two classroom observations for teachers concerned about specific students and helped craft interventions for a profoundly autistic kindergartener at a district Individualized Education Plan meeting. I tried to get updated information on Johnny, but no one knew anything new.

At the end of the day, I gave an in-service to the junior high staff about making sense of self-injurious behavior and responding to a few of the girls who were cutting. While not a topic which would get me invited to a cocktail party, it was still important information about a hard to think about topic and one not a lot of people had studied. I tried to outline the ways self-injurious behavior was radically different from suicide and how our responses to each of these situations are important and different.

I find this topic brings out a visceral response for many people and can elicit anger toward the kids who are hurting themselves with what seems like needless corporal injury. I find it helps when school staff understand cutting as a way to cope when feeling overwhelming pain and a strategy to gain control when feeling powerless to stop the pain. By cutting, a person can localize the pain to one spot, the place being cut, and exert self-control over the intensity, duration, and depth of pain. I shared alternative ways to give kids more affirming ways to be in control of their lives and to handle emotional pain. Several teachers thanked me profusely for the information and tangible suggestions for responding in these situations.

As I headed home, I noticed Lucille had transformed our mailboxes from the birthday ensemble to a Halloween focus with the boxes now resembling jack-o-lanterns with the opening to the box lined up where the mouth would be. It was sweet.

I was whistling a cheerful little tune as I gathered my things from my car and stopped to get my mail. However, the music stopped abruptly with the insertion of Maxine Edward's pervasive negativity and criticism.

"You there, stop!" she commanded with authority. "Your beast tried to steal my intimates again." She fast walked over to me in pale pink chiffon blouse and maroon polyester beltless slacks with her white hair, like usual, piled high atop her head. She continued without a hitch, "I had rigged bells to my clothesline to tell me if there were any shenanigans in motion and that's how I stopped your thief. This is wholly unacceptable, and I believe I made it absolutely clear you will be held financially responsible for any crimes committed by your beast!"

I had no response to this because I knew no response besides acquiescence would be heard. I think Maxine may have been hoping for a verbal altercation as she seemed to lose a little steam when I didn't respond or argue back.

"Well, again, you know how I feel, and my expectations are clear. You and your cat will respect my property and personhood!" She turned and marched away quickly. Her purposeful and angry departure was framed by the beauty of her lush flower garden. The contrast was striking.

I was so surprised by Maxine's kamikaze attack I didn't notice or hear Lucille coming up behind me.

"Remember, lovey, this is all about her and has nothing to do with you."

When I turned to her with a look of disbelief, Lucille seemed to consider something for a moment before speaking in her quiet, breathy voice, "However, because you keep catching her ire, it might help if you know a little bit more about her." She was almost embarrassed as she explained, "I've been thinking about this a lot, and it might help you to hear some of Maxine's background. I don't think it's gossip exactly as everyone else in town knows this stuff already," she added with an apologetic laugh and a little blush.

I was silent and she must have taken this as agreement as she launched into her story.

"Maxine's mom was a gifted musician; she both sang and played the piano and I think she may have tap danced a bit in the local talent show. She was famous in these parts. She'd been a friend to my mother."

That was all it took to sidetrack Lucille.

"Have I ever told you any of my mother's story? She was a debutante from a well-known east coast family. Mother had a fascinating life, particularly the parts about traveling to Washington DC with the Republican delegation in 1918, and of course how she met my dad because of the mine cave-in back in 1923. Boy, it sounded like an awful accident with lots of loss for this community."

I was catching on Lucille could recount a situation in twice the time it took for the event to occur. I wondered if I should let her ramble or try to bring her back to Maxine's story. She seemed to notice my pondering something and fortunately brought herself back on track.

"Oh well, we'll have lots of storytelling time and I was going to tell you about Maxine, right? You've just got to know she has had a tough life since her earliest days. If something could go wrong, it seemed to do so for her and her family. My dad used to say her family was a lightning rod for disaster." She paused, "Wait, do you know what a lightning rod is? I don't think young people have any experience with these." She said the last part more to herself than me. Lucille carried a concurrent soliloquy with herself during most of our conversations.

To educate me, she explained, "We get monsoon storms in the summer and the electrical activity is dramatic. In the past, we used to have more lightning rods around town to try to redirect any strikes into the ground to prevent fires. Fires were destructive before modern firefighting techniques came into being. Did you know downtown Nugget has burned down three times in the past hundred years?"

I looked back at my house briefly, but it was enough for Lucille to catch, and she brought herself back to her story again.

"My goodness, I know I can tell a long story, there's just so many interesting parts of life, don't you think? I was talking about Maxine though, wasn't I, and not how lightning rods work?" She seemed to gather her thoughts with "Maxine, yes. Let's see now… Her father left the family when she was in elementary school, and her mother worked hard to keep the wolf from the door. Providing even the basics for her kids was hard."

Her brow furrowed and she looked sad before continuing. "Her mother died soon after this and Maxine had to leave school to raise her younger siblings, a brother named Alfonzo, and a sister named Emily. Everyone used to say Emily was sharp as a tack and quite the looker. Did you know Nugget had more men than women for the first 50 years or so? Being good looking was important in those days, not that it's not noticed now. But with so few women, I bet you could have had the face of a bulldog chewing a wasp and still had men fight over you."

I gave a big sigh and shifted my mail and briefcase between my hands and looked longingly at my front door again. If Lucille noticed my nonverbal cues, it didn't impact her storytelling.

"Maxine loved school, so this was a hard sacrifice for her to step away from her education, but she did it. My mom tried to offer her some help raising her siblings, but she was dreadfully proud and had been raised to be self-sufficient. She would accept little help from anyone. She and her sister took in washing and her brother would chop firewood and sell it. To her credit, she did a good job raising her siblings even being poor as church mice. At her insistence, they both finished high school, then her brother worked for the mines in their underground operations and her sister went to teacher's college and ended up working at an elementary school in Phoenix."

Lucille got thoughtful again and paused in her story. She seemed to skip forward a bit in time when she added, "We all wanted good for Maxine when she got married to Lorenzo. That rogue was movie-star handsome. Maxine was significantly older at the time; I think 26 or 27."

I decided to not tell Lucille I was 32 years old.

"Maxine's marriage appeared happy, but then she found out that scoundrel gambled them into bankruptcy and didn't leave her two pennies to rub together. He lost all his funds and then bet away all her hard-earned savings." She looked pensive before shaking her head and summarizing, "A light purse is a heavy curse."

The Our Lady of the Hills Catholic Church bells started ringing from the square marking the hour as 6:00 pm. Lucille heard this, turned toward the sound, and exclaimed, "Oh my, so late already? I need to get home. My show is starting." She turned away and started heading to her television as she called over her shoulder, "See you later, alligator. Oh, and don't worry, I'll finish the story another time, Zoey."

I knew that would happen and wasn't worried. Instead, I felt I just needed to breathe a moment following these encounters before I could enter my home and really rest. As I turned toward my front door, I noticed the cat had emerged from somewhere and, like a true gentleman, was escorting Lucille to her abode.

SIGN IN WINDOW OF ZINTHER'S APPLIANCE REPAIR:

If we're not meant to have midnight snacks, why is there a light in the fridge?

AS READ IN THE NUGGET NEWS:

Anonymous Boston Philanthropist Gives Sizable Gift for Whortleberry Park Renovations

Chapter 21

Stolen Underwear

I came home to the cat asleep in my recliner. Amazingly, while regular felines still invoked terror, this one no longer scared or surprised me. I think his massive size, three legs, persistent presence, and complete disregard for my fear made it easy to think he was something besides a cat.

Also, as I was beginning to expect after most visits, I was able to find at least one pair of reallocated underwear within the sanctity of my abode. This time it was a lacy pink high-leg brief with a Victoria Secret label. Sometimes the panties were my underthings, but more often these entailed a surprising number of intimates not originating from my home.

For the first two months, I cringed when I found a pair and then threw the underwear away... they were not mine, they were used, and they were sometimes unwashed. However, after depositing over a dozen pair in the trash, I realized this represented a significant financial investment in underclothing and someone was probably looking for their panties.

So, I asked myself a question which had never taken residence in my thoughts: what should I do with all the stolen underwear found in my home?

Some of these pieces appeared expensive as evidenced by super soft fabrics, name brands, and a few pair all in lace. While I considered my options, I began to wash the underwear, fold them when clean, and keep them in a cardboard box on a shelf high in my closet. By the time I had gathered about 25 pairs, there were men's briefs and boxers (what my sister erroneously taught me were called "tighty whities" and "hangers"), boxer briefs, and trunks. There were women's hipsters, classic briefs, thongs, French cut panties, control top briefs, and even a G-string. The cat appeared to prefer brightly colored pairs with only one white and two tan pieces in his stash.

When I was a little girl, I collected stamps and coins, then later baseball cards. As an adult, I began to acquire fine pottery. For these reasons, I could appreciate the fun of the hunt and the targeted quest, as well as respect the careful selection and the obvious preferences the cat displayed in his choices. I wondered if perhaps setting a few pair out would curb his craving for additional items to add to his collection? I started to leave three or four pairs on my recliner after I washed them. While this worked to slow the cat's acquisitions, his stockpiling didn't stop entirely. When a friend unexpectedly stopped by to visit me and saw the assemblage of men's and women's intimates on my chair, her questioning look was enough to make me stop accommodating the cat in this manner.

As the cardboard box in my closet began to fill, I started to think of the box as a collector's cabinet and would occasionally bring it out and leave it open on the floor for the cat to peruse. I could tell if the cat went through the box when I was at work because some of the pairs would be unfolded, and a few moved to other rooms when I returned home. If he slept on them and there was evidence of cat hair, I rewashed the underwear before putting them back in the box.

"Holy cow! This has got to stop," I told the cat when I came home to find three new pairs in my living room. I didn't know how to get the cat to quit his compulsive gathering and, truthfully, still couldn't figure out how he was getting into my house so the idea of me controlling his thievery was laughable.

"This collection is becoming overwhelming and, no matter how much you like them, these underpants need to be returned to their rightful owners," I tried to graciously explain to him. He trilled and blinked languidly before stretching a paw in my direction and rolling on his back.

As I considered how best to return the underwear to their rightful owners, I had an idea and pulled out paper and colored markers and started to make fliers for the neighbors.

ARE YOU MISSING UNDERWEAR? THE BIG 3-LEGGED CAT APPEARS TO BE STEALING INTIMATES AND BRINGING THEM TO MY HOUSE. I WANT TO RETURN THESE TO THEIR RESPECTIVE OWNERS. PLEASE STOP BY ZOEY TROST'S HOUSE AT 630 N. CUPRITE STREET TO CLAIM ANY UNDERWEAR THAT'S YOURS.

The first neighbor appeared two days later. She seemed apologetic and embarrassed (as was I!), so I brought out the box and asked her to go through them, then discretely turned my back. She cleared her throat a few minutes later to indicate she was done sorting through the box. Because she didn't have any underthings in her hand, I was disappointed, but then I noticed multiple bulges in her coat pocket and the box looked a little less full.

"If you notice any other intimates missing, please check in with me. I don't know why he's gathering underwear or how he's getting in my house, but I'll wash any pair I find and put them in this box."

"Thanks," she said quietly with her eyes averted as she quickly turned to go.

Because I washed the underwear, I was aware of what had been in the box. After she left, I noticed the pink and lavender French cuts were missing, as well as one of the lacy pairs. Yep, if I was to try to guess underpants preferences, those seemed to fit her. We psychologists have all sorts of ways of classifying personality types, though I had yet to read any studies documenting a link to underwear preferences.

The following day, two other neighbors came over. The middle-aged husband and wife thought the entire experience was a hoot and joked about the cat, me, and the panties throughout their visit. The man found several of his missing boxer briefs in a lovely Prussian blue.

"Now I can't blame the washing machine for eating my briefs anymore!" he said with a laugh. "Hey, would you mind if I take a few extra pair for some of my buddies at the Ringtail Lodge? They're going to bust a gut when I tell this story to them."

I felt my face redden as I considered this narrative spreading around Nugget and then realized that ship had already sailed, it was likely too late to do anything about the situation as the story was invariably already making the rounds. With my luck, they were saying the cat was mine and my name was linked to the tale of purloined undergarments.

I sighed, then responded, "Why don't you wait a few days to see if other people claim their underthings first and then you can have as many pairs of underpants as you want."

Later, I wondered if guys would wear someone else's used underwear if they could get a pair for free?

Eww, gross!

Over the next three days, five other neighbors came by and claimed their underclothing. Their underwear preferences on the most part were not surprising, except for one neighbor: Maxine. My uptight, constantly negative, always complaining, dreadfully brittle neighbor went home with all the leopard print and tiger striped thongs, as well as the only G-string in the box.

SIGN SEEN AT NUGGET EXTERMINATORS:

Scorpions are nature saying, "Screw you, I'm combining lobsters, spiders, wasps, and nightmares!" Fight back! Set up your exterminating appointment today.

HEADLINE IN THE NUGGET NEWS:

Local Doctor Invites Public to View Underwear Collection:
"A 3-legged cat brings pairs to my house almost daily"

Chapter 22

The Joy of a Baby's Cry

Kim stood in her kitchen with her hands on her hips wearing a satisfied smile and her "cleaning clothes": filthy jeans, a ripped "Nug's Nugget Nook" yellow t-shirt, and a kerchief holding her hair back. She gave a big sigh, then stopped to sniff the lingering scent of her lemon and pine-scented cleaners, then leisurely twirled. She wanted to look at every inch of her just-cleaned, entirely sparkling, and now spotless home. She had just spent three hours scrubbing every inch of her den, dining area and kitchen. This was truly a beautiful sight! She had played sports in high school and learned to savor victory whenever success came. She knew in her heart of hearts this was one of those moments.

Who would have guessed back in high school how good a clean house would feel or that she ranked this accomplishment right up there with winning the state championship? While her home felt good when picked up and hygienic, it was the rarity of the event which gave the situation such value. With three kids, a large dog, and a husband all going in different directions, it was hard to keep up with all the cleaning.

The miracle of today was made possible because Kim and her friend, Diana, were trying their newly launched "preschooler exchange" program. While eight-year-old Gunnar and five-year-old Olivia were at school, Kim and Diana decided to each give one another two afternoons a month without their respective three-year-old. This meant Tucker was at Diana's house for three hours. After two kids, you might think Kim would know a few tricks for keeping up with a preschooler, but because she now had three kids and a dog, she just didn't have the time or energy to attempt any of them.

She decided to cap her successful cleaning accomplishment by taking out the trash and, when she was taking the bag out to the can, she happened to notice a big yellow patch in the lawn. In the division of household duties, she and John had decided she oversaw the inside of the house, and he would be responsible for the outside. However, feeling magnanimous, she decided to help him and hooked up the sprinkler while dragging the hose out to the dry spot. She turned the water on full force to give the lawn a thorough soaking and noticed their five-month-old puppy run to joyously play in the water as she stepped into the house.

When back inside, she again looked around her clean kingdom and smiled. Today was an exceedingly good day!

You may wonder why anyone would get a large dog when responsible for the care of multiple small children? In fact, this was a question Kim asked herself often, particularly on the days the dog was exceedingly rambunctious or destructive. How this situation occurred is a story all on its own.

John loved animals of any sort but was particularly enamored with dogs. He had two big golden retrievers in high school, Jack and Rose, and they accompanied him everywhere he went, except school and church. In looking back, Kim thinks the dogs are part of why John was so normal when his mom was so… well… not normal. She considered Marge pathologically self-centered and observed his mom appeared blind to all her children and their needs. While this devaluing might have driven another kid toward bad friends or drug use, John had his dogs as his safety net. The dogs were utterly devoted to him and seemed to fill in some of the gaps left by his mom's dramatic lack of mothering skills.

When John and Kim started dating, she quickly learned going anywhere with John included being with Jack and Rose. This was fine with her as she liked dogs in general and loved these dogs in particular. The dogs were such a part of their relationship John decided to propose by having Jack deliver the ring while Rose wore a sign asking if Kim would marry their dad. She of course said "yes" and leaned into John's embrace. The dogs expected to be hugged as enthusiastically as their dad to commemorate the occasion and jumped into the mix, knocking the newly engaged couple to the floor to the chorus of their humans' laughter. Appropriately for the wedding, they dressed Jack in a bow tie and he served as their ringbearer, and Rose had white roses attached to her collar while wearing a backpack filled with flower petals that slowly fell to the ground as she proceeded up the aisle.

While golden retrievers usually only live until about age 12, these dogs surpassed the norm. All the same, John was inconsolable when Jack passed just a month before their first child, Gunnar Alexander, was born. Rose must have felt the same as she mourned herself to death and passed three months later. John wanted to get another dog right away, but Kim asked him to wait as Gunnar suffered from cholic as a baby and then was frequently ill as a toddler. He waited, but then it was Olivia Noelle's turn to be the baby in the family while Kim juggled the care of a baby and toddler. Following this, Tucker James came along a few years later. John kept asking for a dog and Kim kept asking him to wait a little bit longer.

For his 30th birthday, John insisted the only gift which would make him happy was getting a dog. Kim was exhausted from caring for the kids and knew the primary responsibility for tending a dog would likely fall on her. John insisted this would not be the case, mainly based on his experience with Jack and Rose. However, the situation was different now with his full-time supervisory job at the mine and sometimes having to travel for work, and the kids consumed most of his remaining energy and care. She tried to hold out a little longer on getting a dog, but John would not be dissuaded and even told her of an article he read about how kids raised with dogs have better social skills, display more empathy, do better overall in school, and even have stronger immune systems.

Because she could no longer block John's push for an animal, she tried to punt and suggested he choose an animal which involved less care. He considered this and suggested a cat, even though he knew before asking it'd be a "no" because Kim was allergic, but he thought it would make a dog more palatable. It didn't.

He then pushed for hamsters, but she hated the smell of their cages. He briefly put forth the idea of a snake, but she informed him in no uncertain terms she would file for divorce the day he brought a snake into their home. His final campaign was for a fish. She couldn't think of any reason to resist this and, by then, had used up all her "pass" cards.

So, a fish it was. Mind you, John still wanted a dog, but was happy to get any animal into the house and thought he could perhaps work his way up to a dog when Kim saw how well he and the kids cared for their little finned friend. The kids were as thrilled as John, if not more so, and badgered their dad about when they could go to get the goldfish. This had to be scheduled as no place in Nugget sold live fish and bringing this creature into the family would involve a three-hour round trip to the big city.

Finally, the fish acquisition day arrived! John and the kids woke early and, unbelievably, he had them fed and dressed by 7 am, letting Kim sleep in for a change. After they left, she waited to hear a progress report and was a little nervous John and the kids might forget they were only supposed to get a fish. Consequently, she was immensely relieved when she got a text from John stating: "Mission accomplished! Kids in car. Fish in car. Heading home."

The car pulled into the driveway 90 minutes after the text and the kids exploded out of the car with excitement, all talking at once. Kim was surprised a fish would garner this amount of enthusiasm, particularly after an hour and a half traveling with a likely boring creature in a small bag of water. John got out of the car more slowly and seemed to hesitate slightly. This made Kim a bit uneasy.

"Kids, remember what we talked about. I'm going to be the one to introduce Mom to Fish." The kids eagerly nodded their agreement while Olivia literally bounced with excitement standing next to her dad. Gunnar, the "much" bigger brother, kept looking into the sun-shaded window near the back of the mini-van with a smile threatening to crack his face.

"Now, Kim, honey, please know I didn't plan it this way. This just sort of, like, happened."

"Uh, oh," she thought and froze where she was standing. Her breathing started to grow shallow.

John had opened the rear hatch and was lifting out a large crate while Gunnar excitedly tried to help. Olivia's excitement escalated to bouncing accentuated by shrill squawks.

"So, these folks were in the pet store parking lot and, Kim, they weren't even selling the puppies, but just giving them away. I couldn't help but look when I heard they were golden retrievers." By this point, he had the crate out and was turning toward Kim. She looked into the cage and saw the cutest ball of orange fluff she had ever laid eyes on! He had a black nose and two button eyes, his tongue was hanging out of a mouth seemingly stretched into a smile, his tail was wagging a mile a minute, and he appeared as excited to join the family as most of the family was to have him.

"Kim, I'd like to introduce you to the newest member of the Winthrop family: this is Fish."

So, this was how a mother of three small children and an at-times childlike husband got a rambunctious, golden retriever puppy. She had made her expectations infinitely clear to John if the major responsibility for Fish's care ever fell on her, then the dog would go to the pound. John started to argue, but Kim cut him off and told him *someone* would be going to the pound: Fish or him. John got the point.

Fortunately, John and the kids had been more involved in the care of Fish than she thought they would be which was pleasantly surprising. John and the two older kids went to puppy school with Fish and practiced the exercises at home. The "men" in the family began to faithfully lower the toilet seat after urinating when they realized the little puppy loved water so much that he would climb in for a leisurely soak in the toilet bowl "pool" whenever he could access it. John developed a "poop patrol" calendar where he and the kids took turns cleaning the yard and he was faithful to groom Fish and feed him when he was not away on travel. However, when John's work took him out of town, a lot of the care inevitably fell on Kim. She loved the sweet rascal, but somedays wished she had a few less creatures for which she was responsible.

With as crazy as her household could get, Kim had set her kitchen timer to 20 minutes to remember to turn off the sprinkler in the front yard. Diana returned Tucker while the sprinklers were on and then, just as the timer went off, Kim was distracted by the arrival of the older kids' school bus. When she went into the house with Tucker and then headed to the kitchen to turn off the timer's loud beeping, the kids got off the bus and exuberantly ran into the house. However, before they closed the front door, Fish determined he had been locked outside for enough time and enthusiastically followed the kids into the house.

True to his name, Fish had been playing in the biggest puddles of water and mud he could find. The dirty dog and clean house were immediately at odds. However, the mud was a minor inconvenience when compared to the water-spewing sprinkler Fish carried in his mouth and brought with him when he joyfully bound into the house. The water was on high, the sprinkler was relatively new and in great working order, and the device didn't realize its services were not needed *inside* the Winthrop residence.

In response to the sprinkler-laden muddy dog's entry, Kim screamed and ran at the dog which made the kids squeal. Fish interpreted their shouts as cheering and jumped even more wholeheartedly into this new game. At their encouragement, he began to circle the living room at full speed bouncing off the occasional chair or sofa before heading into the kitchen, spraying water mixed with mud and dog hair every step of the way.

Kim could not catch the dog or get the kids' attention to help her stop the dog, so she improvised a quick Plan B and stomped on the extra-long hose being dragged into the house, grabbed and kinked the line to stop the water, and held the green snake of destruction firmly with both of her hands. Her immobility and Fish's forward mobility met a point of response predicted by Newton's Law of Motion: Kim did not move, so Fish lost hold of the sprinkler as he continued sliding full speed toward the kitchen counter, finally coming to a complete halt when his wet body slammed into a cupboard door. He shook off his dramatic stop flinging mud and hair as he shook and then was up and wagging his tail in seconds. While he was recovering, Kim quickly pulled the now-free-of-a-dog hose and sprinkler toward her and out of the house before turning to the spigot and angrily twisting the water off.

John came home a few minutes later to an exasperated and wholly deflated wife in a filthy house with his dog and children relegated to the back yard. He was going to ask what happened, but then looked again at Kim and wisely decided to ask the kids instead.

When he heard the story, John sent Kim to the backyard with a glass of wine while he and the kids tried to erase the most egregious insults to the clean house. He had just invited Kim back into the now merely dirty house when there was a quick two-knock warning and the front door opened as John's mother, Marge, let herself into their home.

This day just went from bad to worse.

Marge was a difficult woman to be around on a good day, but even worse when the day was full of challenges. She looked at Kim first and then around the dirty house with a look of disgust, making a tsk'ing sound while shaking her head in disapproval. John tried to stop her from making any comments on the condition of the house, but it would be easier to stop a warship heading full steam into battle.

"Oh, my goodness, Kim. This house is not experiencing its finest hour, is it? You do realize the state of a house reflects the state of mind of the occupants, right? Cleanliness also influences the development of your children's brains and character. I think it's a lot more important to prioritize cleanliness than you appear to be doing. Cleanliness is next to godliness, you know."

Kim's jaw was tight, her fists were clenched, and – if the deepening red of her face was any indication – her blood pressure was rising. She usually had amazing self-restraint when situations involved Marge, but today all bets were off. John tried to redirect his mother with the "hilarious story" of the dog and the sprinkler while leading her from the room, but she would not be deterred. Marge brought the conversation back to the filthy house and then seamlessly segued into one of her favorite topics: the selfishness and poor judgment displayed by Kim (and only sometimes including John) for having three children and a dog in a world marked by overpopulation, environmental degradation, and financial crises. She said all humans needed to show more self-control (obviously not including herself), but this was especially true of Kim and John.

Tucker was tired from his play date and had lost a shoe. Though he did not understand what was happening, he could sense his mother's growing wrath which led him to burst out in tears following by loud and incessant wailing. Marge tried to raise her voice to be heard over the distraught preschooler. Olivia also was overwhelmed by all the activity and emotion filling the day, compounded by her grandmother's raised voice as she attempted to finish her rant, and how angry her mother appeared, so she started to cry. John sent Gunnar out of the room with a jerk of his hand on the off chance he might cry as well. He noticed Kim's fists now included white knuckles, so he moved his body physically between his wife and mother to try to shield an already-overwhelmed Kim from the onslaught of emotions ricocheting around the room.

Marge shouted above the melee, "See, this is exactly what I am saying! Listen to this cacophony. You need to know, I can barely stand to come over here when there is a child crying, though I will say an infant crying is even worse than this horrible ruckus!"

Over the chaos and crying and noise, into the afternoon of frustration and destruction, amidst a moment of judgmental criticism, a clarion moment of understanding seemed to pierce through the darkness like a ray of hope. John and Kim slowly made eye contact to see if they were both catching the message. They were. A miniscule smile crept onto both of their faces as the absolute insanity of the day quieted a little bit.

As they pondered the revelation that Marge couldn't stand to be around a crying infant, their shoulders relaxed, Kim unclenched her fists, and the light seemed brighter as time slowed. Marge's voice faded to an almost inaudible background as hope flooded their hearts.

Little Emma Joy was born nine months to the day later. Kim was delighted to discover this was the most boisterous and vocally gifted infant she had ever met.

HEATED INTERCHANGE OVERHEARD AT GAS & GO:

Older exasperated woman: "I don't have the time or the crayons to explain this to you."
Older clueless man: "Well I think you should act your age, not your shoe size."

AS READ IN THE NUGGET NEWS:

John Winthrop proudly announces a new family addition: Fish is a delightful 5-month-old Golden Retriever puppy gifted at chewing shoes and finding mud puddles.

Chapter 23

My Mystery Dinner Guest

As I settled into my new job and new hometown, I increasingly missed the depth of connection and years of history I shared with my friends and family in California. I hadn't appreciated my strong support system until it was gone.

One morning not long after this realization, I had finished my Bible reading and was diving into prayer when I heard God plainly direct my steps.

"Make some crock pot chicken, you are going to have a dinner guest tonight."

I knew that voice!

While some Christians believe God stopped communicating directly with humans after Christ was resurrected, I knew differently. Prayer is a two-way conversation and I have heard God's voice clearly on numerous occasions. I know it's in my head and not audible to others, but I also know it is not a voice of my creation. God has warned me of dangers, directed me to correct errors, urged me to reach out to specific people, laughed with me in joy, and comforted me on many occasions. Except when stopping me quickly in dangerous situations, God's voice was usually calm, deep, steady, and clear. I loved to hear it, even though I didn't always like what the voice said when correcting me or directing me to do something I didn't want to do.

I had experience over the years of both following God's direction to blessing and ignoring it to my detriment. I learned God's voice became quieter when I didn't follow the directions right away. At one time, God directed me to give a woman $250 when I didn't have much money and didn't feel I could do so and still pay rent. While I said "yes" to the directive and planned to be obedient, I delayed giving the money as I tried to figure out how to corral that much cash. God prompted me again and I again put God off. When I realized the third time God's voice was now so quiet as to be almost inaudible, it scared me, and I gave the money I didn't think I could afford to the woman. She revealed she was planning to commit suicide later that day because she felt completely overlooked by God and the church community, but my gift changed her plans.

Not surprisingly, I had enough to miraculously pay my rent, too.

So, going back to my earlier prayer, hearing God tell me to make slow cooked chicken wasn't completely out of the ordinary and I knew to follow the directive, even if I didn't know how it would exactly play out. I completely trusted God would bring the right person or persons with whom to share a meal and I was thrilled to see who this was going to be and how the evening would unfold. While not the distinction of a summons to the White House, I was delighted to receive this invitation to a dinner party initiated by God and possibly more thrilled as it was all joy and no stress, meaning I didn't have to worry about what to wear, or the etiquette involved in meeting a head of state.

I am not known for my cooking skills, but even I can't screw up crock pot chicken most of the time. I chose a recipe that had always been successful. I excitedly got out the appliance, prepared the food and plugged the pot in. I even straightened up a bit and ran the vacuum preparing for a festive gathering.

I anticipated a wonderful evening of fellowship and approached with eager anticipation each person who overlapped my path through the day. It was the feeling of a child awaiting gifts Christmas morning, with no one else aware its Christmas. To identify my guest(s), I wasn't sure if they would mention needing dinner or if I should ask, so I just started inviting people.

"Hey, Sally, do you have dinner plans? I put a chicken in the crock pot and would love to share a meal with you and your husband."

"Oh, how nice. Thanks, Zoey, I'd love to, but my mother-in-law is coming to dinner at our house tonight."

"How about you, Jenny? Interested in dinner?"

"No, thanks, Zoey. I already have dinner plans."

"Noel? Dinner?"

"I'd like to but can't do so tonight. I'm studying for a big test for my online master's class and will be up all night preparing."

"Nick? Dinner plans?"

"Thanks for the invite, Zoey, but I coach a youth football team on Tuesday and Thursday evenings."

"Jose?"

"No, gracias. My mother requires we all eat dinner together as a family."

The rejections of my dinner invitations continued all day, but I wasn't discouraged. I knew God had never failed to come through and wouldn't stand me up. If not someone from work, then maybe someone will call me, or I'll get a message, or someone will just show up at my home.

When I got home, I had no notes or messages. I prepped a salad and set the table for two, then waited. The cat was scratching at my front door, something he had never done, so I went out to see what was happening with him.

Once I stepped in my yard, I saw her: Maxine.

With horror, I spoke out loud, "No, God, no. You can't mean her! That's the last person I want to share a meal with." I shook my head vehemently and crossed my arms over my chest, digging in with my firm "no."

To my surprise, she turned around and went into her house.

I sighed with relief, "Whew! That was close. I knew you couldn't possibly mean her."

Then she came out again into her flower-filled garden.

"Ask her."

"Really, God? This is not what I had in mind," I explained. I don't think my expectation was a surprise to God.

That morning I had read a great passage by C.S. Lewis where he said, *"Christian love, either towards God or towards man, is an affair of the will."* The quote came back to me highlighted and in bold font. Darn it!

"Oh, alright already. I'll ask her," I grumbled with as little enthusiasm as I could muster. I may have been more cheerful heading to my last root canal appointment.

Before I lost my nerve, I marched across the street, plastered a smile on my face, and began to talk, "Hey, Maxine. Do you have dinner plans?"

She stepped back surprised, like I had thrown boiling water on her.

I plowed on. "I've been slow cooking some chicken all day, made a nice salad, and have a fresh loaf of crusty French bread. I definitely have enough for two and wondered if you'd care to join me?"

"What do you want from me?" she asked suspiciously with a furrowed brow. Her face and body posture revealed a level of indignation and paranoia appropriately reserved for when a thief demanded you hand over your wallet. "Are you selling Amway, Tupperware, Mary Kay cosmetics, vitamins, or essential oils? Because I'll tell you right now, I'm not buying."

"No, Maxine, I'm not selling anything."

"Then what do you want from me?" she spit back angrily.

"I just want your company," I answered honestly. "I've been a little lonely away from my family and friends. I prefer to eat with others. Somehow the food just tastes better."

My honesty seemed to surprise her.

"This is just chicken. There are no strings attached," I said as I opened my arms to show empty hands and a nonthreatening stance. "If you are interested in joining me, you're welcome in my home. If this doesn't work for you, no problem."

Inwardly, I was hoping she might stay hostile and aloof, then refuse to come to dinner, but – of course – that's not what happened.

"Okay," she scowled, "I'll come. I've been weeding and pruning my flowers for the last few hours, so I need to clean up. I'll be at your house in ten minutes."

She turned toward her house before I could respond, but I nodded my assent all the same. It's a good thing her back was to me because my face held a look of absolute shock and barely contained dread.

Good to her word, Maxine knocked on my front door exactly ten minutes later. She came in, slowly looked around the room with a critical expression, then shook her head with displeasure.

"This is not what I expected a doctor's home would look like."

I felt like a failing student who just screwed up my remedial summer school class.

Before I could ask what she was expecting, she ran a finger along a shelf noting the dust, looked disparagingly at the new donation of hair left on the couch by the cat, and even sniffed to check the odor of my home.

Yikes! Not the social skills of a normal dinner guest.

She laid her sweater on the back of a chair, marched to the table, and sat forcefully. As she was opening the napkin to spread on her lap, she looked at me expectantly.

I blinked a couple of times and then got moving. I had the salad and bread on the table already, so all I had to do was plate the chicken. When I opened the crock pot, the tantalizing aroma made my mouth water and I hoped this might be the positive thing needed to start to turn the tidal wave of negativity that Maxine carried.

"Are these Wedgewood?" she asked looking at my china when I set the plates on the table.

"Um, I'm not sure," I answered with surprise. I grabbed an empty bread plate, flipped it over to read the manufacturer's information, and then nodded. "Yes, you're right. They are."

"These were my mother's favorite pattern," she offered. "I wish I could have kept her collection, but they had to be sold off." She stopped herself and seemed shocked she had just revealed something personal. She quickly shifted the conversation away from herself.

"You have a lot of books. Have you read all of them?"

"Yes," I responded after swallowing a bite of chicken. It was delicious if I do say so myself.

"I love to read," I continued, "and have since I was a young child. Do you enjoy reading, Maxine?"

"Nope. I hate it," she retorted succinctly.

Knowing she had been a top student, I somehow doubted she hated reading, but over the years I suspect she walled off that pleasure. This made me sad.

Believe it or not, the conversation went downhill from there. She criticized the food, my housekeeping skills, the car I drove, and my negligence as a pet owner.

At this point, I didn't even try to tell her he's not my cat.

She then went on to speak negatively about local and national politics, the weather, the economy, and the laziness of teenagers these days. She was angry and sharp as she criticized people trying to pass gun laws and was wittily incisive in her condemnation of foreign cars. She was intolerant of immigrants, vehemently supported the death penalty, fervently opposed abortion, had no patience for people who got caught up in drug use, and came out against GMOs and pesticides.

The breadth of her knowledge was impressive, and she backed all her strongly held opinions with convincing research studies and lots of statistics. She may say she hates reading, but she appeared to be doing a fair amount of it. I was impressed with her intellect, even if I held differing opinions on some of the subject matter. I realized it was a travesty she couldn't continue with school and had to drop out to raise her siblings. She seemed smart enough to have gone as far as she might want in academics.

When there was a brief lull in her diatribe, I thought I could redirect the conversation to something more positive by asking about her flowers. "I've heard you win awards for your flowers, Maxine. Have you always had a green thumb?"

"Yes, I'm famous for my flowers, but this is probably the last year I'll bring home any prizes. You know why?" she asked me with intense scrutiny.

I shook my head. Honestly, I had no clue.

"Because of you!" she spat angrily while pointing a gnarled finger at my face. "You moved here and brought that reprehensible beast to my neighborhood. Your cat has found a way to destroy my blooms at their finest, dig up heirloom bulbs, and break flower stalks. It's a shameful and degrading way to end a gardening success story."

I decided to not ask any more questions and only respond to her prompts from here on. However, though I tried to engage, my role was inconsequential in the conversation. She segued from topic to topic without prompt and I thought it was like turning on a strongly

Welcome to Nugget

opinionated talk show and then passively absorbing the information for 90 minutes. At one point, I cleared the dinner plates and served up some ice cream. I didn't even have a chance to verbally ask if she wanted any, just showed her the container and pointed at a bowl questioningly to which she nodded while she continued to speak.

Finally, the food had been consumed, the dishes cleared, the leftovers boxed up, and we were both standing.

"Well, this wasn't awful," Maxine concluded in final judgment. "Next time I'll cook and show you what a good meal should taste like."

At that, she gathered up her sweater and the little Tupperware of extra chicken I was sending home with her. I could not respond to her dinner invitation (if that was what that was?) but managed a wan smile.

She then let herself out of my front door and closed it firmly. When she finally stepped off my porch, I plopped into my recliner exhausted, took a huge breath, and let my head loll backwards dramatically before starting my debrief of the evening with my Event Coordinator.

"Alright, God. That was a painfully awful evening. Is that what you had envisioned?" I paused but didn't hear a response from God. "Truly, that had to earn me sainthood points," I grumbled, feeling a bit self-righteous in my tolerance of Maxine's negativity and my offering of gracious hospitality.

Then I thought about how much I fought the directive and realized I wasn't exactly the model of obedience, so I revised my personal assessment, "Well, maybe reluctant sainthood points."

I contemplated the evening a bit more, including my negative attitude toward my guest, my judgementalism of her opinions and dress and table manners, the complaining prayers I was mumbling under my breath the whole evening, and revised again, "Okay, reformed sinner points."

Nope, to be honest, even that was too gracious. Enough with the games, I needed to come clean. "Goodness, alright already, God! Perhaps I'm a sometimes-reformed sinner?"

God seemed to wait a bit to see if I had any other revisions to make.

"Nope, that's it. That's all I've got," I admitted.

"I'll tell you who you are, Zoey," God responded with a tolerant chuckle. **"You're my child, my beloved daughter, a priceless treasure I hold close in my heart."** Because that was not at all what I expected to hear, God paused to let me take the message in before closing with a wing dinger aimed straight at my heart, **"I love you, Zoey. I am proud of you. You are my delight."**

I responded the only way I could. I bowed my head and burst into tears.

AS SEEN ON THE TIPSY STEER'S LIGHTED MARQUEE:

"Coffee, you're on the bench. Alcohol, suit up."

HEADLINE IN THE NUGGET NEWS:

Four in ten children in Nugget schools hate math.
Principal remarks, "A majority of kids is a big deal"

Chapter 24

Talking about Food

Olivia raced into the kitchen, sliding to a stop in her pink flamingo patterned socks. "Mom, I'm hungry," whined the perpetually famished five-year-old.

"I fed you yesterday, young lady," Kim responded nonchalantly while wiping cheerios and milk from the kitchen table.

"Mommy! That was yesterday."

"What? Are you expecting to eat every single day?" Kim asked her daughter feigning surprise as she passed to the kitchen sink to rinse her rag.

Olivia smiled and explained, "Mommy, you're supposed to feed us not only every day, but several times a day."

"Who made that rule?" Kim complained. "I think it's asking a whole lot to expect food every day. Plus, I don't want to raise entitled children," Kim responded while starting to make lunches for the kids for the following school day.

"You are the mom, this is your job," educated the 3 ½ foot tall teacher.

"Well, when is my term up?" asked Kim.

"Your 'term'? What does 'term' mean?"

"You know, when does this duty end? I wasn't asked if I wanted to do this, so I must have been elected. Was I voted in for a two years or four years term?" Kim asked with a straight face. "I just want to know when I am done. When can I step down from this responsibility?"

Olivia seemed to consider this question carefully but wasn't sure how to respond. She needed some help.

"Hold on, Mommy. I'll be right back," Olivia said as she ran from the room.

Olivia had Gunnar with her when she returned. "Tell her, Gunnar."

"Mom, you are a mom, and this comes when you choose to have kids."

Olivia piped in, "You choose to have kids?"

Gunnar and Kim both nodded at her question. Gunnar is logical in his thinking and speech and wasn't done explaining the situation to his mom, so he didn't want the conversation to shift to talk about babies. Before this happened, he hurriedly continued.

"You have mom duties until you raise us up and we move out of the house, like when we go to college or join the military." Kim had no idea he even knew about military service.

"So, then I'm done?" Kim responded.

"No, you are the mom forever, but as we get bigger, we can start to cook for you and take care of you when you are really old, like when you're 40," promised Gunnar.

Kim worked hard to not smile at his statement.

"Hmm, that sounds fair, I guess. If some relief is in my future, then I suppose I can stick with it a little longer."

"Good," said Gunnar.

"I'm hungry," repeated Olivia.

Kim sighed, smiled, and headed to the pantry for some noodles.

A few days later, it was Gunnar's turn to talk about food.

"Mom, I'm flusterated."

"'Flusterated', huh?"

"Umm hmm. I mean, when do we get to decide what we're having for dinner?" eight-year-old Gunnar earnestly asked his mom. His hair was mussed from play, and he was dressed in blue jeans with a large rip on the right knee and a Spider Man t-shirt. Like always, regardless of the weather, his feet were bare.

"What do you mean when do you decide?" countered Kim as she stopped sweeping the kitchen floor to look at her eldest child.

"Except for our birthday dinner, you decide on every meal and don't even ask us what we want," complained her eldest child.

"Son, you get a choice every single meal: it's take it or leave it," explained Kim. "When you are the one making the money, doing the shopping, and cooking the meals, then you get to decide. Otherwise, you just need to be grateful you get to eat anything at all."

"But couldn't you give us even a little bit of a choice?" Gunnar continued to advocate.

"Sweetheart, you seem to have confused our household for a democracy when this is a solid dictatorship," Kim responded cheerfully while starting to change out the almost overflowing kitchen trash bag.

"But, Mom, Michael's mom lets the kids each decide one meal a week. They get to say what they want to eat and they're even younger than I am."

After a big sigh, Kim queried, "So, you want to eat at a restaurant? You want a menu?"

"No, not a restaurant, but just a choice about food," continued Gunner.

"If I was running a restaurant, I would expect a sous chef to help with prep, line staff to help with the cooking and plating, and both a bus boy and dish washer to handle clean-up. Are you planning to take on those tasks?" she asked Gunnar.

"I don't know what those things are. I want to just eat and then help clear the dishes off the table," offered Gunnar.

"Also, if I am running a mom eatery," Kim continued, warming to the concept. "I expect tips from all my customers and nothing stingy either, like those insulting Christian pamphlets people leave after church rather than cash. Have you ever tried to buy groceries with a 'Four Spiritual Laws' leaflet?"

"Mom, you know we don't have money to pay you anything."

"And why is that exactly? You're not working, you're not out hunting game or gathering nuts and berries, you just show up expecting to eat."

"Mooommm, we're kids! We go to school, and you raise us until we're adults," Gunnar wasn't sure, but he hoped his mom was teasing him. But he also wasn't ready to give up on his request, so he added, "I just think it would be nice to have a choice every now and then"

"Okay, I'll take this under advisement," Kim promised. When she saw his confused face, she clarified, "I'll give this idea some thought."

The next day, Kim called the kids into the kitchen to make an announcement.

"Because your brother requested this, tonight you kids get to decide what we eat. I will give you a choice of three things and you have to discuss it and then agree between yourselves on one and only one selection."

"Thanks, Mom!" gushed Gunnar.

"Yeah, thanks, Mom," added a surprised, but pleased Olivia.

"Where's my dinosaur?" asked Tucker dressed in his "oatmeal bear" costume from last Halloween, oblivious to the interchange.

"So tonight, you get to decide between escargot, liver and onions, or macaroni and cheese."

"What's escargot?" asked Olivia, wanting to make a good choice and needing to better understand her options before committing to a selection.

"It's an expensive French delicacy of snails cooked in a butter and herb sauce. You usually sop up the butter, herbs, and snail juice with crusty French bread," Kim mentioned over her shoulder as she emptied the dish washer. She could see the kids' expressions on the copper pan on the counter and was watching without their knowledge.

"Yuck! Snails. No way," Olivia decided.

"What about liver and onions?" queried Gunnar.

"Oh, beef liver is soaked in milk, then fried in butter and served with sauteed onions. It smells awful, has a weird texture when you try to chew it, sort of sticks to the top of your mouth, and has an overwhelming and not very tasty flavor. However, it's extremely good for you so that makes all the other things okay, even though your house will smell awful for a day or two afterwards."

"Ugg, really? It sounds gross," considered Gunnar.

They both knew what mac and cheese was, so they asked no further questions. The two older kids got together to discuss these three options quietly. They looked at Tucker to see about including him, but he was oblivious and playing with his now-found dinosaur. They then looked back at each other, Gunnar made a face and Olivia nodded in agreement: the decision was up to them. Their discussion lasted less than a minute before Gunnar became the spokesperson and turned to his mom, "We've made our selection," he announced with formality. After a slight pause, he announced, "We choose mac and cheese."

"If you're sure that's what you want," replied Kim with an even bigger pause to allow them time to change their minds. They both nodded, so she said, "Alright, it's mac and cheese. I'll put the water on to boil and start to grate the cheese."

The older two kids left the kitchen with big, satisfied smiles.

SIGN SEEN AT COPPER KIDS' DAYCARE:

Hell hath no fury like a toddler whose
sandwich has been cut in squares
when they wanted triangles

AS SEEN IN THE NUGGET NEWS

Deputy Sheriff Lures Runaway Potbellied
Pig Home with Soft-serve Ice Cream:
"I'm glad I had a vanilla cone handy"

Chapter 25

Square Dancing

Even with my growing friendships with Lucille and Kim, I realized most of my interactions were with people at work or in the community whom I would consider no more than acquaintances. After more than three months of living in Nugget, I didn't know any other single people within ten years of my age outside of work. This town seemed to have lots of kids and some teens, then jumped to people in their 50's or above. I could not figure out where to look for the single people in their 30's and 40's.

Because I needed to make friends closer to my age and get out of the house more, I decided to attend an open dance night for the local "Belles and Beaus" Square Dance Club. I've never been a good dancer, but the flier said beginners were welcome. This is the reason I was walking into the fellowship hall of Our Lady of the Hills Catholic Church on a Thursday evening. Maybe the people my age who were not at bars were out dancing?

Unfortunately, I immediately felt out of place when I entered the church hall as most of the people there were senior citizen couples, and all were in fancy square dance outfits. They looked great. The men were dressed in western pearl-buttoned shirts, jeans, hats, hand tooled leather belts with big buckles, and boots. The women wore coordinating square dance dresses (many in gingham and all with lots of tulle), special dancing shoes, and ribbons in their hair. Every eye was on me when I entered the room in blue jeans and a white tee-shirt, and several people came forward to greet me enthusiastically, including a half dozen people I had met at First Congregational. With all this attention, I didn't feel I could turn around and leave immediately; consequently, I decided to stick around and give it a try.

There were only a few uncoupled people in the room, and I was paired with a man named Big Ed who was at least 50 years my senior. He was an excellent dancer and responded reflexively to the moves sung out by the caller. I had a hard time keeping my right and left apart (truly a handicap in this type of dance) and didn't know how to do the turns. The caller seemed to be speaking a foreign language with allemande left, chain down the line, promenade, dosido, ocean wave, four ladies' chain, men sashay, star right, weave the ring, sweep a quarter, and many more. However, even with my lack of coordination, I enjoyed the dancing, though I was not skilled at it and repeatedly threw off my square's formation. All the other dancers were gracious toward my mistakes.

I almost started to relax into the dancing, but then Big Ed started an "organ recital" telling me about his heart procedures, knee replacement, TIAs, and gall stone issues. He told me about medical tests, outpatient procedures, and inpatient surgeries; however, he kept circling back to his heart issues as most profound. I found myself trying to review my CPR training for how to restart a heart that has stopped beating, but this was not something my brain could do while concurrently trying to follow the caller's directions to "flutter wheel", "box the gnat", and then "cross run".

When another older guy named Walter asked me to partner with him, I thought it might relieve my stress about possible medical emergencies for Big Ed and so I said "yes" to him. However, he almost immediately brushed against my breasts as we were setting up our squares. I was shocked and felt disbelief at what just happened, but he didn't appear to even register his actions. I told myself there is no way a man would purposefully do inappropriate touching like that in a setting as open, well lit, and full of his friends and neighbors as this was. It had to have been an accident. As women are socialized to do, I wrote off my discomfort and sense of violation and gave him a "pass" for what I decided must have been an accident.

However, I quickly realized he did a whole lot more touching than Big Ed had done and more than other dance couples seemed to be exchanging. Because I was feeling increasingly uncomfortable and my personal space felt violated, I decided to stop dancing with him at the end of this song.

Over by the punch bowl, Linda Augustine elbowed her friend, Karen Bucher, so hard she spilled some of her punch.

"Did you see that?" Linda asked with eyes wide with disbelief.

"What?" Karen looked around with concern as she took a napkin to the punch on the sleeve of her blouse. "Did I see what?"

With disbelief, Linda relayed, "You know the new girl? I just saw one of the men brush her breasts with his arm while they turned."

"Wait, say no more, I bet donuts to dollars I can guess who did this. It was Walter Wagner, right?"

Linda looked amazed. "How'd you know?"

Karen lowered her voice to a conspiratorial whisper and they both glanced over their shoulders to see who was near them before Karen continued.

"I once spoke to his wife, Agnes. You know her, right? She is seated over there beneath the big crucifix. You've probably seen her at the post office where she used to work."

They both glanced quickly toward the wall and saw Agnes sitting with a horrified look as she watched the dancers with a particular focus on her husband. Her glass of punch was frozen midway between her lap and her mouth as she sat ramrod straight and intensely observed what was unfolding on the dance floor.

"We were talking about our husbands as we helped prepare a fundraising dinner at the Elks Club. We'd both had a few beers by then." They both surreptitiously looked at Agnes again before Karen continued.

"She said her husband had roving hands with other women and she seemed to think all men did this. I told her my Louie did not touch other women, but she just laughed like I was joking." Now they both looked at Walter with a scowl and then back at Agnes before continuing.

"I knew they had high school exchange students staying at their house and, maybe because of the beer I'd consumed, blurted out a question without thinking. I asked her how she managed to keep Walter's hands off the young girls who lived with them."

Linda's eyes widened as she took in the risk and outrage of possible child sexual abuse in their town. "What did she say?" Linda asked with interest.

"She said he had a 'type' and she just made sure to never host a student who met his physical preferences."

Linda was fascinated and horrified at the same time. How could this happen without the international student agency being aware? Also, was Walter able to keep his hands off the girls or had Agnes deluded herself?

"Did she say what 'type' he liked?" she asked.

"If I remember right, it was thin, well endowed, white girls with blue eyes. Just like what Agnes looked like when she was younger."

Both women turned their attention to Zoey on the dance floor as Walter managed to cunningly caress her neck and shoulder. They realized she fit every criterion on Walter's checklist. With growing alarm and the appalling draw of watching a car accident occur, they saw Walter grab Zoey's butt and raised his eyebrows with a flirty smile. She responded by slapping his hand away and saying something they couldn't hear, and then left the dance formation midway into the song, grabbed her purse, and ran from the room with a flaming red face.

Across the hall, Agnes paled and slowly lowered her punch glass without ever taking a sip.

I fled the building with my face burning with shame and embarrassment at how much I put up with before deciding enough was enough. I ran to my car, jumped in, started it, and backed out of the parking space even before I registered where I was.

As I headed home, upset by Walter's audacity and awash with my own sense of violation and rage, I shifted my fury between him for his actions and me for not listening to my gut. I realized I didn't have time to make sense of what was happening as I was trying so hard to keep up with the caller's quick directions. My inexperience at this type of dance was part of what happened, but the bigger part was I didn't trust my own intuition.

Unfortunately, like most women in America, I had experience with multiple episodes of groping and sexual harassment. After each incident, I tried to use logic to figure out if there were any clues I missed, what I could learn from the situation, and what I would do differently in the future. Through all these incidents, I had made safety plans to prevent myself from ever again enduring the horrible feeling of violation. However, tonight when it really mattered, I silenced my inner voice and didn't listen to my self-protective warning bells.

I would've never predicted this, but my self-recrimination was stronger than what I felt toward him probably because I could not control his actions, but I could control my own.

As I continued to try to process the experience, I suddenly saw flashing red lights behind me. I hadn't been paying any attention to my driving and didn't have a clue why I was being stopped by law enforcement.

I dutifully pulled over and put my hands in the two and ten o'clock positions Papa had taught me to do to show the officer I meant no harm to him or her. The police car's lights were on high and shining in my side mirror, so I couldn't make out any details about whoever was approaching me.

Starting to talk before my face was fully visible, the officer said, "Good evening, ma'am. Do you know why I pulled you over?"

While I didn't know my offense, I was shocked to realize I knew the man.

"Hi, Officer Peshlakai. It's me, Zoey, the lady you helped with the cat problem." I gave a half smile and a nod of appreciation. I was relieved he appeared to recognize me. "I'm sorry, but I'm upset, so I wasn't paying attention to the road. I probably shouldn't be on the road, but I'm just trying to get home."

"Hey, Zoey. Good to see you again." He gave me a big smile, then furrowed his brow with concern. "You say you're upset. Are you okay?"

"I will be, but I'm still outraged at the liberties a guy at the square dance just took." Then, looking away and speaking more to myself than him, I added, "I probably should've sat for a while to calm down before I started driving, but I just wanted to get away from there." Returning my focus to Officer Peshlakai, I added, "I'm really sorry I wasn't focused on the road."

"You said someone took liberties with you? What happened, Zoey? Do you need police involvement?"

"Oh, I don't think it was bad enough to warrant police action. I mean, he didn't expose himself or try to rape me. It was more subtle, but still feels awful all the same. He touched me in ways I didn't like, and I kept making excuses for him, so I let it happen repeatedly."

"He touched you inappropriately more than once? At the square dance? Were you in a back room or hallway?"

"No, that's just it. It was out in the open and during the dance! I couldn't believe someone would be so blatant, so I figured the first few touches were accidental. It wasn't until he grabbed my butt I realized it wasn't accidental."

"Unwanted contact like you describe is called groping and it's illegal in Arizona. If someone grabs or touches you with the intent to injure, insult, or provoke you, it constitutes assault. You don't have to put up with this, Zoey. I can help you file charges against the man. Would you like my assistance in this way?"

"I'm not sure, Officer Peshlakai. I still can't believe it happened and I'm so angry I didn't listen to myself when my interior warning bells were going off. It kind of feels like I'm responsible somehow. I think I need time to process what happened. Besides, I don't even know his last name."

"This is Nugget. It would be easy to figure out."

I was feeling overwhelmed and shocked about this whole situation. "May I have some time to consider this?"

"Sure, you can. There is a two-year statute of limitations in sexual assault cases, but I will tell you the sooner you file, the better. A prompt investigation usually results in better evidence which will help with a conviction. If this man is found guilty, it is a Class 3 misdemeanor, and he can be fined up to $500 and/or spend 30 days in jail."

I stopped to try to take this in. I didn't realize I could file charges against someone for groping. I also thought $500 seemed way too low a fine for such presumptuous behavior that hurt me all the way to my soul.

"Zoey, you have time to consider your options and I'll gladly discuss these more with you if you wish." He gave me a kind smile and a little nod, then shifted back to the reason for his initial traffic stop. "I pulled you over because you barely slowed at the last stop sign. I think they might call that a 'California stop', but it doesn't work here." He paused to let his comment soak in, then added, "Though I might not have stopped you at all, except your license plate light was out as well and I wanted to let you know so you can get the bulb replaced."

At this point, my feelings of shame over what was done to my body and embarrassment at being pulled to the side of road in a small town where everyone knows everyone (including their cars) collided. I hit my limit for 'bad things in a single day' and started to blink back tears. Officer Peshlakai noticed, frowned, and tried to soften his reproach.

"One of the great things about Nugget is people walk the downtown every evening. Stop signs become imperative, particularly with folks pushing baby strollers or walking dogs."

"I'm so sorry, Officer. Like I said, I was distracted; however, I know it's no excuse. I promise to pay more attention to the road signs."

His brow furrowed as he looked more intently at my face trying to make a judgment about whether I should continue the half mile home. He must have decided in the affirmative when he took a half step backward and added, "I'm going to give you a warning about the stop sign violation and tell you to get your lightbulb repaired in the next 30 days or you will likely be cited."

I was so relieved I started to cry. As the tears started to roll down my face, I sniffed and quietly said, "Thank you."

With a kindly expression, he added, "You take care of yourself, Zoey. Let me know if I can help in any way and I'm sorry you had such a rough evening. Get home safely, rest, and I'm sure things will look better in the morning."

I nodded gratefully and the tears quickened as his kindness washed over me. When he stepped back from my car, I turned on my blinker, slowly pulled away from the curb, and headed home to take as long and hot a shower as my skin could tolerate.

**COMMENT BY THE CHIEF OF POLICE
OVERHEARD WHILE HAVING LUNCH AT
NUG'S NUGGET NOOK:**

I find it ironic the colors red, white,
and blue are the colors of freedom
until they're flashing behind you.

AS READ IN THE NUGGET NEWS:

**Estelle's Introduces New "Cinnamon Crunch
Salted Caramel Delight" Muffin**

Chapter 26

The Morning After

I still felt awful the morning after the groping incident, so I decided to go for a long run to clear my head. However, rather than clearing my thoughts, they just became more jumbled.

Did I do anything to make him think his touch would be welcome? Perhaps it was not processing quickly enough how uncomfortable his progressive strokes made me feel and not stepping away? I felt objectified as if he was taking ownership of a thing, not dancing with a person. Was there anything I could have done differently to protect myself?

Why didn't I trust myself? I overrode the warning bells in my head and in my body. Why did I decide his actions were accidental when they felt so awful? With all I have studied and all the people I have counseled, I knew better! Why did I let this situation continue as long as I did?

Also, did anyone else see what happened? If they did, I hope they didn't think I encouraged this behavior. Are they talking about this incident in the community? Will I be able to tell if people think poorly of me or treat me differently? But, maybe if they're talking, they will confront Walter and hold him accountable for his actions. Actually, if anyone is talking, Lucille is likely to hear it and let me know. I just don't want to ask her or involve her in something so unpleasant if I can help it.

I then thought back to all the groping incidents I endured, and the memories flashed like a strobe light: as a teen at Dodger stadium, in the back hall of the hotel where I worked banquets, on the New York subway, in the pool during a scuba lesson, and even in college working a part-time job while I studied abroad. While I didn't always know who the perpetrator was, I did in some cases and simply was ignorant I could hold them responsible for their actions. I always felt humiliated by these incidents and powerless. In each I wondered if I had brought it on myself in some way, fully accepting the "blame the victim" mentality common over the last 20 years. I tried to sweep the incidents under the rug and pretend they didn't happen. However, the wash of nausea I felt now as I experienced the culminative damage of these violations let me know the "under the rug" solution had never worked.

I also thought about where God was during each of these incidents. When I was researching child sexual abuse, I had a lot of questions about how an all-powerful and all-good God could let these heinous acts happen to voiceless and defenseless children. I delved into autobiographies about the holocaust and then, closer to home, the Japanese internment camps and genocidal campaigns against Native Americans in my home state of California, trying to understand how people kept their faith when dehumanized and horribly abused.

In my quest to answer these questions, I discovered the concept of theodicy and read various theologians' writing on the topic. In a nutshell, if (1) God is all powerful, all good, and all knowing, and (2) God made all things, then (3) how does evil exist? How do we vindicate or make sense of an all-loving God who allows evil and doesn't stop victimization?

Not to be overly dramatic, I understand my various groping incidents and threats of sexual violence are no where near the vicinity of genocide or human trafficking or horrific child abuse. But, believing God is ever present, it begs the question of why God appears to intervene in some situations and not others. In the end, I decided to stand on God giving humans free will to do good or evil, and the comfort of having a suffering Savior who is present with us in our darkest hours, weeping both with us and for the choices being made by the oppressor.

Though, to be honest, I didn't want God to have any compassion for Walter this morning.

I kept running until I could lower the intensity of my self-criticism from a nine to a six (on a scale of ten) and direct most of my indignation toward the grown fool who had acted so selfishly and inappropriately. As a new person in town, I wasn't sure if I wanted to press charges, so

I decided to talk to my attorney sister about this. Also, there were so many things pulling for my focus, I didn't know if legal charges and a possible court appearance were how I wanted to use my time or energy. I looked forward to getting my sister's legal opinion when I could talk to her by phone.

When I got home, I kicked the newest pair of purloined underwear in my house to the side of the hallway, brewed some coffee, put on soft classical music, grabbed my Bible for my morning devotions, and took my Bluetooth speaker outside to sit on my patio. I let the beauty of the morning act as a balm to my ragged soul. Just as I started to feel the warmth of the java and focus on the variety of bird calls surrounding me, I heard a cheerful, "Yoo hoo!"

Lucille turned the corner as she entered my yard with a bright smile, sparkling eyes, and then waved at me with her cane which was sporting a new feathery cat toy attached by a string to her handle. She was focused on safely navigating my uneven stone patio as she headed my way and didn't seem to notice my dark mood. However, it was hard to stay angry and self-reflective with the infusion of her cheerfulness. All the same, I still needed a few minutes to transition to having company, so I decided to ask about the new toy attached to her cane to give myself a little more time to transition into interacting with her.

"Hi, Lucille. What's this new contraption on your cane?"

"Oh, honey, your boy simply adores this toy! I've tried a whole bunch of different ones with him, but this is his favorite, so I decided to start carrying it with me so I'm ready if he's feeling sporty and wants to pounce and tumble after these feathers."

I thought of her limited food purchases, regular Meals on Wheels deliveries, and frequent reports of gratitude for the aged-out bread and cookies Jimmy's made available for free at the Senior Center. I was concerned for how her love for the cat might be impacting her financially.

"You're not buying toys for the cat, are you, Lucille?"

"Oh, don't worry, honey. These won't break the bank. I'm not paying full price." She plopped herself into my open patio chair, barely fitting her generous backside into the confines of the metal chair rails. After leaning her cane against the side table, she explained, "These are from a toy basket at the animal rescue place. I buy them for only 25 cents each. It's an absolute steal." Here Lucille gave a proud smile. "Even if he doesn't like them a lot, I feel like I'm getting such a bargain."

I was a little relieved to know she wasn't skipping a meal or not picking up her medication to finance what I was beginning to comprehend may be an extensive collection of cat toys. However, just as I breathed a sigh of relief, she continued.

"Saving all that money gives me extra dollars in my pocketbook and I don't want it to burn a hole, so I splurge it in a different way. Did you know how much your boy adores salmon?"

I didn't see that coming. I shook my head and sputtered out, "What did you just say?"

"He likes tuna as well, but salmon is his favorite. Now don't worry yourself about calories and such, I only buy the fish packed in water and not in oil."

"Wait, are these cans of salmon and tuna-flavored cat food?"

"Goodness, no! Who knows what's in that stuff? I saw a news story about a nail found in one can, metal shavings in another, and even cock roach parts in some cans. No, I wouldn't expect him to ingest animal parts or contaminants. I care too much about our sweet boy to see him possibly suffer."

I could imagine the big lout sitting at Lucille's table at the place she regularly sets for him eating salmon out of a porcelain bowl. Suffer? Hardly.

"Be reassured, Zoey, I also make sure the fish is low in mercury, sustainably sourced, and wild-caught."

I shook my head. Who was this? The Lucille I knew ate discarded Pop Tarts and cookies, bought 44-ounce soda pops when on sale at the gas station, and regularly called a cup-of-noodles a full meal. Low in mercury and sustainably sourced? Seriously?

I didn't point out the dramatic difference in what she put into her body versus what she felt was appropriate for a wild cat's consumption, so I shifted my observation to her last comment and remarked, "Lucille, I didn't take you for an environmentalist."

"I'm not sure about environmentalism, but I do know I want the best for our little lump of love. He is such a treasure and he's always grateful for the treats."

Yes, I bet he was. Wild caught tuna and salmon. I didn't buy that level of quality for myself and all this time the "little lump of love" was enjoying fine dining.

"Also, did you know he likes broccoli?"

"What?"

"Once a month, the food bank brings boxes of fruits and veggies to the Senior Center. This past month's box included broccoli and I accidently dropped some on the floor. Of course, our big boy found it immediately and began to play with it. I was enjoying his antics when he decided to taste the toy and must have liked it because he ate all of it and then looked to me and meowed for more."

"He wanted more broccoli? Really? I didn't know cats would eat vegetables."

"Oh, he loves all sorts of things, Zoey. I discovered his passion for bacon and cheesy eggs but found he will not eat just regular scrambled eggs. He'll eat oatmeal but is not as fond of it as he is cottage cheese. He also surprised me when I found him drinking my Sanka."

"Lucille, are you saying the cat drinks your coffee?"

"Yes, sweetheart. He seems quite the fan and might even like it better than his saucer of milk."

I had no response to this and just shook my head trying to take this new information in.

Lucille sighed loudly and smiled before adding, "Zoey, I know I don't have to tell you, but I just adore your cat."

SIGN POSTED NEXT TO CASH REGISTER IN GLORIA JEAN'S DIVA SALON & BOUTIQUE:

Always wear your invisible crown.

AS READ IN THE NUGGET NEWS:

Nugget NRA Hosts Annual Turkey Shoot

Chapter 27

Processing the Violation

The first person I talked to about the incident at the square dance was Kim. John had the kids at the park, so she and I were alone at her house while I did some laundry. Like a true friend, she was outraged when she heard what happened and thought Walter should be punished.

"That's not okay, Zoey. I don't care how much of an old fart he might be, even ancient guys know you don't touch women like that." She humphed in frustration as she considered the situation.

"Kim, I don't know if anyone else saw this and I let it continue longer than I should have," I admitted.

"It's not your job to catch on to other people acting like jerks. It's up to them to not be buttholes in the first place."

While inelegant, I found her comment true.

Kim continued, "I hate when men think they're entitled to touch whomever they want or act inappropriately with looks or words; however, I've just put up with this nonsense my whole life. However, now that I have a daughter, I don't want to sit back and expect her to 'just take it'. I need to make this world a better and safer place for her and other young girls."

"You know, Kim, I hadn't thought about this having an impact on anyone besides me, especially not someone like Olivia. You've added a wrinkle I hadn't considered as I try to figure out how I'll respond to the groping."

Kim then referenced an earlier comment I had made, "So you're not sure if anyone else saw this codger touch you?"

"No, I have no idea. I wasn't looking around and I ran out of there after it happened."

"Well, that's something we can fix," replied Kim. "While I don't know anyone in the square dance group, I can start to ask around about the old goat."

"No, please don't, Kim," I requested. "I'm not sure how I want to proceed yet and don't want this information spreading around the community."

When her face reflected confusion, I added," I don't want the added talk or attention while I'm also weathering Dr. Hinman's negativity. I don't know how he might do it, but I believe with all my heart he'll find a way to use this incident against me."

My papa somehow knows when things are bothering me. It's almost spooky. I don't know how he does it, but he usually knows something is up even before I tell him. When we were next on the phone, he asked early in the conversation, "Mija (*my daughter*), what is brewing in your corazon (*heart*)? I sense you are carrying a heavy weight."

I had suspected he would know, so I was kind of prepared to tell him about the groping. While not a comfortable topic to discuss with a father, I also trusted him implicitly.

"Papa, I went to a local dance and an older man touched my breasts. I didn't trust my instincts and wrote it off as an accident. The grace I gave him let the groping continue and he touched me in other places. This made me feel even worse when I finally caught on to what was happening and left the building."

My papa is one of the most patient men I know, but his anger at hearing this was sudden and passionate. "This is not right! That man must be held accountable!"

"That's just it, Papa, I don't know if I want to press charges or get the police involved."

"Yes, law enforcement is appropriate," he countered. His assessment felt less like a pursuit of justice and more like an act of delegation with someone in authority stepping in when he could not advocate for me himself.

"I'm considering this, Papa. I want to talk to Kat before I decide anything," I explained.

He then offered another solution. "Zoey, I can leave here immediately and be in Nugget in ten hours. If you want, I will confront this man for you. He will not abuse you again," he declared emphatically.

"Thank you, Papa, but I think this is something I need to figure out for myself. However, please know I appreciate and will consider your offer."

"Mija, this incident, plus the bullying and lies from your boss. It is enough, si (*yes*)? It is time for you to come home."

"I'm considering this, Papa, and praying about it. Truly, I am. However, God's leading to come to this place was so strong, I'm not willing to pack up yet. I think there's a reason I'm here."

"Ah, mi amore (*my love*), you have a good heart, but some people will take advantage of this. I don't want this to happen to you."

"I know, Papa. I know. Thank you," I said with sincerity. "Also, I know I say this a lot to you, but it's true: I'm so glad you are my papa, and I am amazingly grateful for your love."

He accepted my decision during that phone call and waited to hear how I planned to proceed or not proceed. However, in subsequent calls he started to again press for me to return to Los Angeles and even got my mom to join in the push, though I think her comments about getting married to stop foolishness like this may have been a bigger priority for her. Papa is nothing if not persistent when he is advocating for his girls.

My older sister, Katrina, understood immediately how awful I felt and had experienced jerks groping her, too.

"What woman hasn't?" she asked more as a statement than a question.

"Kat, I don't need your experience as a woman," I clarified a little impatiently. "I need to know what you recommend as an attorney."

"My specialization is tax law, Zoey, you know that; however, I studied criminal law in school and have friends who practice in that arena." She paused and thought about the situation before asking, "You know this could result in a long and drawn-out legal battle, right? Do you have credible witnesses?"

"I'm not sure," I answered truthfully. "The room was full of people, but I don't know if anyone was looking at me or him. Even if they thought they saw something, they might write it off as unintentional contact like I did."

"Did anyone talk to you about the situation after it happened?"

"I didn't stick around long enough to give them a chance to talk to me. I just wanted to get away as quickly as I could."

"I understand you getting out of that space, but witnesses matter," Kat emphasized. "Without witnesses, it's just a 'he said, she said' situation. With this guy being older, I bet he is more established in the community and might be believed over you."

I tightened my mouth as I considered my tenuous new friendships and relationships at work and around town. Would I be believed? How respected was Walter?

"Another thing," my sister added. "In a small town, your accusation is going to be talked about and tried in the court of public opinion, even if it never goes into a courtroom or before a judge. Do you want that attention and added stress?"

It only took me a millisecond to decide I did not.

We were both quiet for a few moments considering other angles before Kat added, "There's a movement afoot to make people more aware of sexual harassment, but this effort is still in its infancy." She then drilled down more specifically addressing the environment in Nugget, "I doubt your little mining town will be up to even a beginning level of sensitivity and awareness of sexual assault and harassment."

I knew my sister was probably right about this. Kat and I had talked about how rural areas don't seem as aware of political correctness as big cities like Los Angeles are.

"Zoey, I think this process would likely be harder on you than the jerk who groped you in the first place," she surmised. "I want to caution you about proceeding legally against this man. Given what you've told me, I would not get the police involved."

"But, as bad as I feel about the groping, Kat, I feel worse knowing this happened and deciding to do nothing to fix the problem which potentially sets other women up to feel as violated as I do." I was thinking specifically of five-year-old Olivia and Kim's admonition to do something to make the world better for her.

"Zoey, I know you want to do what's right, but not every battle is yours to fight. You've got a lot to deal with adjusting to your new town, trying to stay under the radar of your obnoxious boss, and intervening to stop self-harm and child abuse among your clients."

In my heart of hearts, I knew she was right. I'm no sloth in confronting inequity and injustice. I fight against these things all the time. However, this topic may not be my battle to undertake.

I made my decision to do nothing for the time being.

My sister added, "Also, remember there's a two-year statute of limitations which can be used if you ever change your mind."

Even talking about all of this made me feel dirty and, after hanging up the phone, I took another extremely long, blisteringly hot shower.

ADVERTISEMENT TACKED TO THE MESSAGE BOARD AT THE HARDWARE STORE:

You know what will make housework a lot more fun? A cleaning lady. Call Maria Guadalupe Hernandez for good house cleaning services at a fair price (Only available during school hours)

HEADLINE IN THE NUGGET NEWS:

Belles and Beaus Square Dance Club Qualifies for International Dosido Competition in Canada

Chapter 28

Feeling Thankful

As the holidays approached, I noticed the cute jack-o-lantern look of our mailboxes had recently been replaced by Lucille with turkeys and fall leaves as we moved into November.

To make plans with my family for the holidays, I spoke to Papa, Mom, Kat and her girlfriend, Eden. No one had really cemented Thanksgiving plans, but Kat and Eden had just moved to Seattle for Eden's new job as a district prosecutor. They were not enthusiastic about traveling when I invited them all to come to Nugget. Papa said he was up for the visit, but Mom balked at ten hours of driving one way and then a quick turn-around after the long weekend. We decided to all do our own thing for Thanksgiving and then to get together in Los Angeles for Christmas.

I later happily realized being in L.A. for a week would also give me a chance to get my hair cut by someone who knew how to cut curls.

A few days later, I was talking with Kim. We knew family dinners were notorious for bringing out the best and worst in families. Because it was Kim's turn to host the Winthrop Thanksgiving meal, she and I both knew Marge would fall in the later of these two categories. However, even with that dumpster fire to anticipate, I was thrilled when Kim invited me to join their family for the holiday.

In fact, her invitation made it into the top ten of my "Things I'm Grateful For" list as I prepared for Thanksgiving and reviewed my blessings during my morning devotional. While I knew the offer was soaked in hospitality and love for me from a dear friend, I also suspected Kim could use some emotional back-up when interacting with Marge. I asked what I could bring, and she asked instead for me to come to her house to help with the cooking, starting the night before the meal.

Welcome to Nugget

Thanksgiving dawned crisp and cool, with bright sunshine emphasizing the gorgeous fall colors of yellow, red, and orange in the trees and shrubs. Anticipating both eating more than I usually do and needing to mediate the stress Marge would bring, I went for a long run in the morning. I saw Eaton and Makin walking Crispy, then Makin flagged me down.

"Hey, Zoey, as a doctor I thought you'd appreciate my new joke. Listen… One day a plumber fixes a damaged pipe in a doctor's house and asks for $200. The doctor balks and says, 'Even I don't make so much money in such a short period and I'm a doctor.' The plumber replies, 'I know, sir. I used to be a doctor myself.'" We all laughed, and Makin seemed to walk with a lighter step as I continued my run.

A few blocks later, I saw Carl walking with something. As I approached, the companion became clear: it was the giant cat.

I shouldn't have been surprised.

I showed up about two hours early to help Kim with the food preparation and table setting. We always ate in the kitchen with casual plates, so I was shocked to see her entertainment selection.

"Kim, your linen, crystal and china are stunning," I exclaimed with surprise.

"All wedding gifts," she said as she passed me to pull out candlesticks to add to the table.

Olivia was ecstatic to be helping with the easier cooking tasks and it was a delight to watch how much joy this brought her. Twenty minutes before the extended family was to arrive, Kim stopped cooking to get the kids cleaned up and dressed in their nicest "dress up" clothes (as Olivia called her outfit). Kim changed into a gorgeous shimmery champagne silk sheath dress and John appeared in a dark grey designer suit. Seeing their finery, I was glad I had decided to dress up for the meal.

Marge and all the other Winthrops arrived within five minutes of each other and very much on time. They were all dressed formally.

As a prophylactic measure, John had already put on some calming Vivaldi in the background, a composer he knew Marge liked. He then took drink orders and opened several bottles of wine for the grown-ups and sparkling cranberry juice for the kids. While he was doing this, I took out the crudité and olive appetizer plates Kim had prepared.

"Hmm, I haven't seen you use your crystal glasses for a while," Marge observed as she scrutinized the house, the table, and the family's clothing choices. "Those are Waterford, right? I think my cousin gave them to you."

"Yes, you're right. You've got a great memory, Marge," Kim observed evenly.

"But the linen napkins didn't get starched or ironed, did they?" Marge quickly followed.

"Again, you're right. You're very observant."

"One must always watch decorum, Kim. Propriety will open doors in this world," Marge lectured primly.

Kim doubted anyone else in town besides Marge would notice if the napkins were ironed (let along starched), but she kept this view to herself. She also knew most of the homes in Nugget were using paper napkins and possibly paper plates today.

People seemed to be having a good time and the kids were actively playing with their cousins when Kim called them all to the table. She had added extensions to the table, but still needed a kids table and a grown-ups table to fit all 21 people. As she knew would be expected of her, Kim had made formal place cards for each seat and people scrambled to find their name and take their place. Marge was at the end farthest away from Kim who sat closest to the kitchen door.

"It's always hard to figure out where to put Marge in situations like this," Kim had confided earlier. "She wants to be in the center or at the head of the table, but she would also be upset if John and I didn't take our places at the ends of the tables as she considers proper for the host and hostess to do." She sighed heavily, "I don't know why I even think about it. Whatever I do will be inadequate for her."

I watched Marge to see how she would respond to being at John's right side, but at the end of the table. She noted her placement and where everyone else was assigned but accepted John's gracious offer to seat her formally and then rested her left hand on John's forearm in a proprietary manner when everyone had taken their seats. I think Kim chose well.

John had already deposited a gorgeous 22-pound turkey on a giant platter at the head of the table. The turkey was browned to perfection and garnished with sage and little pearl onions. It was lovely and could have graced a Martha Steward *LIVING* magazine cover which was something I told Kim ahead of time in anticipation of a slew of criticism at the table. She seemed to appreciate hearing this. I helped bring in the food with Kim, another thing we discussed with Marge in mind. It was decided John was more valuable as a buffer and focus for Marge at the table.

Kim had scoured *Southern Living* and *Bon Appetite* for recipes and simply outdid herself. She prepared, with Olivia and I acting as her sous chefs, an herb-roasted turkey with lots of butter, a white wine and rosemary gravy, cornbread dressing with sage and pork sausage, sour cream mashed potatoes, broccoli and cauliflower gratin, bourbon yams with a toasted marshmallow topping, roasted squash with goat cheese and cranberries, and a crispy brussels sprout salad with a citrus-maple vinaigrette. She had given one sister-in-law a recipe for salted caramel-apple slab pie and another a recipe for ginger pumpkin pie. The third sister-in-law always brought two pecan pies and Marge brought an oversized traditional pumpkin pie from Estelle's. Kim had rich French vanilla ice cream for an a la mode addition for those who didn't want her handmade maple-vanilla whipped cream.

I would be shocked if any table in the community was as well dressed as Kim's or had such succulent food choices. It was the tastiest Thanksgiving dinner I had ever had, and I had no idea this hidden talent hibernated within my friend. Kim's cooking was extraordinary and most of her guests let her know.

Of course, this was not the viewpoint of Marge.

While even she couldn't slam the beauty of the table, she spoke out about some people present needing to stay mindful of carb counts and healthy choices. She then passive-aggressively slammed the amazing dishes by lauding the value of simple food choices (plain turkey, plain potatoes, plain yams) that spoke to our true American heritage without fancy spicing or flavors being added that might confuse people's palates. She also vociferously expressed her view there was not enough food for all the people present and offered to skip eating if it would help everyone else get fed.

I think she was trying to get Kim to eat less with her whole self-sacrificing "I'll not eat" routine and, personally, I would have accepted her offer of martyrdom out of pure spite. However, Kim was much more gracious and directed everyone to fill their plates as full as they would like. She said there was enough for all and offered to pull out frozen pizzas if people were still hungry after this meal.

Marge frowned and shook her head disapprovingly to even imagine frozen food (and pizza at that!) ever gracing a Winthrop holiday table.

I was upset at Marge's rudeness and tried to shift the tone of the table. "Kim, this is the best Thanksgiving meal I have ever eaten!"

"Thanks," Kim said with humble gratitude for the honest acknowledgment.

"How did you learn to cook like this? If a recipe has more than four ingredients, I'm intimidated. I don't think I could have done any of these dishes."

"My grandmother was a renown cook in this area, regularly bringing home 'Best in Fair' awards from the annual county fair. She's the one who taught me how to cook. In fact, she was teaching me techniques until about a week before she passed away."

Knowing fame and community recognition was important to Marge, I strongly suspected she had known Kim's grandmother. Feeling malevolent toward her because of her cruelty to my friend, I asked, "Did you know Kim's grandmother, Marge?"

Marge gave me a frown and a hesitant, "Yes, I did." Her reluctant answer suggested she wondered where I was going with this.

Having heard from Kim that Marge didn't ever cook the family Thanksgiving dinner and always had it catered, I feigned innocence and asked, "Were you ever fortunate enough to try out any of her recipes when you've cooked your Thanksgiving meals?"

The entire table grew silent as every eye turned toward Marge. They knew the answer and assumed I did not. Several looked my way quickly to see if the explosive bomb of a question was accidental.

Welcome to Nugget

While Marge craved attention, she didn't like what she was getting now and gave me an intense and angry stare while the silence deepened.

When she did speak, Marge didn't talk to me and pretended she hadn't heard my question. Expertly, she shifted the attention away from her lack of cooking skills to her sizable knowledge of wine with a comment to John, "Is there anymore of this lovely Chardonnay? It tastes like a Chartreuse Vineyard warm weather grape with its lower acid and opulent fruit flavor. Is this the award-winning bottle I gave you for your birthday?"

I know my actions were petty, but I felt a smug satisfaction at unsettling Marge and turning her attack away from Kim. If I knocked Marge down a few pegs, it seemed only fair with all the ways she was unfairly disparaging Kim. I know, not nice, but it seemed appropriate in the moment.

I had one other small moment of satisfaction when I saw how upset Marge became with what Tucker was being allowed to eat.

After he turned four, Tucker hit a picky eater phase. He seemed particularly sensitive to food spiciness and texture. Despite Marge's anticipated and then realized criticism, John and Kim had already decided to not fight this at the holidays and just let him eat whatever he wanted for this one meal.

When I looked over at the kids' table to spy on Tucker's thanksgiving plate, it made me smile. He had served himself a mound of cranberry-orange sauce, a pile of sliced black olives, and a little mountain of sugar cubes. I agreed with John and Kim that Thanksgiving was about much more than nutrition and, more importantly, Tucker appeared thankful for what he had before him.

As the meal progressed, Marge monopolized the conversation with talk about longstanding family traditions and what other notable families in the community were doing for the holiday. If anyone else tried to add anything to the conversation, she repeatedly interrupted with "I was talking" or "Nobody listens to me!" Though all but Marge loved the scrumptious food, I think everyone at the table was relieved when the meal was over, and the family took a break from eating (and from Marge) before enjoying the pies.

The kids all ran for the Winthrop kids' toys while half of the adults went with John's dad, Hal, to check on the ball game and the other half went out in the brisk and beautiful weather to walk a few blocks to help their food settle. I stayed and helped Kim clear the table of the dinner dishes and set out dessert plates and coffee cups.

"How dare she slam you, your meal, and your hospitality," I exclaimed angrily when in the kitchen helping Kim rinse and stack the dinner dishes. Maybe because Kim wasn't reacting to Marge, I felt doubly angry on her behalf.

"Oh, Zoey, come on. There's absolutely no surprise in Marge's behavior and I would have thought something was wrong if she wasn't trying to put me down every other minute. Besides, if I got upset every time she was inappropriate, I would be eternally angry. I don't want my Thanksgiving joy hijacked by her actions and my anger."

"It's just wrong," I continued halfheartedly, unwilling to give up my outrage on my friend's behalf.

"It's Marge," she concluded with composure.

With that, there wasn't anywhere else I could take my indignation. I tried to follow Kim's lead and let it go, but—to be honest—I wasn't entirely successful.

SIGN ON MARQUEE AT TASTY TIDBITS DONUT SHOP:

I hate when I think I'm buying organic vegetables and then get home to discover they're just regular donuts.

AS READ IN THE NUGGET NEWS:

Statistics show teen pregnancy drops off significantly at age 20: "Our prevention efforts are working!"

Chapter 29

Interaction in the Park

Besides being addicted to Nug's Nuggets and – more specifically – his secret sauce, I was almost dismayed to discover Estelle's Sweet Delights' scrumptious muffins. These giant baked confections were billed as breakfast, but they could have passed easily for dessert which is probably why I loved them so much. I found myself thinking about them at work and today woke up craving a concoction called a cinnamon crunch salted caramel delight. To be honest, I may have been dreaming about this muffin.

To support my planned indulgences for the day, I slathered on sunscreen, put on brightly colored clothing for roadside safety, grabbed my sunglasses, and went for a long run. I planned it so my six-mile route went into the hills around Nugget, then looped back into the downtown. I wear a Velcro armband to carry my phone and listen to music while I run, but it also has a tiny pocket for a key or cash. Today it had money tucked inside it for Estelle's muffin and a vanilla latte from No Doze.

Like most things done in a small town, my running habit was something the community both noticed and commented on. My jogging and especially my speed routine of timed sprints was humorous to some of the older residents who teased me about it when our paths crossed while I was exercising. They offered predictable lines like "So where's the fire?" or "How badly did you hurt him to have to run away so fast?" or "There's a speed limit around here, young lady." Makin once told me a joke when he saw me during one of my runs, "You know, Zoey, I like to run, too, because whenever I go running, I meet helpful people, like paramedics."

Other people were perplexed by my behavior and told me, "You know you don't actually have to run because you're already thin." They never seemed to catch on I could eat what I wanted because I ran. As expected, Makin also found frequent ways to tease me about being thin. Still other people, usually younger, seemed to admire the discipline it took to get out and move consistently.

This morning, several people honked and waved as I went through my paces. I smiled and returned their greetings. In what has become my new normal because of the cat, one man flagged me down to ask if I had found any underwear with pterodactyls on them (I had not... yet). About half a mile outside downtown, I started my cool-down walk and then, when I came to the delightful town square, I used a shaded bench for my stretches. When I had stopped profusely sweating, I felt presentable enough for an outdoor table or maybe a return to the park with breakfast on a bench, so I headed toward my intended destination: Estelle's Sweet Delights.

As I started to leave the park for the three blocks walk to the bakery, I looked across the expanse toward my preferred hangout area and something caught my eye. After an anonymous donor gave funds for park improvements, Nugget Public Works staff fixed the large park fountain and had the foresight to put benches among the largest mature trees which provided the most shade from the crushing heat. This section was back from the more trafficked part of the park, so it was quieter and to me more restful. I was a little disappointed when I saw my favorite bench behind the bandstand and closest to the large, multi-tiered fountain appeared occupied. However, as I looked closer, I thought the person might be Carl and then was shocked to realize he appeared to be talking!

I changed my trajectory to covertly get a little closer to see if this was possibly true. Yes, he seemed to be talking or at least his mouth was moving, but he was too far away for me to hear. Unfortunately, no one was sitting with him, so this might not be a great sign, but a break from his years of silence still seemed like an improvement. I was about to turn away when something moved in his lap. Wait a minute, what did he have there? I moved a little closer until I could see this wasn't a something, but rather a someone: a giant three-legged cat with an M on his forehead, tufted oversized ears, and a thunderous purr. He was stroking the cat and talking to him while the cat seemed to snuggle in, knead his pants leg, and even quietly trill back to Carl like he was carrying on a conversation.

Well, I'll be dipped!

I finally turned away to get my muffin and coffee and walked from the park with a pleased smile, incredulously shaking my head at the miraculous healing power of compassion.

Good job, cat.

POSTED ON EBENEZER BAPTIST CHURCH'S MARQUEE:

The first to apologize is the bravest.
The first to forgive is the strongest.
The first to forget is the happiest.

AS READ IN THE NUGGET NEWS:

```
Research Shows Oxygen is Good for your
                 Health
```

Chapter 30

Light Extravaganza

Christmas is one of my favorite holidays and I discovered Nugget did it justice. I loved the small-town celebrations of a light parade, neighborhood decoration contests, Christmas bazaars by two of the churches, a Christmas carol sing-along at Ebenezer Baptist where people from all the churches came, a youth production of A Christmas Carol, and then the magical first sprinkling of snow. Being from Southern California, this was a new experience and I loved it, but decided to stay home for the three hours or so before the snow melted as I didn't know if it would affect the safety of the steep roads. I had no clue how to drive on snow or ice.

Lucille also loved Christmas. She decorated every inch of her house, wore Christmas-themed clothing all through December, and really outdid herself with our mailboxes. She opened the doors and built a little cardboard bridge between the two mailboxes, then transformed the interior of the boxes into a stable with Mary, Joseph, wise men, shepherds, angels, sheep, and an oddly shaped cow. She added a star on a long pipe cleaner over the boxes and craftily held off from telling me it would light up. Instead, she got me outside the first night to discover the star had a sensor that turned on a tiny battery-powered light when it grew dark. The mailbox stable had an empty manger she insisted could not hold the little plastic Jesus until December 25th.

I wasn't sure how the post woman was going to fit our mail into the box around this crowded menagerie, but somehow, she figured it out. I also covertly checked if the figures were taped or glued down. They were not, so I prayed there were no winds strong enough to blow the people and animals out of the mailbox stable and checked them each morning as I went to work.

Welcome to Nugget

As a part of my Christmas shopping, I visited Patriot Firearms to purchase a holster for Lucille's Smith and Wesson .357 Magnum revolver. I did not want her to resort to her bathrobe tie or another Jimmy's Grab and Go bag if she needed to have access to her gun. The staff were extremely helpful as we debated the merits of each option they had and how it might fit onto the upper railing of a walker. One younger staff member even walked a quick block home to borrow his grandfather's walker so we could try out the various holsters before I decided on my purchase. I just knew Lucille would love this gift.

I made plans to drive the ten hours home to Los Angeles the day after school got out for winter break. My sister had moved to Seattle a few months ago and was coming down to L.A. with her partner, and Papa's mama – my abuela (grandma) - was going to be here from Costa Rica. Papa loved to have the entire family together. We spent quite a bit of our phone conversations discussing possible sleeping arrangements, as well as a rough schedule of favorite holiday traditions and how to make accommodations for Abuelita when we went into the mountains to cut down our Christmas tree, toured and rated neighborhood light displays, visited the Los Angeles County Zoo and Botanical Gardens for Zoo Lights, and had our Christmas Eve picnic at the beach.

Because I don't want to cheat Thanksgiving of any holiday limelight or let the commercialism of "Xmas" overtake my favorite family meal, I try to not start anything Christmassy until after Thanksgiving. However, this year I began wrapping gifts weeks before leaving as I eagerly anticipated seeing my family after months of separation. I felt my holiday violation was justified with all the planning I was doing with Papa and because I still held off decorating or playing Christmas music until the day after Thanksgiving.

Nugget Hardware was sponsoring a raffle to raise money for the Little League team, and they were selling tickets for 2500 feet of colored exterior lights. I wasn't interested in exterior Christmas lights but bought a ticket all the same because I pledged years ago to support every fundraiser advancing child ventures, be it wrapping paper sales, or raffles, or hand-lettered lemonade stands. To my shock, I heard on the radio my name was pulled out of hundreds of entries.

I didn't own a ladder or know how to put up exterior lights but figured I could improvise if need be. I borrowed a ladder from a work colleague and then offered to decorate both Lucille's and my houses. This seemed only fair with her year-round decoration of both of our mailboxes.

Lucille clapped with glee at this offer and talked about it for days. On "Light Extravaganza Saturday" as she was calling it, she bundled up and remained outside with me talking and telling stories the entire time I worked. Her breathy voice was hard to hear when I was on the ladder, and I asked her to speak up. She agreed to be louder, but she kept talking at her normal quiet volume. I don't know if she can go louder even if she wanted to do so.

There was nothing fancy to my strategy, just attach lights to the eaves around the outside of each of our houses and along the paths to our front door, but her enthusiasm made it seem like the Mona Lisa was being painted. I finished as dusk fell and, at her suggestion, we grabbed lawn chairs and moved these to her driveway, played Christmas music on my Bluetooth speaker, bundled up further with hats and lap blankets, and sat outside enjoying the lights for two hours after finishing up.

Because Lucille had announced she was going to be responsible for the evening's refreshments, she had been grabbing triple her normal cookie stash from the Senior Center. She divided her selections into her favorite cookie tins from the 1960s and '70s and gave me all the details of who gave her each tin and even what cookies were in them originally. Once full, she gave me a cannister heavily weighted with the lemon cookies I favored, kept a container for herself with most of the Mallomars, and saved a special tin with the broadest selection of choices for tonight. She also provided hot chocolate for the humans accompanied by a saucer of milk and some crunchy cat treats for the beast.

It was a lovely way to commemorate my favorite holiday and, I suspected, would be a part of my Christmas tradition in the future.

OVERHEARD AT THE NUGGET SENIOR CENTER:

"There's a pretty good chance I'll end up being one of those senior citizens who randomly bites people."

AS READ IN THE NUGGET NEWS:

Building Burns to Ground During Safety Inspection

Chapter 31

The Wrong Car

On the same evening Lucille and I were celebrating Light Extravaganza Saturday, Marge, Kim, and John attended one of the sold-out showings of the award-winning community youth theater group's production of Charles Dickens' "A Christmas Carol." Unfortunately, Hal couldn't attend because he had a "holiday gathering" with work colleagues, something John suspected involved poker, Nug's nuggets, and several bottles of single malt whiskey.

The entire youth production was impressive with outstanding acting and costumes, but most striking was the decision to move the stage to the middle of the room with theater patrons seated in a big circle around the acting area. John and Kim both felt this evening's quality of entertainment could give a big city production a run for its money.

Though they knew most of the kids and would have liked to stay to congratulate the cast and visit with friends, they had to skip the reception entirely because they needed to get home quickly: their babysitter had an algebra test the next day.

Marge no longer drove after dark, so she needed a ride home and Kim and John planned to drop her off on their way home. She stated almost immediately she "absolutely must make a quick stop at Jimmy's for a quart of milk." Even knowing their time crunch, Marge was unswayable and insistent, so they pulled into the grocery parking lot knowing acquiescence was easier than trying to convince her otherwise. They also knew Marge's shopping was never simply a quart of milk. Being the holidays, the lot was packed so John said he would keep the car running and wait for a parking spot to open while Kim went in with Marge.

Welcome to Nugget

The quick stop for milk ended up being 25 minutes and three bags of groceries later before Kim could get Marge out the door. Marge was talking about a scandal at her church and Kim was only half listening as she looked for John's white SUV. When she spotted the vehicle parked down the second row, she pointed Marge in this direction.

Marge came to a dramatic point in her story and said with a flair, "And then I said, 'We will not have poison served to God's people in his holy church!'"

"Wait, what? Weren't you just talking about muffins from Estelle's?"

"Exactly! Aren't you listening to me?" She began to shake her head remorsefully with the neglect she had to bear, "No one listens to me when I talk."

Kim silently thought, "How can we not listen? You never allow anyone but yourself to say a word!"

"So, as I was saying, the new girl coming to church works as a clerk at Estelle's Sweet Delights. She's been bringing the 'day old' muffins to church, you know the ones which don't sell on Saturday?"

Kim nodded and said, "Wonderful! I bet people are thrilled to get them. Those are the best muffins in town. Also, her donation solves your challenge of how to pay for treats at coffee hour."

"No! You are missing the point. Aren't you listening to me? Those muffins are filled with sugar and made with gluten. They will make people sick!"

"Marge, you buy Estelle's muffins to bring to parties. Didn't you bring them to the baby shower at church a few weeks ago?"

"That was completely different! It was a celebration, not church."

"Wait, so coming to God's house is not a celebration?"

"Of course not. Goodness, didn't your parents explain this to you when you were growing up? Everyone knows you come to church as a sacred duty. We *celebrate* God at Christmas."

"So, it is okay for you to poison people with sugar and gluten when you bring the muffins and the occasion is a celebration, but it's not okay when the new girl brings them to coffee hour?"

"Exactly, it's just like…."

Kim doesn't hear the rest of what she said as Marge quickly got into a white SUV with the motor running.

Unfortunately, the vehicle was not John's car.

Kim didn't realize she was no longer walking with her until a few seconds later.

"…and that is why I will not allow this dangerous behavior to continue as long as I am the chair of the coffee hour snack team." Marge slammed the door shut, looked over at the driver, and screamed!

"Who are you? What have you done to John? Get out!" She started to whack the man sitting in the driver's seat with her oversized and punishingly heavy handbag. He put up his arms to defend himself, but she was faster and stronger than one might guess for a woman of her age.

Kim tried to get her out of the car but discovered the passenger door was locked. She banged on the window to get her attention and Marge screamed louder and hit the driver even harder, screaming, "You will not car jack me!" She then began a litany of "Get out! Get out! Get out!", punctuating each command with a blow from her weaponized handbag.

The man did the only thing he could do.

He got out.

Because Kim could not get Marge's attention on her side of the car, she ran around to the driver's side and approached the stunned driver who was standing outside his car rubbing his upper right arm. Kim quickly said, "Sorry" to him as she tried to get Marge's attention by speaking through the open door. "This is not John's car, Marge! You are in the wrong car. You need to get out. This is the wrong car! Marge, get out of the car!"

Finally, this registered enough for Marge to reach for the door handle and exit the vehicle. However, she still didn't comprehend the situation. She stomped around the vehicle at double-time and charged the young man, wielding all 5'2" of her stature. As she approached, he involuntarily stepped back from her. Fortunately for him, she had shifted from swinging her handbag to using her jabbing index finger to accentuate her message.

"How dare you do this to an old woman! You should be

ashamed of yourself. What would your mother think? This is an outrage. An outrage, I say! No, not an outrage, this behavior is beyond that... it is criminal!"

He stood there blinking, trying to figure out what was going on and how he got into the center of this mess.

Kim tried to get Marge's attention to redirect her from her thundering war path. "Marge, he didn't do anything to you. YOU got in HIS car! You scared him and then attacked him with your handbag. Marge, you did *him* wrong. You need to apologize."

"What? Did you say 'apologize'? Apologize... the very notion! I will not when I am the aggrieved party. In fact, how dare you even suggest such a travesty, Kim. This young man scared me nigh unto death! He needs to answer for his actions."

At this point, Kim had her by the elbow and was trying to get her to step away from the terrified man. As Marge continued to fume and spout off about "young people these days", Kim told the man, "I'm so sorry! Really, really sorry."

She repeated the apology a half dozen times.

A few weeks later, Marge was leaving Estelle's Sweet Delights with her friend, Edith, after buying a dozen muffins to take to the funeral luncheon for Johnson Smith. As she stepped outside the door, the young man was walking down the sidewalk toward her, and they both saw each other at the same time and froze.

Unfortunately, Marge unfroze first. "There! There he is, Edith. The man I told you about. The one who tried to kidnap me."

The young man's eyes grew wide, his face paled, and he raced across the street to the other sidewalk with a look of terror on his shocked face. Once there, he ran -- full speed, engaging all muscles, sucking air as his heart rate surged, and glancing over his shoulder to be sure she was not on his tail. Illogically he believed if any old person could catch him, this crazy biddy would be the one.

Marge and Edith shook their heads with disgust as they watched him flee before continuing a passionate discussion on the way to the funeral home. They covered the horror of crime coming to Nugget, reviewed self-defense and ways to prevent kidnapping, identified potential criminals targeting the elderly, and concluded by delineating the many things wrong with young people these days.

They were shaking their heads with looks of disgust as they pushed the funeral parlor's doors open.

SIGN POSTED NEXT TO CASH REGISTER IN GLORIA JEAN'S DIVA SALON & BOUTIQUE:

A recent study found women who carry a little extra weight live longer than the men who mention it.

AS READ IN THE NUGGET NEWS:

Man stabs mother-in-law with squirrel:
"I just couldn't take it any longer."

Chapter 32

Getting Fit

I really enjoyed my adopted family with John, Kim, Gunner, Olivia, Tucker, baby Emma, and Fish. They brought such joy to my life, and it was amazingly satisfying to be included in mundane and daily acts.

One evening as we did the dishes after a carb-rich spaghetti and garlic bread dinner, Kim shared how badly she felt about all the weight she had put on. She said each pregnancy left her a little heavier and she didn't feel good about it.

"I'm embarrassed to be out of breath climbing a flight of stairs. That's just pathetic!" she chided. "I know I would feel better if I lost a few pounds, but I'll be buggered if I'm going to give Marge the satisfaction of thinking she got me to start dieting," Kim declared.

"Could we do this sort of on the down low?" I queried.

"How so?" Kim asked.

"If you want, we can start to hike every weekend, or you could jog with me in the morning or just after work, but never in her neighborhood. You will likely lose a bit of weight, feel stronger, and the aerobic exercise will help your breathing with exertion. If you keep wearing your current clothing, I bet she won't notice if they start to get baggy," I summarized. "Besides, I would just love your company."

She smiled and considered this.

"I like it, Zoey," she said with a slow smile. "I have a jogger stroller and could probably fit both Tucker and Emma in it." As she considered the logistics of jogging, she realized, "This would be good for Fish, too. Maybe he'll burn off a little energy."

That decided it. We were on.

"What do you think about starting with walk-jogging a mile a few days a week?" I asked.

She nodded and then hesitantly revealed something she said she had shared with no one. "A few months ago, I decided to silence the voice of Marge in my head and lose 10 pounds." She seemed to then move past embarrassment to report, "So far, I only have 13 pounds to go."

She had a huge smile when I guffawed with surprise at her one liner. Comedic timing at its best.

We started walk-jogging a few days later. Because she was out of shape, we decided to run a block, then walk two blocks, then run one, etc. This was a good start for our first mile. We also decided to add a tenth of a mile a week to our distance. This increase was so incremental; it didn't feel overwhelming or scary and we agreed to reconsider our plan if it wasn't working. As her lung capacity grew, Kim could run and talk more easily. I was thrilled because I enjoyed hearing about the kids' antics and Kim was a great storyteller.

We also took all the kids and Fish on some of the weekend walks and hikes. As he grew better at voice recall, we started to let Fish off leash to bound up and down the hills along the trails. With some freedom, he ran at least three times the distance we hiked which helped to tire him out. He also was able to find any puddle, stream, pool, or mud hole within a tenth of a mile of the trail and always took himself for a cool-down soak when he found such a treasure. This was true when we hiked in warm and cold weather, including him swimming in the creek while it was snowing. Kim had numerous towels in the back of her minivan to try to reduce the moisture and mud Fish brought with him.

We also started to let Tucker out of the stroller to run along for some of our in-town walks to tire him out a bit, too. This didn't always work well though and sometimes was more tiring for us. Today he tried to run into a busy street.

"Tucker, you can't run in the street," corrected Kim loudly with a scowl of alarm as she grabbed the active preschooler.

I could tell she was both surprised at his fast movement and was masking her fear for his safety with a bit of irritability.

"I want to run in the street!" cried the four-year-old, something he had not considered a moment ago but now decided was the driving purpose of his life.

"Nope, you are too little to be in the street. The cars may not see you and if they hit you, you will have big ouchies which will make me very, very sad," explained Kim.

"I'm too little for everything," declared the tiny boy with disgust. "Gunnar and Olivia get to do everything."

"Sweetheart, even your sister and brother can't run in the street because they are too little, too."

Kim watched Tucker process this surprising information and then consider his own choices. He had the debate skills of a future attorney, and she was curious where he would go next as he rarely let a rule go unchallenged. His brain was practically whirring as he ran through possibilities and then asked, "How old do I have to be before I can run in the street?"

"You must be 18 ½ years old," answered his mom promptly and definitively.

He thought about this and, while not exactly sure how far away that was, he knew he now had an actual end point to this ghastly restriction on his freedom. Knowing the prohibition would end made it bearable. Plus, his older brother and sister were also prevented from this desired activity by the age restriction. Somehow, it was enough.

"Okay, Mommy. I will wait until I am 18 ½ years old," he acquiesced.

Kim smiled as he ran off down the sidewalk to join his older siblings.

We continued our exercise plan and started to call it our "group therapy" time, especially if another friend joined us while we exercised. I thought Kim was doing great, but she didn't feel like it even after losing a few pounds and gaining some muscle.

"I'm in a constant battle between wanting a hot body and wanting a hot fudge sundae," she told me.

Though I laughed at the imagery, I took her comment seriously.

Welcome to Nugget

"You know, Kim, as we focus on fitness, maybe it's not just about exercising our bodies, but maybe we also need to look at our self-talk and body image. What do you think?"

"I think you're on to something, Zoey. Even when I lost some weight between Olivia and Tucker, I still felt like a fat person when I looked in the mirror which was disheartening and I eventually gave up on my healthy eating choices," she huffed a bit as the trail steepened, then she continued. "Not only did I fall off the diet wagon, but I dragged it into the woods, set it on fire, and used the insurance money to buy ice cream."

I loved her sense of humor. Her levity was both a relief and kept putting things back into perspective when life became discouraging or too serious.

"We can do this, Kim. Let's start to think about it. Maybe we need to schedule an occasional spa day for our mental health. When's the last time you had a massage?"

"Umm..." she looked up and to the left while pausing as if thinking, then answered dramatically, "Never!".

I was shocked at this simple pleasure and health routine my friend had never experienced.

She continued with exasperation, "Come on, Zoey, with the cost and energy that goes into being a mom to small children, the closest I'll ever get to a spa day is when the dishwasher opens, and the steam smacks me in the face."

"Nope, not an acceptable answer, Kim. I'm your friend and I say you need 'me time' while managing the Winthrop household zoo. You deserve this, Kim, and it will help you to not only feel better about yourself, but also be a better mother." I nodded as I added emphatically, "We're doing this. I'll get more information and then we can schedule a day."

She wiped sweat from her brow and nodded her assent as Fish ran ahead of us with a large stick in his mouth and we continued up the steep hill.

AS SEEN ON ST. LUKE'S EPISCOPAL CHURCH'S SIGNBOARD:

Blessed are the curious, for they shall have adventure!

AS READ IN THE NUGGET NEWS:

Odessa Girls Give Nugget Varsity Softball Team a Whooping

Chapter 33

A Suicidal Pipsqueak

After the joy of the holidays, it was hard to have a good attitude when I returned to work after Christmas break.

The days were darker and the weather colder. The holiday lights and decorations were gone. I caught a little cold and many of the staff and students were absent for similar reasons. Worst of all, Dr. Hinman was around the office more and I found my anxiety increasing just imagining an interaction with him.

Miss Geller was able to finally get an update on Johnny and we learned his brain injury had impacted his ability to speak and walk. With the tyrannical father out of the picture, his mother had moved the family to Phoenix to be closer to the physical therapists and speech therapists who were working with Johnny. We continued to pray for his progress, were angry at the abuse, and mourned all he had lost through the assault.

Adding to the heaviness were some big challenges with several of my other clients. One fifth grader lost his mom in a house fire when a Christmas candle was left unattended. A teen client had a flare up of her anorexia following the food splurges of the holidays. A junior high boy was arrested for shooting at (he repeatedly corrected the "at" to "only toward") a police cruiser and another pre-teen was arrested when she got caught shoplifting on a dare. Finally, a kindergartener I just loved came back from the holidays with his usual joy missing from his face and eyes. I later discovered he had been sexually abused by a family member.

I had to work hard at my self-care to not take my anxiety about Dr. Hinman and my concerns for the children home with me. It's sometimes difficult to not ingest trauma when I empathize with the pain of my kids, something psychologists call vicarious traumatization. There's also the risk of burn-out and compassion fatigue with the intensity of the needs around me. My "red flag" warning that I'm not doing a good job keeping work and home separated is if I start to dream about my clients.

Perhaps because of these extra stressors, I surprised myself when I realized I was looking for the cat now when I came home. Mind you, I didn't want him in my house and didn't want to touch or pet him, but I somehow felt reassured if he was on my porch or patio.

During this dark season, the news only got worse.

One of my seven-year-old clients, Andrew, attempted suicide last night. Seven-years-old! How did he even figure out the concept of killing himself? He has two teenaged siblings, so perhaps he heard about self-harm from them or learned about suicide from one of the movies they watched?

I heard the news when I arrived to work and was dumbfounded. Reportedly Andrew was being treated at Phoenix Children's Hospital because of ligature injuries to his neck and, as the day progressed, we got more information about the incident because our janitor was a cousin to the elderly woman who saved the little boy's life.

This neighbor had seen Andrew playing alone in his yard from her kitchen window. When he took some of the plastic-coated clothesline off the support poles and wrapped cord around his neck, she figured he must be playing some sort of game and thought nothing of his actions. However, a few minutes later she was horrified to see him get on his bicycle and pedal as fast as he could down a steep hill. The clothesline jerked him off his bike and he lay motionless in the dirt.

She ran as fast as she could out of her house and over to the child. By the time she got there, his little face had turned purple, so she quickly unwrapped the clothesline and was relieved to see him start to breathe again and get his color back. However, he remained nonresponsive even when she called his name and shook him. She hollered to another neighbor to call 911 and gathered this little guy into her arms and pulled him up onto her lap. She rocked his diminutive body, cried out to God for help, and wept with worry until the EMS team arrived and could transport him to the hospital.

I had been working with Andrew for a couple of months and had seen him the day before this incident. He was happy and playful with me during our session. Was there any indication of distress in our interactions? Did I miss some clue or warning? Because of likely Fetal Alcohol Syndrome, he had almost no impulse control and phenomenally poor judgment. This must have played a part in the incident.

Oh, my goodness! The more I thought about the situation, my heart broke even more for this little scallywag whom I dearly loved. I thought of his mother who already carried tremendous guilt for her drinking when pregnant with him and wondered how she was doing. I couldn't call the family because they didn't have a phone, so I considered calling Phoenix Children's Hospital because it was likely his mother was there. However, I knew they couldn't reveal any info about the child without a signed release from the guardian and probably wouldn't be able to bring Mom to the phone. I suffered all day worrying over Andrew and his family, as well as rehashing my time with him to see if there had been any warning this was coming.

At about 2 pm, I was notified Dr. Hinman wanted to speak to me. My stomach fell and I instinctively knew this was related to Andrew's suicide attempt and would be turned against me. When I went to Dr. Hinman's office, I met Delvinia's eyes in the reception area and she gave me a worried glance while tightening her mouth and slowly shaking her head. I felt like she wanted to say something to me, but Dr. Hinman's office door was open, and she could not speak freely. He appeared to have been waiting and watching for me.

"Miss Trotter," he said with disgust. "Enter," he commanded authoritatively. I moved into his chamber and stood near the door.

"Close the door immediately," he directed. He did not offer me a seat and I felt like I wanted to be able to bolt if need be anyways. He addressed me confidently from a relaxed position seated behind his desk.

"You almost killed a child yesterday," he began. This was more direct and egregious than I expected even from him, and his comment threw off my equilibrium which was already shaky with the day's unfolding drama. I said nothing.

"How do you explain your failure to protect this child? More importantly, why should I allow you to continue to work here after this catastrophe?"

I blanched and tried to take all this in. I was already blaming myself for not catching any clue the child was moving toward self-harm and this direct accusation from the highest authority at the school was more than I could handle. I blinked and started to sweat.

He noticed my discomfort and increased the emotional heat. "So, answer me! Why should you continue working here!" he angrily demanded.

I did not want to cry in front of Dr. Hinman, though I think he was aiming for that reaction. I felt the tears start to pool behind my eyes. I was also too emotionally flooded to speak or try to answer from a place of logic. I remained silent and my silence was interpreted as an admission of guilt.

"Exactly like I thought," he snarled. "You cannot answer for your actions because they are inexcusable." He smiled in victory and followed with, "I think you should submit your resignation and start packing your things immediately."

I don't know how, but a tiny light went off deep in my subconscious. He wasn't firing me, but he wanted me to quit. Something was off here. If he really thought this was a sackable offense, he would have jumped gleefully on it. He was trying to pressure me to resign on my own. I needed to slow this down and think about it.

I knew I had not made a mistake with this child. I also knew you can never predict and prevent every suicide attempt. People make choices and our actions are not always logical. I reminded myself this community had been rocked by suicides which was why I was brought here: they need help. I was the most qualified person in the entire county to address this challenge and I had been doing this well as evidenced by a slowing in attempts across the district and no completed suicides.

I took a big breath and stepped back mentally from the accusation and recommendation lingering in the air. Almost in a state of dissociation, I found myself looking down on the office and the two of us interacting and could feel myself emotionally pull away. Somehow this was not about me, but about Dr. Hinman and I may lose my job today anyway. I wanted to turn the KGB interrogation spotlight away from me and toward him. With this realization, I uttered my first words since entering the office and asked a question I'd had for months but seemed inappropriate when I was trying to just do my job and stay out of his line of sight.

"Sir, what in your background has caused you to have such a hatred toward counseling and a vindictiveness toward me? You made up your mind to despise me before I set foot on campus, and you've treated me with contempt since our first greeting." I paused to watch his face transform from triumph to surprise. He huffed loudly, his eyes narrowed, and his face began to redden.

I continued, "Do I remind you of someone? Have you had bad interactions with psychotherapists in the past?"

As he watched the focus turn from me to him and realized his plan to get me to quit was not working, I could feel him cycle from surprise to disappointment to anger and then to rage.

"Who exactly do you think you are, young lady?" he shot back with a raised voice as he stood up from behind his desk. His voice got even louder as he shouted, "How dare you challenge me? How dare you question my background."

I wasn't sure how this was going to end, but somehow against all odds I remained calm as he spiraled into rage. However, my calm seemed to fuel his fury further and he started shouting demeaning comments laced with obscenities. I kept an expressionless face until he formed a fist and started moving quickly from behind his desk toward me with a menacing look. I could tell he had spiraled out of control and was no longer thinking clearly and wondered if he was going to physically assault me. I needed to get out of there quickly.

Just as I turned to go, Delvinia opened his office door, quickly took in the scene which she could hear from outside the office, and threw the entire interchange off balance with, "Excuse me, sir. You must not have heard me knock. The school board president is on the line. Do you want to take the call, or should I take a message?"

He stopped moving toward me abruptly, pursed his lips, breathed heavily, and miraculously his intense focus shifted away from me as he took in her message.

In the few moments this was occurring, Delvinia moved into the room and stepped between Dr. Hinman and me. With her hand, she gently grabbed my sleeve and casually pushed me further behind her and out of the office while appearing to focus entirely on Dr. Hinman in a professional manner awaiting his direction.

He spat out, "Take a message!"

"Thank you, sir. I will do so," she replied calmly and gracefully exited the room after me.

In an urgent whisper, she then told me, "Go, girl, go! Get out of here. We've just got to give him time to calm down. I will find you, sugar."

I thought Delvinia's comment about the school board president being on the phone had been a ruse, but she suspected Dr. Hinman was gunning for me and had called the board president reportedly to follow up on the last school board meeting minutes. However, as she predicted, Dr. Hinman had begun yelling and she had interrupted the school board president with a concerned, "Oh my goodness, what's going on in there?" comment as she held the phone toward the yelling superintendent's office. Dr. Hinman's words came through loud and clear. She quickly excused herself with, "I'm sorry, sir, but let me see what's going on in Dr. Hinman's office" and then left the receiver off the hook so the school board president could hear what became even clearer as she opened the superintendent's door.

Good to her word, she found me later after Dr. Hinman had reported he needed to go home, and she saw him peel out of the staff parking lot in his Escalade.

"Girl, I know he is hounding you and trying to get you to quit," she said with sympathy when she came to my office later with two cups of herbal tea. Her kindness and proactive intervention were more than I could bear. I sipped her welcome gift and the tears I had been holding back came flooding out. She let me sob for a bit and even pushed the tissue box closer to me. When I was only crying and no longer weeping, she started to talk again, and I listened.

"Zoey, you've got to realize something: Hinman doesn't have anything to use legally to fire you and he knows this. This is the reason he is trying to pressure you to quit." She paused to let me take her words in. "You are well liked by the staff and students, parents have been praising your work to the school board, and your professionality has been exemplary." She paused to let me take that in, then added, "Remember, sweetheart, your value doesn't decrease based on someone's inability to see your worth, no matter how big his title or ego may be. So, hang in there, Zoey. A lot of people are pulling for you."

She gave me a wan smile, but it was coupled with a determined look, "Girl, don't let Hellman have his way. Don't you dare let that twit win."

By the end of the day, I was bone tired from the bad news and emotional assault I had endured. I drove home in a trance, noticed two pairs of men's tighty whities in my patio and left them where they lay, went into my house, dropped my briefcase and keys, then started to get into my pajamas. The time was only 4:30 pm, but I wanted to curl up in bed immediately. I knew I should probably eat something first, so I shuffled into the kitchen and consumed a pathetic dinner consisting of several big spoons of cottage cheese while I put the kettle on to make myself another cup of tea. I wanted the emotional comfort of ice cream and probably would have eaten the entire carton if I had some, but I didn't and was too tired to head to the store. I put the food away, then washed my face and brushed my teeth.

As I was getting into bed, I noticed the massive cat stroll by my bedroom nonchalantly. He looked my way briefly before stopping to clean his leg and moving on. I swear the boy now walked with a casual air of entitlement when inside my home.

Wait, what the heck was the creature doing in my house yet again?

I got up with a groan, picked him up (which I could do now without trembling), and unceremoniously tossed him out the front door. I locked the door and checked all the windows. How was that darn cat getting into my house? I didn't have any working brain cells left to dedicate to solving the problem now but planned to revisit this issue tomorrow. I was comatose almost before my head hit the pillow and slept a deep and dreamless sleep.

A car alarm was going off and I could barely breathe!

What was going on? What happened? Had I been in an accident? Did my car go over an embankment? Was I pinned by the car?

I tried to make sense of my surroundings. The setting was dark and cool, but I felt a lot of heat around my chest. Perhaps an injury from when the car landed on me? I tried to wiggle free but could not move an inch.

I could smell burning metal but did not see flames. I seemed to be alone and hollered for help but didn't hear any response. The car alarm was deafening and incessant, going off over and over and over. Good gracious, turn that alarm off! The ruckus was making it hard to think.

I realized the car could have cut me in two when the vehicle landed on me, so I guess I was lucky to still be alive and breathing, though getting air into my lungs was exceedingly difficult to do. The smell of burning metal worried me, but I couldn't seem to get out from under the car. I hoped the auto wouldn't burst into flame with me stuck there. Maybe I could dig myself out from under the vehicle? What am I lying on: is the ground asphalt, dirt, pine needles, or something soft I can move?

I was already scared, but then I panicked as something soft started to touch my face!

What's happening? What touched me? Is it an animal or a plant or something else? How can this thing touch around my eyes without me noticing, particularly with my eyes open? Why can't I see anything?

My heart started to beat so quickly; I woke myself up.

Huh? Are you kidding me? None of that was real? I was asleep?

I tried to orient myself, slow my heart, take bigger breaths, and calm down.

Good gracious, all this terror was only a dream. I am going to be fine.

But wait, I still can't breathe, still hear the unceasing alarm, and still smell burning metal.

What the heck?

As my eyes finally focused, I realized I was looking directly into the eyes of the massive beast. The cat was inches away from my face and kept batting me lightly on the cheek and around my eyes (fortunately, with his claws pulled in so he didn't scratch me). The difficulty breathing was related to his huge body pressing down on my lungs. The car alarm was amazingly in sync with the cat opening his mouth and, as I continued to wake up, I realized the cat WAS the alarm! I had never heard the cat make a single sound louder than a quiet chirp or the rumbling purr he frequently gifted to people. Otherwise, never a noticeable meow, yowl, hiss, mew, caterwaul, or growl. This thunderous sound was coming from the cat! He was directing his voice toward me and for some reason he would not stop yelling.

As he continued to bat my face, sit on my chest, and sound an alarm, I realized the burning metal smell had not gone away when I woke up. In my defense, I sleep deeply and wake slowly so sometimes I take a bit of time to come to consciousness, but I finally caught on...

Holy cow! Something is burning!

I unceremoniously shoved the cat off my chest and sprang out of bed. I raced through my darkened house toward the smell and found a burner on and my silver tea kettle glowing a bright red secondary to extreme heat. Oh my gosh, I never made my tea! The metal was making odd crackling and popping sounds. The spout cover containing the tea pot whistle was open, so the whistle could not warn me when the water boiled or as the pot grew scorching hot as the water evaporated and the metal continued to be exposed to flame.

I was nervous to get near the kettle as I didn't know if the container would burst into flames or possibly explode sending metal fragments flying. Suddenly I was aware of how thin my pajamas were and that my bare feet were exposed. Though I had no protection, I just couldn't wait to put on shoes or change into more protective clothing. I put my arm over my face, leaned in to turn the burner off, and then jumped backward to get away from the stove in case the kettle exploded.

I wondered if I should take the tea pot off the stove and move the kettle outside to cool, but I didn't want to jostle it even a little bit as the pot looked volatile with the metal glowing a bright and angry red. Fortunately, the crackling sound appeared to be quieting once I turned off the burner flame, so I decided to let the tea pot cool right where it was.

As I now assessed the situation with an entirely awake brain, it started to dawn on me how serious this threat had been. If a fire had started, the blaze would have blocked my access to the only door in the house. The windows were high and small in my bedroom, and I would have had a hard time climbing up there without the little step ladder which unfortunately was stored on the other side of the stove and fire. I realized I needed to make better emergency exit plans for myself for the future. This had been a close call amidst a precarious situation.

No matter how tired I was, I was upset with myself. How could I have left a burner on? This was a potentially life-threatening mistake. Then, as I continued to think through my lack of evacuation plans and watch the red-hot tea kettle, I realized I was trembling and wanted to cry. I stepped away from the kitchen and pulled a fuzzy blanket around myself as I plopped into my recliner, pulling my feet and legs under myself as I tucked the blanket firmly around my quaking body. I then started to thank God repeatedly for his protection before bursting into tears.

I was on my second Kleenex when I felt a paw on my leg. The cat had come over to the recliner and gotten on his back legs to better reach me. I looked into his massive furry face and realized his eyes appeared concerned and radiated kindness. Without thinking, I set the Kleenex down and reached for the cat, pulling him into my lap while making space for him in a little nest between my folded legs. He settled right into the furry blanket and began his thunderous purring. I thanked God for his provision of this fuzzy guardian angel and then thanked the cat for his clear thinking and unceasing efforts to rouse me.

I wrapped my arms around the beast, nestled my face against his neck, and scratched under his gigantic chin. I could feel my heart beat slow and my spirit calm as I began to match my breathing to the steady rhythm of his comforting purr.

AS OVERHEARD IN PILGRIM'S PHARMACY:

"I'm looking for a moisturizer that hides the fact I've been tired for the past ten years."

HEADLINE IN THE NUGGET NEWS:

Hero Cat Prevents Fire:
"He simple wouldn't stop yelling until I got up."

Chapter 34

Stopping the Madness

The school board president was on the phone with the school district's attorney.

"But, Jim, I heard it all! He was yelling, calling her obscenities, and trying to bully her into quitting. This supports all the complaints we've been getting about Dr. Hinman. It's proof his behavior is inappropriate. I heard him myself."

"But, Don, were you there?"

"I was on the phone listening!"

"Were you physically present in the room?"

"Why would that even matter? I know his voice, I trust Delvinia, and I heard enough to confirm the Board's suspicions and the community's concerns."

"It matters because a defense attorney will appropriately call this hearsay. You did not see Hinman speaking. It could have been someone with a similar voice. You did not confirm he was speaking to another person in the room. He could have been talking to himself or practicing lines for a play or listening to a podcast on speaker."

"But we know that's not the case, Jim!"

"You may know it, but what you are telling me will not hold up in a courtroom. I've reviewed his contract. He was astute in his negotiations and put in some ironclad guarantees, including the unheard-of stipulation you pay him two years' salary if he's terminated for any reason barring criminal complaint. Don, have you all considered he may be trying to get fired?"

"I know you're probably right, Jim. The board knew this was not standard contract language, but we were desperate to get leadership in place before the school year started."

"Do you all even have the money that would entail? Really, it would've been smarter to leave the seat empty until you found a more qualified candidate."

"We know that now, but we felt strapped at the time. You remember Ann had been diagnosed with cancer and was likely stepping off the board. Eric's wife was getting worse with her early-onset Alzheimer's, and he was going to be less involved, if not resign as well. It was not a good time."

"I know, but it has created a mess now."

"Another thing is Edward Swanson was an excellent superintendent and the Board had gotten a little lackadaisical in our duties because he carried so much of the responsibility and did it well. To have all the district leadership return to us when we were already hit with such big health crises among board members... well, we jumped when we were offered what we thought was a miraculous answer to our prayers."

"Yes, I do understand. That's water under the bridge now, Don. We know hindsight is 20/20. And, if you give me a few minutes, I'm sure I could come up with other folksy sayings to describe the situation. Let's just move on from here."

"Thanks."

"I know we've talked about this, Don, but has anyone put their complaints about Hinman in writing? When we talked last time, you said you'd had at least a dozen verbal complaints, but no one was willing to put their statement in writing or testify if this became a legal matter. They were all too scared of the man. Has that changed?"

"This is Nugget. It's a small town and the people who live here are all going to shop at the same store, go to church together, have kids on the same Little League teams, and... well, everything. No one wants to make waves in the community, so they stop when asked to give a written statement. No one except Delvinia has given us anything that will hold up in a personnel law review, but the community still wants the Board to fix the situation."

"Get something solid, Don. Get something I can use in court. Better, get evidence of something criminal in nature. That's your ticket to freedom in this situation."

AS OVERHEARD IN THE BAKING AISLE AT JIMMY'S:

"Don't ever let a recipe tell you how many chocolate chips to use. Girl, you measure that stuff with your heart."

AS READ IN THE NUGGET NEWS

Chicken caught running on Main Street in red pants: Officer exclaims, "I didn't even know they made clothing for chickens!"

Chapter 35

Reconnaissance

I needed to run some errands downtown and the weather was gorgeous, so I decided to walk. The distance wasn't far but included several steep hills, so I threw a water bottle into my backpack along with a package I needed to mail and my shopping list. I put on sunglasses, kicked a new pair of underwear off my welcome mat, and waved to Lucille who smiled brightly at me from her kitchen window. Maxine may have nodded slightly when she saw me pass her garden, though in truth her acknowledgement of me was more her frown deepening into a scowl as she looked up.

As I walked down our hill, I noticed my newly decorated Valentine's-themed mailbox and knew I would need to thank Lucille later. I also thought about hiding some valentine candy in her holster, an item she proudly declared was "the most thoughtful gift anyone has ever given me." Her holster was now a permanent fixture on the right side of her walker for quick draw readiness and so she would be "set to go at a moment's notice." A different type of prepper, I thought with a smile.

Fortunately, I had never seen a gun in the holster yet.

About a block later, I stopped to take a picture of a particularly gorgeous Christmas cactus in bloom when something in my peripheral vision caught my eye. Was something moving behind me?

I turned to see the beast about 20 yards back. Was that darn cat following me? As I stopped to study the creature, he sat down disinterestedly on the pavement and began to clean his fur. With his back turned toward me, I could not scrutinize his face. Hmmm, maybe he wasn't following me, and his presence was merely a coincidence? I guess it didn't matter one way or the other. He didn't belong to me and could go wherever he wanted.

But I was curious to know if I was being followed. I walked another half block and stopped at a bank of roses to casually look sideways. Yes! There he was, still about 20 yards behind me. I walked a bit further and then furtively looked over my right shoulder. The little scoundrel was sneaking behind me, going in and out of bushes and driveways as if hiding. He knew exactly what he was doing and stopped walking whenever I stopped and then purposefully avoided eye contact. Why would a cat follow a person? I had never heard of this behavior before.

With my curiosity even higher, I wanted to see what he would do as I entered the downtown area. I popped onto Main Street and turned left to head to the post office. The furry behemoth continued in my footsteps. When I went in, he waited patiently near the front door like a faithful dog. I snuck a peek out of the post office window to see if he would move, but instead he stretched out like he owned the place and relaxed on the front steps. He garnered a half dozen pats and pets from people passing by and many seemed to talk to him like they knew him. The other post office patrons who saw me spying on the massive cat gave me judgmental side-eyed looks.

As I was finishing my transaction, Carl came into the post office, screamed loudly, and turned twice in a circle before stopping and looking around vacantly. No one appeared alarmed and three people in line behind me greeted him simultaneously with a "Hey, Carl." I hoped the loud noise had not scared the cat, but when I looked outside, he hadn't moved so he either didn't hear it or wasn't easily alarmed.

When I left, I pretended to not see him and continued to No Doze Café. The cat followed me to the coffee shop, waited patiently for me to get my iced mocha, and then lay in the sun two tables over pretending to neither see nor hear me as I watched folks passing by and greeted people I knew. A couple individuals stopped to pet the cat and he would roll over lazily to allow them access to his tummy. If they stopped petting him, he would casually put his paw on their hand until they continued again. I heard several people I didn't know make comments about his massive size and missing leg, but most were focused on how friendly and loving he was. Men and women fawned over the feline, and he soaked the attention up like a sponge.

When I finished my drink and headed to the market, the cat followed me for a few doors, but then detoured when he popped into the screened entryway to Castaneda's Deli after someone exited. I backed up and watched from outside as he politely went up to the glassed meat display case, stood on his hind legs, waited to be noticed, and then was served a few slices of something (turkey or ham?). The cat waited for Mr. Castaneda to come from behind the counter before he rubbed up against his work pants and got a few strokes.

Mr. Castaneda appeared to signal for someone and then a few minutes later, Mrs. Castaneda came from the back room leading her hunched over, white haired mother-in-law who sat on the bench near the front door. The cat seemed to know what to do and jumped up beside her, put a paw on her lap and settled in. Obviously, this was not a first time visit for the cat! After being pet for a bit and given a nonstop litany of "Bueno gato… bonito gato… mi angel," (*"Good cat… nice cat… my angel"*) he rubbed against the elderly Mrs. Castaneda's pink cardigan, jumped off the bench, then headed back outside.

As I passed their screened door, I stopped when I heard Mrs. Castaneda tell her daughter-in-law, "Cuando mi gato ronronea me hace sentir feliz porque me tiene confianza." (*"When my cat purrs, it makes me feel happy because he trusts me."*)

"Si, Mama" (*"Yes, Mother"*) she agreed with her mother-in-law.

"Cuando los gatos están relajados y contentos, hacen un movimiento como que amasan pan. Es muy tierno." (*"When cats are relaxed and happy, they make a movement like kneading bread. It's very sweet."*)

I missed speaking Spanish with my family and felt my heart warmed by hearing the endearments about that goofy cat.

Once on the sidewalk, he stopped and looked around sizing up the people close to him while licking a paw. When he saw me standing nearby, he turned his head and dramatically ignored me. I started again for the market and – no surprise now -- again the cat followed me, but only for about 100 feet before he stopped. I stepped around a corner, then stopped to peek back at him to see what he was up to. Would he eventually saunter my way? He did not.

I felt a little foolish being downtown with a steady stream of cars passing while I furtively spied on a cat which was not my own; however, I felt the piece of humble pie paid off when I saw the cat get up, move to the edge of the street, look both ways, wait for a car to pass, then cross to the south side of Main where he waited expectantly outside Gloria Jean's Diva Salon & Boutique. Not sure what he was waiting for, his intent became clear when someone exited and then held the door for him. When he ducked inside, I had to know what was going on!

I crossed over and tried to casually watch the cat through the big plate glass window. He appeared known and liked within the shop. He made his rounds to all the women sitting under hair dryers and rubbed against their legs until they pet him. He then examined and batted at a few piles of hair Gloria Jean had swept into the corner in the hair salon side of her boutique before hopping up into a styling chair. Women seemed to be watching him and laughing. Gloria Jean appeared to ask the client on whom she was working something, the client nodded, and then Gloria Jean went over to the cat and pulled out a special comb from the drawer under the mirror. I was stunned when she began to carefully comb out the cat while talking to him the entire time. No one seemed to think this unusual, most of the women were nodding and smiling, and occasionally he would roll side to side to give Gloria Jean the access she needed for a full grooming experience.

One of the women must have noticed me watching outside the window because everyone turned at once and greeted me with smiles and waves. Gloria Jean pointed to the cat with her comb, then motioned me inside. I didn't want to be linked to the beast any more than I already was, but ignoring the invitation would be rude, so I stepped into the shop.

"Oh, Zoey, we've been wanting to thank you for sharing your cat with us," Gloria Jean gushed. "He's a regular, coming in every few days for a comb out, and we just love him. Amazingly, he lets me comb out mats in his curly stomach fur and in his neck ruff, then lets me spritz him down with my water bottle when I need to clean dirt from his fur. He doesn't even blink with the water, so you've trained him well."

"Thanks, but I didn't train him. He's actually not my cat."

"I have always wanted a cat," a little blue-haired lady exiting the hair dryer chimed in. "But my husband was allergic. I come in weekly and always hope your cat will coordinate his visits with my appointments."

"Does he?" I asked, immediately wishing I had not been suckered into this conversation.

"I think so. He's only missed one appointment in the past few months. I always bring him sliced turkey which may help him remember or at least move my appointment higher on his busy social calendar."

While we had been talking, Gloria Jean had finished the cat's comb-out, rubbed a tiny dab of mousse along his racoon-like tail to smooth out the fluffiness, and then returned to the client on whom she had been working when the cat arrived. Nonchalantly the cat jumped down from the chair and made his way over to a middle-aged woman who appeared particularly beaten down by life. He jumped up into her lap like he owned her, turned in a circle, then plopped down for a cuddle after curling his now stylish tail around his body like a blanket. He gently kneaded her skirt and she began to absentmindedly stroke his fur while wiping an errant tear from her cheek.

Gloria Jean lowered her voice to a whisper, "See, he did it again. Amazing! He's really a phenomenal cat."

"He did what?" I asked in a quiet voice before sneaking a glance at the cat cuddled on the sad-looking woman's lap.

"Out of all the people in my shop, he chose the one woman who most needed love today and whose heart had been wrung dry by her verbally abusive husband. Such a horrid man, really. Joanne wouldn't take comfort from us, but she's soaking up your cat's kindness." Both Gloria Jean and her client had serious expressions, but slowly nodded their support for the cat's choice.

"Zoey, I never know whom he will chose to share his affection, but he is always right," Gloria stated emphatically. "Sometimes I understand his choice before he goes to the person, other times I learn later why she needed extra care. A few days ago, he chose Harriet. She had just learned her youngest son would be going to prison for selling drugs, and she was heart sick over the situation, but seemed better able to face her circumstances after your cat loved on her for a while."

One elderly woman getting a bouffant waved me over as I was leaving and said, "Such an amazing cat! Thanks for sharing him."

Not only did I not know he was a regular at both Castaneda's Deli and Gloria Jean's Diva Salon & Boutique, but I had no idea he knew how to cross a street safely, enjoyed comb-outs and allowed water spritzing, and was gifted as a therapy cat who could give comfort to those most needing encouragement.

SIGN POSTED AT THE CHECK-OUT COUNTER OF NUGGET PUBLIC LIBRARY:

"Poets have been mysteriously quiet on the subject of cheese."
G. K. Chesterton

HEADLINE IN THE NUGGET NEWS:

Robertson's Vegan Cousin Visits from Sweden: Mayor states, "I sure hope she likes chicken nuggets."

Chapter 36

Tastes of Nugget

Sometimes people say you can have too much of a good thing, but that was not the case with chicken nuggets in Nugget, Arizona. The success of Nug's Nugget Nook inspired other local restaurants to carry their own Nugget nuggets selections.

The Italian restaurant offered lightly breaded oven-baked nuggets with a marinara dipping sauce, though in-the-know locals knew you could also order off-menu and ask for their Alfredo sauce as a delicious nugget dip. The Chinese restaurant deep-fried their nuggets to an ultra-crunchy wonton-like finish and served them with a soy and rice wine sauce. The Mexican restaurant coated their nuggets in the same cornflake mixture they used for their deep-fried ice cream and then offered salsa or guacamole as a dip. Finally, the East Indian buffet offered both a tahini and peanut-based dipping sauce, but both were a little too exotic for many of their older customers' tastes; however, younger people loved them, and the nuggets stayed on their menu all the same.

Because of all the variations, the battle for best local nugget was fiercely contested. To capitalize on the rivalry and in celebration of Nugget's amazing spring weather, the Chamber of Commerce sponsored a "Tastes of Nugget" chicken nugget festival drawing people from three counties. Someone's relative visiting from Sweden came to the festival as well, but refused to eat any nuggets, so they weren't officially counted.

All the restaurants, clubs, and social groups put up booths and Walmart quickly sold out of shade canopies. Attendees could buy "nugget punch passes" for the number of chicken nuggets they wanted to try across all the booths. The Chamber president found a copper splash vaguely chicken nugget-shaped and had a "Best Nugget" plaque crafted which would be awarded with a $500 cash prize.

The battle was on!

The Nugget High School Marching Band Booster's Association offered a serious contender for "best nugget" (crispy exterior, moist and delicious interior with a homemade thousand island dipping sauce) which was surprisingly good, and people wondered if the judges would be emotionally swayed by the kids needing to make money for their new band uniforms. However, to avoid partiality, the Chamber brought in out-of-area judges and had them choose the winner from a blind taste test to silence any complaints of favoritism, nepotism, or grift.

At the end of the festival, people waited with bated chicken-scented breath for the announcement of the winner. The tension in the crowd grew when this year's "Miss Nugget" stepped to the microphone, the Chamber president handed her a yellow sealed envelope, and the Nugget High School marching band snare drum started a drum roll. As she ripped open the envelope and pulled out a single notecard, I saw Harriet and Joanne from the beauty shop take big breaths, then hold them with the suspense.

"And the winner is... Nug's Nugget Nook!"

Everyone agreed this selection was the best choice that could have been made across all the entries. It seemed fair and fitting as Nug was Nugget's nugget pioneer.

Still riding high from his award, Nug attended the state fair a few weeks later and accidently misread a girl's "Hugs, Not Drugs" t-shirt as "Nugs, Not Drugs." This idea stuck with him, and he mulled the saying over every which way but Sunday.

About ten days later, he woke in the middle of the night with an epiphany: he would use his $500 prize money to host a "Nugs, Not Drugs" campaign for the junior and senior high school students!

His campaign was well received and then became personal to Nug when his friend Kenny's love of cannabis spiraled out of control, and he was arrested for stealing his neighbor's pygmy goat while high. Kenny was extremely remorseful, offered to brush the goat and clean his pen for a year, agreed to speak to kids about avoiding marijuana during the next "Nugs, Not Drugs" campaign, and was allowed off with probation primarily because he was truly penitent.

Unfortunately, Kenny couldn't seem to say "Nugs, not drugs" in his personal life, kept smoking pot which gave him unbelievably sticky fingers for all sorts of useless items which, unfortunately, had value to someone. Kenny kept reoffending until he eventually ended up in court-ordered drug rehabilitation services. His friend's challenges broke Nug's heart.

When Nug had three successful years of "Nugs, Not Drugs" campaigns under his belt, the local mine's corporate office offered to put up the cash to support the campaign's fourth year and from then on, his "Nug's, Not Drugs" campaign included free t-shirts for each student who attended an anti-drug/pro-nuggets rally in Whortleberry Park.

These became highly collectible items featuring a new creative representation of his shop each year as drawn by a local student. The honored artist was awarded a year's free nuggets as a generous prize and the winner became legendary among their fellow students – a little of this was their artistic acumen, but their fame mostly related to the miracle and wealth of a year's worth of free nuggets which might be shared on-the-sly with friends.

They say imitation is the highest form of flattery and Nug enjoyed this in many ways. Not only did other restaurants begin to sell chicken nuggets, but Zeke Robertson one year tried to launch the sale of a new line of high-end area rugs in his flooring store with a "Rugs, Not Drugs" campaign. Unfortunately, this didn't take off because teenagers were the pulse of Nug's campaign and kids simply didn't get excited about floor covering.

SIGN IN THE BREAK ROOM AT CRUZ AND SONS' FUNERAL HOME (TAPED WHERE NO CUSTOMER COULD EVER SEE IT, BUT AGAIN TAKEN DOWN IMMEDIATELY BY GRANDMA CRUZ):

Being cremated is my last chance for a smoking hot body.

AS READ IN THE NUGGET NEWS:

Canazuela Sentenced to 48 years in Federal Prison for Multiple Crimes: Prosecutor announces, "He's not going to see the light of day for a very long time."

Chapter 37

Guard Cat

I needed some groceries and knew the weight would be more than I could comfortably carry home, so instead of walking I headed to my car for a quick trip to Jimmy's. I kicked aside a lime green pair of men's briefs at my front gate and drove the two minutes to the market.

I was reviewing my list as I walked toward the front doors, so I didn't notice Dr. Hinman as he exited the store until we were face to face. I had successfully avoided him at work for the past few weeks which wasn't hard as he seemed to hide in his office or find meetings he needed to attend in Phoenix. Unfortunately, I couldn't see a way out of this interaction though.

"You!" he sputtered when he realized who I was.

"Good morning," I uttered out of habit and not good wishes, involuntarily both stepping back and leaning away from him.

It almost seemed like he had been waiting to cross paths with me, because his eyes started to gleam when he told me, "Ms. Trotter, I believe it is time for your six-month job review and I have quite a few deficiencies for you to correct to be allowed to continue your employment." He smiled with self-satisfaction and malice.

I cocked my head and looked at him with disbelief. "Sir, if you don't even know my name, how can you possibly know the quality of my work?"

His face grew red, and his brow furrowed as he took a menacing step toward me. "You dare to continue to question me? Insubordination will get you fired."

His increasing anger and how close he was now standing to me caused a flashback to him coming around his desk at our last confrontation. I was sure he was going to assault me then and knew our interchange had further enflamed his hatred for me. My face grew white as I returned mentally to the still traumatizing incident and tried to figure out how to keep myself safe right now.

Dr. Hinman saw my fear and misread it, thinking it was something he engendered right then and there with his arrogant implementation of authority. He smiled victoriously and stepped even closer to me.

I leaned backward and he started to whisper threateningly while jabbing the air with his index finger, "Yes, now you're starting to get it. I am the boss, and you will respect me. In fact, you will..." However, he stopped talking and looked confused when he heard a deep guttural growl coming from somewhere near his kneecaps.

When he looked down, he met the intense stare of a massive, three-legged, cat-like beast. His tail was lowered and rigid, with the end slowly twitching side to side; his ears were swiveled down and pointed backwards; and his back was arched. His body seemed to emit waves of aggression and dominance. Dr. Hinman had no doubt this brute would attack and seemed to be waiting for the slightest misstep on his part to justify the action.

He had never seen a cat of this size. It couldn't possibly be a domesticated cat, but he didn't think it was a wild cat. Because he wasn't sure what it was and could sense he was in danger, he unconsciously curled his shoulders inward to protect his core and to appear smaller to the creature and less of a threat. In addition, he slowly stepped backward to create more distance between the beast and himself.

One step wasn't enough "respect" per the cat's expectations, and he began to excruciatingly slowly step toward the now anxious man never breaking eye contact, but added a deeper and more menacing growl, a fluffed-out tail, and with the hair on his back puffed up. I didn't think the giant cat could look any bigger, but he now appeared twice as large and more frightening than I had ever imagined possible. With narrowed eyes, the creature slowly took one more step forward and started a loud yowling... the kind you hear before a cat fight starts.

Some people noticed the giant cat at the store's entrance and others were drawn by the frightening yowl, but all stopped when they took in the scene. With a fascinated disbelief, every person stayed to watch the unfolding drama, several people whipped out their phones and started filming the interchange, and comments could be heard between strangers.

"Is that the three-legged cat who belongs to the new doctor? I didn't believe it could be as big as people said, but it's huge!"

"Quick, Bob! Come here. You must see this to believe it."

"Yowza! This creature is bigger than my dogs and they're 35-40 pounds. How is that physically possible?"

"Dude, that cat looks royally pissed off. I wouldn't want to be the older feller doing the face-off."

"Do you think it's a house cat or maybe a bobcat?"

"Hey, what's going on? What was that horrible sound?"

"Dang, man, what's up with the angry beast and, wait, does he only have three legs? Totally weird."

"Good lord, what a massive cat! What's happening here?"

It took a while for people to register anything beyond the overwhelming presence of the cat. When they caught on there were humans involved with the cat, they reluctantly looked away from the behemoth. However, when they shifted their gaze and beheld Dr. Hinman's eyes wide with fear, they were surprised and then pleased a famously unpleasant man was finally getting what he was due.

Most silently cheered the cat on with quick nods and quiet comments to other spectators. When they realized the cat was confronting "Hellman" to protect the new doctor, they were even more impressed, and several people took note to never treat the new lady poorly if it might inspire this type of behavior from the cat toward them.

Because public appearance mattered to him, Dr. Hinman registered the growing crowd while not wanting to break eye contact with the cat. When the cat added an ear-splitting screech and hiss to his repertoire, began thrashing his tail back and forth, and extended his claws, it was enough. Regardless of how he might appear to others, Dr. Hinman turned and ran to his car, leaping inside and slamming the door shut. He raised his head up slowly to look out the window to see if the cat was at his door. During his escape, the observers at the store's entrance began to laugh at him and cheer for the cat.

The cat ran after Dr. Hinman for three steps before stopping to be sure his enemy was ensconced in the vehicle and not returning. His tail kept flicking angrily from side to side. When the cat felt the threat was contained, he turned toward me and fast stepped his way back to my side with his amazingly fluffy tail straight up and swaying like a victory banner. He slowed as he got close and began to purr loudly while weaving in and out of my legs, claiming me with his scent, and slowly rubbing his fluffed-up fur back down into a more normal position.

Total strangers talked among themselves, and people were slow to disperse, but eventually did. I was in absolute shock.

Holy cow! What just happened? And more importantly, how do I protect myself from Dr. Hinman's retribution when he catches me without a guardian cat at my side?

SIGN ATTACHED TO THE CITY LIMIT MARKER:

Remember, kids: "Nugs, not Drugs!"
Campaign proudly sponsored by
NUG'S Nugget Nook, Nugget, AZ

HEADLINE IN THE NUGGET NEWS:

Luz Marietta Cruz Celebrates Her 104th Birthday: "Daily our mortuary helps people facing death while my mother continues her death grip on life"

Chapter 38

The New Hairdo

As expected, Lucille heard about the confrontation in front of Jimmy's from the lightning-fast gossip that circulated around the community and was at my gate when I got home. She once told me "A lie will run a mile before you lace up your sneakers" and it felt like local gossip might be on the same award-winning track team.

Lucille demanded a blow-by-blow playback on every part of the interaction and had already picked sides before I said a word: Dr. Hinman's words and actions, my response, "our heroic cat's brave stand against injustice", and "Hellman's humiliating retreat." I obliged and she offered comments and pointed observations throughout the entire story. Again, the retelling with Lucille was two to three times as long as the actual encounter.

"What really burns my biscuit, Zoey, is the entire community knows how inappropriate that little twit is being. How can the school board let him continue?" She was sputtering in anger and her whispery, breathy voice seemed slightly louder in response to the injustice. "His bullying behavior toward you and others is the straw that broke the camel's back in my mind. Maybe they will finally do something after this nastiness." She inhaled quickly and puffed on her exhales. I could tell she was still thinking about this insult on top of his history of disrespectful behavior toward me.

Again, I sent up a prayer of gratitude for the people God had brought into my life here in Nugget, folks who will rally for me when most needed. I flashed between Delvinia, Lucille, Kim, and others as I offered my thanks. To my surprise, the giant cat's face also came to mind.

Life went on in Nugget and with my work with the Nugget

Unified School District.

I was thrilled to learn Miguel was doing so well that he was selected to go to the State Spelling Bee where he came in third place. I met regularly with Andrew both in my office and in his classroom. He continued to struggle with impulse control but had done nothing else to try to hurt himself. Three of the four junior high girls who were cutting had stopped and I think distanced themselves from their friend who suggested this idea in the first place.

Delvinia heard another update on Johnny, and she shared with the team. He had regained his speech and mobility, but still had numerous challenges related to his facial injuries and brain damage. I suspected this may be something with which he would struggle for the rest of his life.

All in all, many of the kids with whom I worked experienced improved mental health with counseling, a few stayed the same, but no one got worse. As can be the case, about a quarter were not having problems themselves, but reflected challenges their parents were experiencing and that improved with parent training.

The teachers reported a decrease in kids talking about suicide at the junior high and high school. This concurred with my subjective assessment of less suicidal thinking among my clients. I was really pleased with this decline but know it's difficult to demonstrate success to others when it equals the absence of something. We had one suicide attempt by an 11th grade girl who tried to overdose after a big fight with her boyfriend, but fortunately she told her mom what she had done, and the hospital's emergency room staff were able to pump her stomach.

Most importantly, no additional children had died from suicide since my position was created.

March flew by and Lucille changed our mailboxes to a St. Patrick's Day leprechaun creations with green sparkly glitter and four-leaf clovers on wires that moved in the wind.

Lucille's cheerfulness was like a magnet for me. I just had to think of her broad face with slightly flushed cheeks to be happy myself. I found her face and spirit beautiful and thought of her when I read a

Charles Dickens quote, *"Cheerfulness and contentment are great beautifiers, and are famous preservers of good looks."*

One day she came over with the cat walking along side. Her holster held a plastic bottle of water and swung gently as she moved. Despite her usually put together presentation, today her hair was a tangled mess. When she noticed me looking at it questioningly, she laughed and explained, "Your boy decided to do my hair today!"

I looked at her with alarm and she laughed again. "It's okay, Zoey. I really enjoyed his attention." She then explained she was watching television and fell asleep. At some point he must have moved from her lap to the back of her sofa because she woke to the unique sensation of having her scalp massaged by a single paw while the cat licked and groomed her hair.

"When I figured out what was happening, I laughed and laughed. That just seemed to encourage him, and he doubled his efforts. I didn't feel I could stop him with him being so proud of his coiffure skills, so I just let him go for it."

At this point, we both looked down at the fluffy creature weaving among our legs. She was right: he did seem proud of himself.

SIGN ON BACK OF PICK-UP IN
THE WALMART PARKING LOT:

FREE KITTENS!!
When women get to a certain age,
they start collecting lots of cats. This
is called many paws.
Be prepared and start your collection
today.

HEADLINE IN THE NUGGET NEWS:

Three Nugget elementary students go to
the State Spelling Championships: They
report feeling "Incredulous,"
"Marvelous," and "Luminous"

Chapter 39

Cooking Lessons

"Mom, what's for dinner?"
"Young lady, how old are you?"

"I'm five-years-old. You know that."

"Okay, so let me do the math… 5 years times 365 days times 3 meals a day equals over 5000 meals." Kim turned to her daughter and asked with a serious expression, "You have eaten over 5000 times and you have not yet figured out how to cook a meal on your own?"

"I can cook!" Olivia defended herself quickly. "I can make cereal with milk, and I can make bread with peanut butter. Oh, and I know how to make chocolate milk," the little girl relayed.

"Well, alright then, I guess you have been paying attention," Kim pretended to reluctantly concur before adding, "but we need to work on you learning how to cook a few more meals." "

"Really? Great!" gushed the little girl.

Not exactly the response Kim expected, but she would go with this and see where they ended up.

"What would you like to learn?" Kim asked her.

She thought for a few moments before telling her mom, "I like when you make Pavlova, macaroni with cheese, drunk chicken casserole, hamburgers, sourdough bread, and pizza," listed Olivia.

Kim was shocked her little kid could pull such a wide-ranging list out of her head so quickly. As Kim considered the complexity of each item, as well as the oven/stove use requirements, she decided to offer some of her own menu items for safe and simple meal preparation in the future. This would be good for all the kids to learn, she decided. But tonight, she would choose from Olivia's list.

"Okay, let's start with pizza, but you must let Mommy or Daddy work with the oven whenever you make this, got it? Agreed?"

"Yes!" replied the tiny girl enthusiastically. Her brown wavy hair bobbed along to reiterate her affirmation.

"Alright, Miss Pizza Chef, let's get started on your first masterpiece. Go put on an apron, then get the stool and see if you can reach the pizza box in the freezer."

Olivia was loving her cooking classes and Kim was shocked by not only her enthusiasm, but her precocity. She started to branch out to more complicated menu selections while still requiring the five-year-old not operate the oven or stove without mom or dad present.

I was at Jimmy's for some salad making ingredients when I heard my name hollered from down the aisle.

"Zoey!" It was Olivia, running toward me.

"Hey, sweetie pie," I replied as I knelt to give her a full hug.

Boy, an enthusiastic greeting is truly good for the soul.

"You gotta come to dinner tonight, Zoey. I'm making pizza, but not frozen pizza this time. I am buying the bread part, the sauce part, and the cheese and pepperoni, but then I am making my own pizza!" Olivia beamed with pride and enthusiastic anticipation.

By this point, Kim had joined us —she chose to not run down the aisle to hug me like the munchkin did. Olivia immediately included her in the conversation.

"Mom, Zoey is coming tonight to try my pizza!"

I hadn't agreed to this yet, but I would have moved mountains to open my schedule if it was booked. As it stood, I was free that evening.

"That's great, honey," Kim affirmed, smiling at her little junior chef.

"May I bring anything to contribute to the dinner?" I asked. "I could make a salad," I mentioned as I pointed to the lettuce, tomatoes, avocado, yellow pepper, and cucumber in my basket.

Kim started to say "great" when Olivia spoke over her, "No, just come, Zoey. I'm making salad, too. And we're having chocolate chip ice cream for dessert."

Kim looked surprised at these revelations but was willing to support the little girl's plans. She looked my way and shrugged.

"What time should I come over, Olivia?"

"You can go to our house now if you want, Zoey. I have my Legos out, so you can play while I cook dinner," she suggested.

"Would it be okay if I stayed in the kitchen with you and your mom while you cook, so I can visit with you?"

"Sure, Zoey. That's okay with me." With that, she turned and skipped toward the produce section.

Kim looked at me with a "What have I unleashed?" look, but this quickly morphed into a big smile tinged with pride.

OVERHEARD AT THE POST OFFICE:

"Insanity doesn't run in my family. It strolls through taking its time getting to know everyone personally."

AS READ IN THE NUGGET NEWS:

Odessa Man Plans to Open Combo Radiator Repair and Nail Salon:
"There will be something for everyone"

Chapter 40

The Speeding Ticket

As Easter approached, Lucille turned our mailboxes into Easter baskets, complete with chocolate malt eggs left labeled for the post woman one day and jellybeans a few days later. The flowers and trees were blooming, everything seemed washed clean after a few light rains, the ground smelled fresh and full of life, and the birds were creating a raucous symphony of song.

I felt my hope reserves refill as the sensory beauty of sights, sounds, and smells accompanied my day. When downtown, I noticed Carl and the cat walking together in the park and felt my heart warm at the image. I also noticed the cat no longer had leaves or sticks in his long fur with his regular comb outs at Gloria Jean's Diva Salon and Boutique, and I could tell which days he went in because he came back to my place smelling clean with a hint of floral perfume and his fur silky soft. As the weather warmed, she asked if it was okay to give him a "hygiene trim" and had been shortening his long fur around his backside and around his toes.

I began to bring a selection of Estelle's muffins to the school every Friday for my colleagues. This was a way to show appreciation for all their hard work, but it also gave me an excuse to enjoy a muffin every week without guilt, using the justification I was practicing solidarity with my peers. Also, though only Delvinia knew this, the muffins were a way to secretly celebrate surviving another week under Dr. Hinman's leadership. Delvinia would sometimes catch my eye when taking a muffin and glance toward his office with a wry smile or hold the muffin my direction for an invisible salute or toast.

After work one Friday, I decided to celebrate the beauty of the region with a drive to the lake. I was singing worship songs at the top of my voice on a road out of town that was infrequently used when my music gained an odd accompaniment: the sound of a police siren. I looked in my rear-view mirror and saw the lights and siren were for me.

I slowly pulled to the road's shoulder and tried to figure out why I was being pulled over.

My buddy, Officer Peshlakai, answered my questions.

"Hey, Zoey," he began.

"Hello, Officer," I responded.

"Do you know why I pulled you over?"

"No, I'm sorry. I don't"

"You were going 20 miles over the speed limit in a 45-mile-an-hour zone. What's your rush?"

I hung my head and mumbled a reply, "No rush, Officer. I was singing a rousing worship song and I think my accelerator foot was joining my praise."

"Worship or no worship, that's too fast," emphasized Officer Peshlakai seriously. "Please know I could ticket you for 'reckless driving' which is a Class 2 misdemeanor or 'excessive speed' for going 20 miles over which is a Class 3 misdemeanor," he looked at my face closely to see if I was catching on to how large this violation was. I think my blanching and bulging eyes demonstrated my comprehension. "However, I'm going to ticket you at 19 miles over the limit, Zoey, but just this time. You should be able to pay a fine and attend traffic school to keep this off your record, but you must slow down," he admonished.

"Yes, sir. Thank you, sir," I responded. I could have cried with relief but didn't this time. "I will definitely be more aware and work to stay within posted limits."

He nodded to acknowledge my pledge.

"While not the way I hoped to meet you, I have been wanting to see how you were doing after the shooting incident with Mr. Canazuela. I'm sorry I was too distracted after the square dance to ask you then, but I've thought about you quite a few times since and prayed for you. Are you fully recovered now?"

"Gosh, thanks for asking. Yes, it was really only a graze, but it was a scary confirmation our bullet proof vests work and need to be worn daily. The bullet grazed the vest and then my inner arm, but it's all healed now."

"I heard you were honored by the Chief of Police."

"Yep, they gave me an Arizona Medal of Valor, though – to be honest – it seems funny to be honored for being hit. However, they focused on the fact I continued to pursue the suspect even after being hit because I was the closest to the scene."

"I'm so glad you are okay, Officer Peshlakai. I was really worried about you when I first heard the news."

"Thanks. I heard you played a part in bringing Canazuela to justice, too, Zoey. Something about intervening at the school?"

"I was trying to protect Johnny, not pursue his father, but, yes, my intervention played a part, though I don't think my part helped as much as it exacerbated the situation. I think we were both doing our jobs that day," I replied before adding an afterthought, "Some days are just harder than others."

"Boy, isn't that the truth," he replied before handing me my ticket. He then asked, "Hey, I've been wondering, how's Mr. Blue Ribbon doing?"

"Who?"

"Your heroic cat. I heard he protected you from a possible house fire and then stepped in to protect you from someone acting aggressive at Jimmy's Market. Pretty impressive!"

"Yes, he surprised me with both of those acts. Why are you calling him Mr. Blue Ribbon?"

"If you entered him in the Arizona State Fair, I bet dollars to donuts he would be the largest, smartest, and kindest cat in the state. Plus, he's polydactyl. Hands down, he would take 'best in show' honors which almost always means a blue ribbon."

"Ah, got it," I said with comprehension. "Mr. Blue Ribbon... I bet he'd like that name."

"You tell him 'Hi' from me, Zoey," Officer Peshlakai said with a smile and his thumbs tucked in his police-issued regulation belt. Then he gave me a little nod, turned, and walked back to his squad car.

Even after the speeding ticket, discouragement didn't seem possible with the beauty of this season. However, I worked for Dr.

Hinman. He continued sly put-downs in passing, tried to disparage me in staff meetings, and always shot hate stares across campus in my direction. I could bear this knowing how unliked and disrespected he was by all staff, but it was still a bit tiring to keep my defenses up.

Regardless of my emotional fortification, I couldn't deflect his poison when he announced to all the staff he had heard an update on Johnny.

"I know many of you care for Johnny and have been rooting for his recovery. However, the news is not good, and prayers are needed for this little boy. He is back in the hospital following complications from one of his many facial reconstruction surgeries."

Looking directly at me, he added, "This poor child suffered needless injury because our staff were not doing their jobs and didn't step-up to protect him." He then looked to the entire room and added, "Let's be sure this never happens again."

His words were arrows that hit my heart and made my shoulders slump.

You'd think by now I would be watching for elderly neighbors in waiting as I pulled into my driveway, either Lucille to bring joy or Maxine to bring anger. But I wasn't. My mind was still focused on Dr. Hinman's comments in the staff meeting and poor little Johnny's condition. I was absorbed with trying to breathe deeply to stop my tears as I drove.

Good gracious, I think I have cried more in less than one year in Nugget than I have the rest of my life combined. What a year.

It was at this moment Maxine sideswiped me with an angry accusation about the cat before I even finished getting out of the car.

"That abhorrent animal of yours has been stalking me when I garden and pouncing on my award-winning bi-color gladiolas," she spit out angrily as she stomped across the street toward me. "He destroyed six prize blooms today. I have to say that…"

To Maxine's disbelief, I interrupted her midsentence.

"Stop! I've had enough today," I said sternly. "I have no room in my head for another problem and nothing left in my heart to give to another angry or mean person. I especially have no room for bitterness and hatred. I cannot listen to you today," I finished decisively.

Maxine's face registered shock, then shifted to anger, and finally landed on concern. The idea of her being concerned (for me?) was an odd concept, but I didn't have the energy to try to unpack that novel concept. Instead, I turned and went directly into my house.

ON THE MARQUEE OF FIRST CONGREGATIONAL CHURCH:

"I believe in Christianity as I believe that the sun has risen: not only because I see it, but because by it I see everything else."
— C.S. Lewis

AS READ IN THE NUGGET NEWS:

Announcing the Birth of Emma Joy Winthrop, a 9-pound 3-ounce bouncing bundle of joy born to proud parents, John and Kim

Chapter 41

A Bad Game of Golf

The beginning of the end for Dr. Hinman came from the quick thinking and top-notch investigative skills of Delvinia's best friend, Joyce Humphrey.

One evening, she was home with her husband, Allred, watching what she considered one of the slowest-moving, most tedious sports on television: golf. She was doing so as an act of spiritual discipline. Last month, she attended a church women's conference and one of the speakers focused on how to infuse new life into your marriage by spending time with your man around his passions. Her presence with him watching this snoozer of a TV show was one of the many wearisome sacrifices she had made over the years for the good of her marriage.

There was a big golf invitational tournament in Phoenix, and it drew the biggest professional names in the field. For some reason it had been delayed this year and this was big news. Now it was back on the air. Reportedly, this tournament had raised over $100 million dollars for charity, drew over 700,000 spectators a year, and was billed as the "greatest show on grass."

Joyce humphed when she heard this improbable claim.

Allred was enthusiastic and had been talking about it for several weeks. For his 60th birthday, their three kids had gotten together to splurge on him and purchased an 85" television which made the televised images larger than life. Allred purred this was exactly the type of event for which this was made. He had recorded the show because it aired during their work hours and besides, he wanted to be able to re-watch the monotony in the future. His recliner was strategically surrounded with a 2-liter bottle of Coco-Cola, several bags of chips and pretzels, and an entire package of Nutter Butter cookies because he didn't want to have to get up to go to the kitchen and miss a single minute of commentary.

Joyce had no understanding of this concept. She saw a trip to the kitchen as relief from this tedious and mind-numbing "entertainment." Though she did not say this out loud, she suspected hell might have large screen televisions endlessly streaming golf matches narrated by monotone commentators speaking at an almost whisper.

She tried to engage Allred about the golfers and their strategies, but he shh'ed her whenever she tried to talk. After about 45 minutes of "action", she found herself struggling to stay awake. She was inventing games for herself where she analyzed the clothing selections of the athletes, tallied grammatical errors by the commentators, and looked for silly hats among the spectators lining the course. She was aghast people pay good money to stand by a tee and watch people swing a club and then you can't even see where the ball lands.

However, her boredom came to a screeching halt at the sixth hole.

The commentator was talking about the skills of the guy currently in second place as he teed off on a hole famous for stymying golfers with a sand hazard just to the left of the putting green. As they talked about wind velocity, distance, and par for the hole, her eyes started to blur until she happened to glance at the crowd standing behind the golfer and saw him.

Pictured directly behind the man, in the front row of the crowd, was someone who looked like Dr. Hinman.

She yelled, "Stop the tape!"

He had forgotten she was in the room with him and startled at her voice. "What?" he responded.

"I said 'stop the tape.' I want you to rewind just a minute or so back."

"Joyce, this is the Waste Management Phoenix Open," he said, as if this statement would mean something to her.

"Allred, you have this entire snooze-fest recorded. You can stop and restart it at any time," she said with more intensity and honesty than she intended. "I need you to stop the tape now. Are you going to rewind, or will I have to do it?"

Welcome to Nugget

Reluctantly, Allred stopped the show and went back until Joyce again yelled, "Stop!"

"There, there he is. Do you see him?" she asked.

Allred had no clue what was going on, who was involved, or even where to look.

"There in the front row in the obnoxiously bright green shirt with the broad purple stripes."

With this explicit clue, Allred could see who she was pointing out and asked with amazement, "Wait a minute now… is that Dr. Hinman?"

"Yes!" Joyce responded triumphantly because she had already spun ten steps ahead of Allred in her thinking.

"The tournament was earlier today, during work hours," Allred reasoned out. "What was he doing there? Did he take leave to attend the Open?"

Joyce nodded sagely thinking about all the questions she wanted answered.

Then he thought some more, "Those tickets are really expensive and hard to get, I wonder who he knows?"

Joyce whipped out her phone and hit Delvinia's name on autodial.

"Girl, where was Hellman at today?" Joyce asked minus her customary greeting.

"Huh? You're asking why exactly?" Delvinia responded, knowing this was Joyce with or without a greeting and trying to make sense of her random question.

"Sugar, I just saw that fool bigger than life on television," Joyce explained triumphantly. "He was at a big-deal golf tournament today in Phoenix."

"What? Ooooh, Jojo, are you sure?" Delvinia asked with surprise. "He said he was going to be at the state capital working on that committee he's on, you know the one that's looking into school funding referendums. That doofus goes down weekly for this group's meetings." There was a pause and a leather scrunching sound as Delvinia sat in her favorite recliner. "Girl, I got to sit myself down for this phone call." Her great grammar sometimes went out the window when she and Joyce got to yammering about something with strong feelings.

With a fast mind and putting on the thinking cap of a devious person, Joyce asked, "Del, do you get the announcements for the meetings or see the agendas?"

"No, I don't," replied Delvinia. "I'd really not thought about it much as I was just grateful he was out of the office almost weekly for this work."

"Well, I believe it's time to check on the 'work' this alleged committee is doing," Joyce announced definitively.

As was not a surprise to either Delvinia or Joyce, they discovered there was no committee looking into school funding referendums. Delvinia went into the travel reports Dr. Hinman submitted for vehicle mileage reimbursement and per diem funds and found none of these reports had the meeting agenda attached as was required by the finance office. When she asked the finance clerk about this, the woman said she had asked once for the agenda and been met with such a fiery rebuke by Dr. Hinman she had been letting it go ever since and just reimbursing him out of district travel funds.

Joyce followed a hunch and thought anyone daft enough to watch golf probably played golf, too. She researched all the best golf courses in the state and then began calling all of them stating she was Dr. Hinman's employee (technically true) and was putting together his business receipts (also true), and wondered if they could help her identify dates he visited their facility and the course fees he paid. She casually commented the golf course was the best place to make connections and seal business contracts and explained any games he played with clients could be claimed as business expenses (also true if he was doing business on these outings). She found he was a regular at the five courses closest to Nugget and they were more than glad to assist one of their best customers.

Delvinia dug deeper and looked at all the out-of-town meetings Dr. Hinman had reportedly attended over the past few months. All but one were fictional affairs.

Joyce was an amazing private investigator and discovered Dr. Hinman had a friend who worked in the administrative offices at Waste

Management and Dr. Hinman had been talking to them about a lucrative contract managing the trash and recycling of the Nugget Unified School District. The fact Nugget was nowhere near any region Waste Management worked seemed inconsequential. These business discussions had resulted in a top tier ticket to the WM Phoenix Open golf tournament.

Almost in passing, she discovered Dr. Hinman's sister was a highly respected psychiatrist in New York City. She also stumbled upon an online family picture of Dr. Hinman, his wife, two lovely auburn-haired daughters, and a goofy black Labrador retriever. She was taken aback and had to blink a few times when she discovered how remarkably similar Zoey looked to Dr. Hinman's wife. It was almost eerie.

Joyce and Delvinia prepared a detailed report with lots of supporting documentation and quietly presented this to the school board president. He called an emergency school board meeting and the scuttlebutt on campus was something big was going down. Delvinia had quietly suggested to Zoey this meeting would be worth her time, so she was there.

While school board meetings usually saw six to ten people show up, there were 43 people in the audience for this meeting. Two of these people were Delvinia and Joyce who looked hopeful and determined. They were dressed in their finest "go to church" clothing with coordinated jewelry, purses and shoes matching their outfits perfectly, Cruz & Sons Funeral home fans, white gloves, and hats big enough to provide shade for a wheelbarrow full of petunias. In all the years of school board attendance, no one had ever seen these two dressed this fine for a work event.

After a quick opening in the general assembly room, the board went into Executive Session in the smaller conference room next door for what the agenda listed as a "personnel matter." After 90 minutes, they called Dr. Hinman into the E-session and spoke with him for another 35 minutes. Throughout this long wait, amazingly none of the attendees left the session.

When the Board came out of the executive session and back into general chambers, Dr. Hinman appeared stunned and pale while the board members appeared either angry or tired and resigned to something unpleasant. The president called the meeting back to order and asked for a motion.

One of the members spoke up, "I move we terminate the employment of Patrick Hinman immediately for dereliction of duty and misappropriation of district funds."

The audience began to murmur and talk among themselves. This was worth the wait.

"Silence in the chamber," the president ordered. "Is there a second?"

There was a quick second by a board member who looked disgusted with the entire proceeding. When the president asked if there was any discussion on the motion, the board presented him with a stony silence. He called for the vote, and it unanimously passed.

Dr. Hinman was fired on the spot.

The board president directed the school security officer who attended all board meetings to accompany Dr. Hinman to his office where he was to pack his belongings immediately. He pointed out three empty cardboard boxes sitting to the side of the auditorium no one had really registered were there until now. The president then asked the security officer to make a note of every item the now disgraced former superintendent removed from the space.

Dr. Hinman scowled and pursed his lips. He looked more enraged than penitent. His face was deep red, his fists were clenched, and he looked to the floor to avoid eye contact with everyone as he quickly left the school board meeting room through a side emergency exit door.

Delvinia and Joyce turned toward each other and held eye contact for a moment before slowly nodding and smiling broadly.

Joyce quietly quoted, "'You shall know the truth and the truth shall set you free.'"

"Amen, sister, amen," Delvinia concurred.

CONVERSATION OVERHEARD AT SENIOR BIRTHDAY PARTY AT NUG'S NUGGET NOOK:

Husband, morosely: "I don't want to be 89."
Wife, matter of fact: "Your only other option is to die."
Husband, cheerfully: "Well, 89 it is!"

AS READ IN THE NUGGET NEWS:

Nugget Superintendent Fired for Golf Addiction: Police Consider Criminal Charges for Misappropriation of District Funds

Chapter 42

Laying Carpet

Zeke Robertson had the only flooring business in town and had been the "go to" source for the community for 37 years. He had interned right out of high school with a true old school professional and learned more about flooring than a college education could have provided. He started by specializing in carpeting and tile work but had branched out early on to include wood flooring and then window blinds, a surprisingly lucrative addition.

Zeke was also in his fourth four-year term as Nugget's mayor.

As the oldest of 12 kids, he felt a lot of responsibility to make sure the other "kids" (all adults in their 50's, 60's, and 70's) were doing well. It was amazing how quickly each of the kids lost their adult authority and accomplishments when talking with their big brother, particularly if he confronted them about any issue. Though they didn't like these conversations, they knew he loved them and wanted only the best for them, so they listened to him when they would listen to no one else.

His youngest sister, Denise, had married three times and each marriage ended dramatically. Her only child, Kyle, was a 22-year-old slacker Denise allowed to live for free in her basement out of a misplaced sense of guilt. She felt his lack of motivation was linked to her broken marriages when actually it was a result of sheer laziness and being spoiled rotten. She was doing him no favors by supporting his current lifestyle.

Zeke spoke to Denise about helping Kyle launch on his own by finding employment because she couldn't care for him all his life. However, caring for him was the one thing she felt she did well in life, so Denise was reluctant to change the status quo. A few weeks later, when her hours at the factory were cut, she needed extra funds to keep up with the bills and Kyle's internet and pizza expenses, so she finally consented to the advice of her older brother.

Not trusting her to go through with setting limits, Zeke organized an "intervention" for Kyle. He and three of the older siblings backed Denise up when she told Kyle he could no longer live in her home for free: he had to either get a job and contribute to family expenses or move out. Knowing his laziness, his uncle and aunts made the situation clear he would not be welcome in any of their basements either. When Kyle complained he could not find work (though he had never looked), his uncle had anticipated this excuse and offered Kyle a position with Robertson's Flooring as a carpet layer and told him he would start the next day. Kyle couldn't immediately come up with an excuse, so he reluctantly agreed.

That night Denise cried herself to sleep because her little baby (all 6'2" and 265 pounds of him) was finally flying the coop (though he would remain firmly ensconced in her basement). Oh, she mused, the burden of parenting and the pain associated with empty nest syndrome!

The next morning, Kyle arrived at work 15 minutes late and looked disheveled in dirty jeans and a torn rock band t-shirt, enhanced by bad breath and uncombed hair. He may have even had some scrambled egg in his unkempt beard framing a sallow face way too pale for Arizona, but reflective of a young man who rarely went out of doors because of his video game addiction. His attitude was sullen, and he looked like he was being marched to his death.

Zeke gritted his teeth, handed Kyle a breath mint and his comb with instructions to use it on his head and beard, and then put Kyle on his own crew for the day so he could keep an eye on him. Kyle was slow and devoid of ambition or initiative. He made many mistakes Zeke felt were probably done on purpose. He tried to give Kyle the simplest jobs with which he could not mess up but didn't fathom the level of Kyle's passive aggressive behavior nor how hard he would work to avoid working.

At 4:45 pm the crew was finishing a carpet replacement in a rental house in Nugget. Kyle knew his uncle routinely worked overtime and wasn't about to agree to extra work if he could help it. In the darkened back corner of a closet, he discovered a space cut in the floor for a vent which had been overlooked during construction. The opening was hard to see and probably unnoticed when the heating and air conditioner crew installed their duct work. He could see the dirt under the house through the hole and felt a slight breeze. Rather than take the time to do the right thing and close the gap in the floor, Kyle knew this would have made the work go past 5 pm so he simply laid the carpet over the gap and tucked the rug into the corner. He doubted anyone would figure this out.

Unfortunately, this rental was Zoey's house.

The carpet in the corner was now untacked and decorated with a thick layer of cat hair where the huge cat was making his entrance at least once a day. The space remained invisible to Zeke when he checked Kyle's work and later to Zoey in all her many inspections of the house.

Additionally, though the broken crawl space cover had been fixed by Makin and held up to the javalinas, no one had noticed the little hole on the southern side of the house leading from the outside to the underside of the structure. Being a hundred-year-old structure built before there were building codes, there was no stem wall and just wood on dirt holding the little house up. The cat had tunneled under the wall after the crawl space access was appropriately closed.

There was no stopping him from finding a way into his favorite place in Nugget.

GRAFFITI INSIDE A MEN'S BATHROOM STALL AT THE NUGGET GYM:

Exercise? I thought you said, "extra fries."

HEADLINE IN THE NUGGET NEWS:

Regional javalinas unusually fertile this year

Chapter 43

The Cat Finds a Home

"Zoey, come quick! It's your cat." Lucille urged breathlessly. She had obviously been watching for me to return home from work and was panting even more than usual in her haste to rush over to talk to me.

"Excuse me?" I was so tired I didn't want to try to explain again the creature was not my cat, but I was also alarmed at the level of agitation I was witnessing in Lucille.

She started to tear up as she explained, "The javalinas... they did it to him!"

Now I was apprehensive. "Did what?"

"Well, he was strolling back to your yard after coming over to my house for tea. Did I tell you we have started to have tea together each afternoon? I switched from Sanka to Lipton's to add a little spice to my life. Also, you know the cat visits every day, right? Once I got the cat treats, he would stay even longer and carry-on lengthier conversations with me. We sit at the table, well, on the chairs at the table, and I set out a teacup for him with just milk while I made a nice pot of Lipton's for myself. I only pretend to pour him a little and..."

"Lucille! The cat. What happened to the cat?"

"Oh, my. I was getting to that part of the story. Goodness! Let me see now, we had just finished tea and he was on his way home when he ran into a herd of javalinas. They had several babies in the mix and you know how protective they are with their wee ones. But, oh, those babies are so precious with their little stick legs and big barrel bodies. They look like they have four little pencils for legs and..."

"Lucille, the cat!"

"Yes, so your cat turned the corner into your yard and ran into this herd. The big ones charged him and one of the biggest ones gored him with its' tusks while the others tried to scoot the babies to safety. I saw the situation unfold from my kitchen window and it was horrible, Zoey, absolutely horrible. I think I screamed." She was blinking back tears and looking into the distance at this point of the story as she re-experienced the trauma during her recollection.

"I grabbed my walker and not my cane because I can move faster with more stability, then I came over as fast as I could to check on him, but he wasn't moving. I knew he needed medical care right away because he looked all torn up, but he was too heavy for me to lift. I know this for a fact, dearie, because I tried, and I couldn't carry him with my walker anyways. So, I knew we needed help. I wracked my brain for someone who still had a car as most of my friends are too old to drive, then I remembered Reeves Davis, the young man who delivers my 'Meals on Wheels' boxes. He's Maybell Davis's next to youngest grandchild and has done really well for himself. He was the star center on the Nugget High basketball team, and I believe he will…"

"Lucille! The cat!"

"Yes, yes, you're right. Once Reeves heard what had happened, he hurried up here with their big, handicapped van, which is a godsend really for those of us slowing down a bit. Well, he helped me get your cat to the vet."

"The cat is at the vet?"

"Oh, yes, sweetie. Don't you worry none as I told the vet you were a doctor and would pay for any expense needed to treat your little love bug. Also, I explained to the front reception lady how close you are to this big boy and how deeply your cat loves you and she nodded understandingly, so she's gotta love a cat like you love your sweetie pie." Lucille smiled benevolently and awaited my gratitude. I was too shocked to say anything.

"Where is the vet, Lucille? Can you direct me if I drive?"

"Sure, honey, no problem. Let me get my sweater and I'll be right along."

I felt strangely unmoored as I went back to my car. You know how time can sometimes slow down or speed up when something important is happening? I felt like I was moving in slow motion and the quality of light around me had changed somehow.

Lucille did a great job giving me directions and we were at Happy Paws Peterinary Clinic in under five minutes. We rushed in... well, "rushed" may be stretching the truth, but we moved as quickly as Lucille could go with a fast shuffle. In typical Lucille fashion, she added lots of extraneous details as she introduced me to the receptionist (Margarita, sister to Estevan who is married to Magdalena who works at the donut shop), vet tech (Haley, still only in high school, but she has a 4.0 and is planning to go to vet school), and then the vet (Dr. Hopper, son of Eric Hopper who worked at the mines with Lucille's husband for 35 years and had hit a Grand Slam at the big Odessa vs. Nugget softball game of 1953). It took forever, but I felt like trying to rush this for her would end up taking longer, so I gritted my teeth.

While Lucille was talking endlessly, I realized the focus was on me from all the people in the room except for Lucille. I felt like a celebrity with all the scrutiny, but also had an awful knot in the pit of my stomach when Lucille finally paused and the vet looked at me with pity and stated solemnly, "I'll take you to your boy now. Please follow me."

Lucille stayed in the waiting room, and I was taken through a maze of examination rooms, a lab, a pharmacy, and an operating theater -- more treatment space than I would have guessed for a small-town veterinary clinic. With the vet tech hovering in the background, Dr. Hopper put his hand reassuringly on my shoulder as he pulled open the recovery room door where the cat was resting.

I caught my breath and stepped back when I saw him! He was almost entirely swathed in gauze and bandages.

"Now, don't worry. I know he looks awful, but he's done remarkably well considering how seriously he was injured," explained Dr. Hopper. "Your boy is a scraper and one of the largest Maine coons, actually largest cat of any breed, I've ever treated. I weighed him at 28½ pounds and very little of that is fat. I think his size helped him and prevented the javalina from killing him." He nodded slightly and looked impressed as he surveyed the cat on the recovery blanket. "He made it through the surgery and is doing amazingly well."

Welcome to Nugget

While I could hear Dr. Hopper speaking and telling me more about what types of injuries he sustained, I was so overwhelmed with the visual appearance of the cat I wasn't really listening to the vet's words. The giant beast somehow looked shrunken and smaller even with the addition of all the bandages. The story of the attack, the types of treatment, and the transformation of the feline into a huge ball of gauze was lost on me as I was struggling to process the situation.

Dr. Hopper continued, "Now we watch and pray there's no infection, but the good news is he is stable now. We'll keep him at least one night for observation."

I looked at him blankly after he finished his report, shifted my attention to the cat, and then shocked everyone by bursting into tears.

The vet and vet tech looked at each other with surprise and concern. "I said he is doing well, really well, and he's stable," Dr. Hopper repeated slowly.

"Yes," I snuffled, embarrassed by my torrent of tears. I realized I was both worried for the cat, but even more relieved he might recover.

"So, why are you crying then?" the vet tech asked with confusion.

"Because he doesn't like to be away from home," I explained with a sob and realized this was true.

As they ushered me out to the lobby, the receptionist whose name I couldn't remember said she needed to start a file for the cat and asked what his name was. I had never given him a name because, until this exact moment, I had never considered him mine.

Pausing for only a heartbeat, I replied with certainty, "His name is Tripod."

And so, it was.

CREDITS

"Don't take life so seriously. It's not like you're going to get out alive." Is a paraphrase of "Please do not take life quite so seriously – you surely will never get out alive." Credited to Elbert Hubbard, 1900.

"Don't look at me (in that tone of voice)" is a song title credited to Gene Watson, 1977.

"If we're not meant to have midnight snacks, why is there a light in the fridge?" is a paraphrase of a joke credited to Deon Cole, 2017.

"I don't have the time or the crayons to explain this to you" is credited to Jimmy Carr, 2015

"Act your age, not your shoe size" is credited to Barbara Schoen, 1967

"The first to apologize is the bravest. The first to forgive is the strongest. The first to forget is the happiest." Is usually attributed to anonymous, but one source links it to Ralph Smart.

"Blessed are the curious, for they shall have adventure!" is attributed to Lovelle Drachman.

ABOUT THE AUTHOR

Thea Wilshire grew up with many cats and is privileged to currently serve a beautiful Bombay named Gidi (Apache for "cat"). Gidi is the boss of two large dogs: Elliott, who is shaped like a baked potato and has the coloring of a s'mores, and Wylie, a pony-sized gentle giant and gifted drooler. Gidi works hard to keep Thea from sleeping past what he deems to be his breakfast time. To learn more information about the author, go to her webpage at www.theawilshire.com.

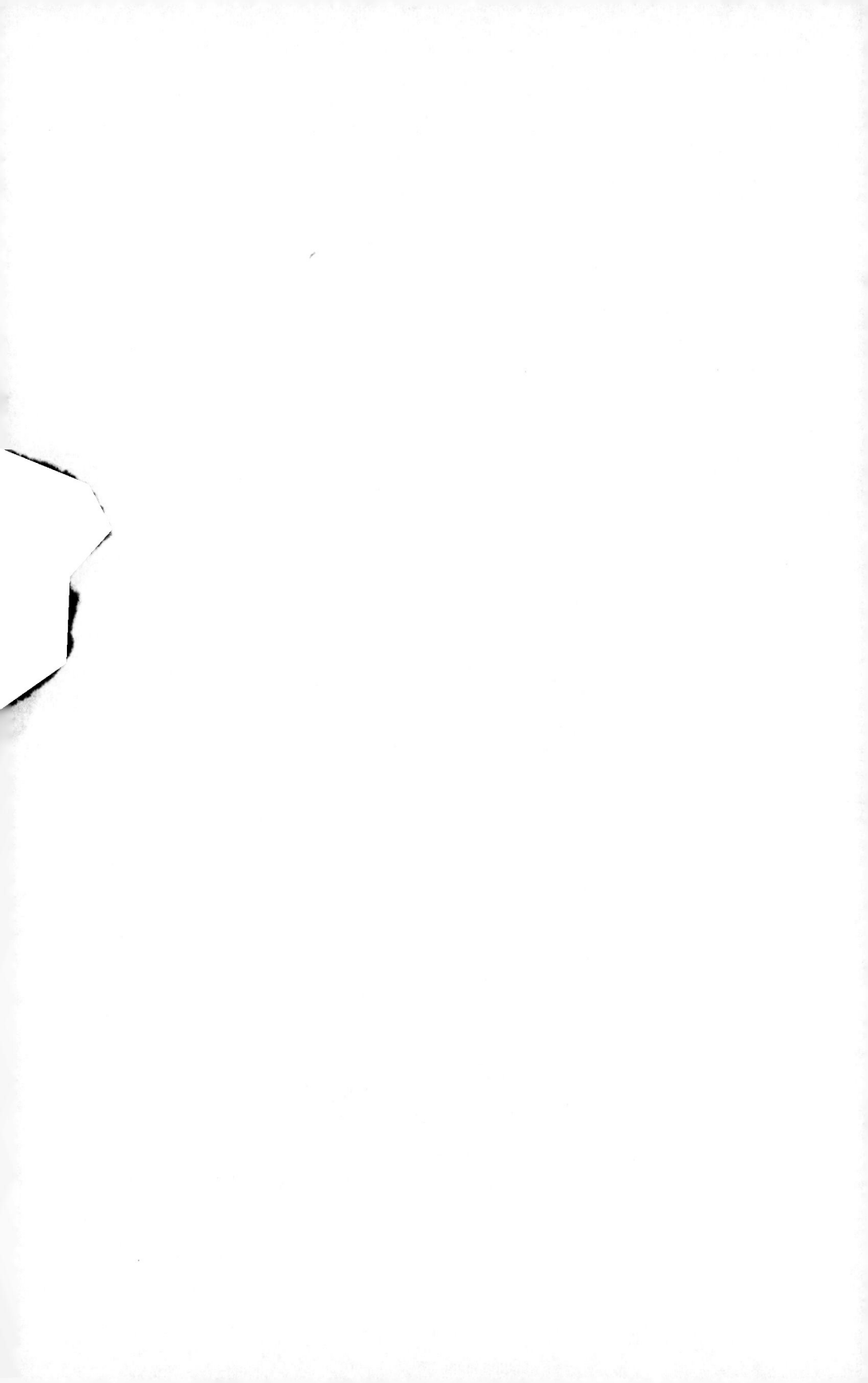

Made in the USA
Columbia, SC
25 April 2024

d6db651a-bfa2-40b5-b9b3-96059237b1d3R01